"A smart, twisty, wonderful novel with all the messy grit of the real world. Devon Wilke digs into complex relationships and finds heartfelt emotion in a story of suppressed ambition and motherly love that resolves in unexpected and profound ways. Just a wow."

—James Parriott, award-winning producer/writer/director, *Grey's Anatomy, Ugly Betty, Patriot*

"*Chick Singer* rocks with dynamic characters whose dialogue pops like a backbeat. Devon Wilke trains a knowing look upon our current frantic and fragmented state, and the music that goes with it. A multi-track saga for these digitized times."

—Junior Burke, award-winning dramatist, songwriter, and author of *Buddha Was a Cowboy* and *Cold Last Swim*

"Bittersweet and deeply felt, *Chick Singer* nails the heartbreak of an artist forced to recalibrate when the heady dreams of youth crumble into the stale compromises of middle-age. But Libby Conlin is not about go gentle. In a world where music, passion, and even sex are pitched as the exclusive domain of the young, Libby fights to reclaim some part of her stolen youth and promise. It's a hell of a story, by a hell of a writer, with characters that live and breathe and stick with you long after the music stops."

—Tom Amandes, actor/director/playwright, *Everwood, The Untouchables, Celestial Events, Brothers & Sisters*

"Lorraine Devon Wilke has masterfully captured the middle-aged angst of a woman who dreamed big, lost, and successfully put her dream in a box never to be opened. It's a page-turner that will resonate with anyone who has ever dreamed big and lost, only to find out that sometimes dreams can come true, just not in the ways you expect."

—**Ann Werner, author of** *Crazy* **and the**
After the Apocalypse **series**

OTHER BOOKS BY LORRAINE DEVON WILKE

After the Sucker Punch
Hysterical Love
The Alchemy of Noise

Chick Singer

A Novel

LORRAINE
DEVON WILKE

Sibylline
DIGITAL FIRST

Sibylline Digital First Edition
eBook ISBN: 9781960573575
Print ISBN: 9781960573704
Library of Congress Control Number: 2025930838

Cover Design: Alicia Feltman
Book Production: Aaron Laughlin

**Sibylline
Press**

For Pete and Dillon, always

"It climbs through you like electricity; up from your gut and through your throat, bursting into the air with such sound and fury you couldn't hold it back even if you wanted to. It rushes ears, explodes senses; raises goosebumps, until they wail and scream and move to the floor, arms flailing, leg pumping, every word shouted in tandem, and when that happens, and you know it was you—your voice, your energy, your electricity—that inspired the joyful clamor, you rise up out of your body in pure exhilaration. And sing louder."

—*Front Man* by Moody Haines

THEN

Los Angeles 1989

S.I.R./Stage 1

Two steel-edged Anvil cases and one microphone stand propped the hulking metal door open, rain splattering like pebbles on the loading ramp. A team of roadies in T-shirts and skinny jeans hefted drum cases, keyboards, amplifiers, and guitars from the Ryder truck backed into the dock, rushing to keep all from getting soaked as they slip-slided in and out of Stage 1. A din of voices and muffled rock music pumped from somewhere inside as instructions were bellowed and some kind of order was found in the mayhem.

Inside the large, dimly lit rehearsal space, techs set up lights and checked sound. The catering team assembled the bar, with hors d'oeuvre tables on one side of the room, chairs in various key spots in front of the stage. Huddled in another corner, drying off boots, belts, and leather jackets, fluffing coiffed and sprayed hairdos, was the band.

The six members of Liberty were paying varying degrees of attention to a set list being cobbled together by Nick Jackson, lead guitarist, band leader, and perfectly assembled '80s rock god, and Libby Conlin, the stunning, sartorially resplendent lead singer. Debate about mood, tone, and flow abounded; arguments about what to save for the encore and who should say what between songs were ultimately interrupted by the breath-less arrival of Damon Holland, the besuited manager who dragged frantic energy into every room he entered.

"Bloody hell, can you believe this mess? It's a madhouse out there; no one can drive in the stuff. We're gonna have to hold off at the top because you damn well know they'll all be late, draggin' in here whining about puddles and crap parking." He shook off his raincoat, threw it on a chair, then took a long, deep breath. "And now for the good news." His grin was smug. "I got the call just before I left. He'll definitely be here."

Libby, cheeks flushed in the generalized excitement of the evening, turned with a blank stare. "Who?"

"Are you kidding me with that? Eric Burrows. Have you not been paying attention, sweetheart? We've been trying to get him locked down since the showcase was booked. He's the big fish, the kahuna, the guy we're going for. Mount Cloud Records, Sony subsidiary—big time, baby. They're hot as hell right now, and word is he's looking for something fresh. He's looking for you guys, so you better slay him tonight!" He pulled her into a hard hug. "Especially you, Miss Liberty!" With that, he marched to the stage barking orders about amber gels and "creating some space for her to move around, for hell's sake!"

The band reacted to his announcement with hoots and high-fives; Libby slipped quietly to a cluster of chairs across the room, her body language tight. Nick followed.

"Got some jitters going?"

She turned with a wan smile. "I'm pretty sure he'll implode if we don't pull this off. If *I* don't pull this off."

Nick, glancing toward their still-barking manager, laughed. "He's all noise, but he knows how this goes. We'll just kick ass like we always do; our friends'll yell and scream, and whatever happens, happens. Main point is to have fun. If it ain't fun; it ain't worth it. Right?" His tone was mock-serious.

She managed a perky salute. "Got it, yes, fun!"

"There ya go."

"What time will Mercy be here?" Libby liked Nick's current girlfriend, mostly because she added much needed feminine energy to the very male bastion of the band.

"At least fifteen minutes late, possibly twenty. The girl's clinically averse to punctuality," he said good-naturedly. "Hey, did you end up inviting your parents?"

"No." Her expression was sheepish. "Decided I didn't need anything else to be nervous about tonight. They think I'm at a freshman orientation event."

"Ah, still convinced you're college-bound, eh?"

"Let's just say my dad would not be happy if he knew I was here." She looked honestly aggrieved by the statement.

Nick squeezed her arm. "I guarantee he'll be real happy when you're at the top of the charts, filling stadiums, and winning Grammys. And if he can't figure out who you are, that's on him. *You* know who you are."

"Do I?" Libby's vulnerability was transparent.

He cocked his head, holding her gaze. "Nah, I don't buy that. You know exactly who you are. You're a star, Liberty, full blown magic stuff, doing exactly what you were meant to do. You open your mouth, you sing, and everyone knows that's true."

She looked up at him. "Yeah?"

He touched her cheek. "All I know is, you kill me. And that's hard to do, I promise."

She flushed at the compliment. "Thanks. Wonder if Eric Burrows will agree?"

"Forget Eric Burrows. Forget your dad. Forget our gasbag manager. You just sing."

A tall blond roadie yelled from the stage, "Hey, Nick, come tell me how you want your set-up tonight. It's tight quarters up here."

"Bart, just put it—oh, hell, I'll be right there!" Nick looked at Libby with a smirk. "Sometimes I can't believe you're dating that guy."

She blushed again. "Sometimes I can't either."

He laughed and jogged to the stage. Her gaze followed, watching as he and Bart quibbled over the positioning of amps, guitars, and pedal boxes. She took a deep breath and stood up; fluffed her crimped hair, straightened her ripped fishnets, pulled her sequined bolero jacket tight and, shoulders up, walked toward the lights.

CHAPTER 1

Los Angeles, 2025

Beachwood Canyon

Bridget Conlin Hart had not been a good roommate. At any age. From toddler to teen to young adult, she'd reigned with such levels of agony and angst that by the time she left for good she'd exhausted everyone in her wake.

Yet here she was again. Weary and worn, separated all of one day from the man she married eight years ago in defiance of parental warnings about potential alcoholism and financial instability, the man with whom she'd built a modestly successful wine bar near Georgetown University; the man whose newly discovered illicit lover (the nighttime sommelier) was rumored to be pregnant and angling to move into the townhouse Bridget had decorated with faith, hope, and creativity. These facts convinced her that her life was cataclysmically over. It wasn't. It just found its way back to her mother's house.

Officially too late to continue the histrionics that accompanied her debrief to said mother, Bridget sat hunched on the edge of the bed wearing misery like a cloak, fragile arms stacked on her knees as if their only purpose was to keep her head afloat. The curtain of dyed black hair shielding her face couldn't hide the red nose and weepy eyes.

The exhausted woman across the room leaned against the wall, pondering why this pale, bedraggled creature had found her way back here. It didn't seem that long ago that the same swollen-eyed girl sat on this very bed screeching that she didn't have enough freedom, that "everyone can just leave me the fuck alone," that she'd be out the minute her diploma was in hand, never to return. She didn't, ultimately, abscond that quickly, but the ensuing years until she did, somewhere in her early twenties, were as clamorous and disruptive as those previous, which made the return surprising.

Libby Conlin sat down on the window seat juggling how best to respond to her daughter's plight. She didn't feel versed enough in recent events to offer useful solace; they'd rarely spoken in past years. When they did, it was always brief, usually sharp, with Bridget's contribution often ambling and pointless. Libby wondered at times if they'd ever known how to talk to each other.

Frankly, they'd struggled to find equilibrium from the moment Bridget was able to stamp feet and parse words, and that hadn't resolved in adulthood. It simply got more distant and with better vocabulary. Now, at this unexpected moment, Libby felt honestly annoyed that her recalcitrant, churlish child, who'd become a recalcitrant, churlish adult, had had the wherewithal to pack her personal belongings, fly from D.C. to Los Angeles, grab an Uber to the house, all without thinking or taking the time to alert her mother of her impending arrival. She was also genuinely saddened by Bridget's clear anguish. Over the last hour, essential plot points had been conveyed with equal parts rage and sorrow, and now the two sat without words, either out of them or simply waiting. The silence went on long enough to become awkward.

Bridget shifted on the bed; reached for a tissue and blew her nose, falling back on the pillow with a deep sigh. "Sorry. Guess

I'm talked out." She glanced over at her mother. "I bet you were surprised to see me at the door."

"I was." Libby betrayed little emotion, offering only a tired smile.

Bridget cocked her head. "But it's okay if I stay for a while, isn't it; at least until I figure things out?"

"Of course. This is always your home. Though I'm curious what your plans are looking ahead."

"I don't have plans. This just happened."

"And you're convinced it's a dead issue? No hope at all, even if you two met with a counselor?" Seth Hart, the wayward husband, was an ass, but Bridget tended to catastrophize enough that the question felt warranted.

Bridget sat up so fast she had to grab the side of the bed to steady herself before bleating, "Mother, she's pregnant! What's supposed to happen after *that*?"

The familiar, surly tone. Libby had forgotten how unpleasant it was to have someone speak to her that way. No one in her current life did, would, and she didn't like it any better now than when Bridget was fifteen. At thirty-five it seemed less petulance and more a true personality flaw.

"Bridget, I've been exceedingly out of the loop on your life, so I'm simply trying to catch up. If I say something wrong, you'll just have to forgive me. You said you weren't sure she was pregnant, so I wondered about the potential of reconciliation if that does prove to be false. Not such a strange question, I think."

Bridget blew her nose again, louder than was necessary.

Libby continued. "You're welcome to stay here as long as you like. I'm just wondering if you have any idea how long you'd like that to be, or if there might be a plan I could help you with. Are you thinking of actually moving back to Los Angeles or is this just a breather?"

"I don't know. *I don't know.* He told me last night she was probably moving in, and I jumped on a plane today. This is as far as I got." Bridget slid back to supine. "And he did say he was pretty sure she was pregnant, so that seems a good enough gauge."

According to previously reported conflagrations over the years, Seth had been known to lie, often egregiously, so maybe not as good a gauge as Bridget thought.

"But they're getting an official test done, correct?"

"What does it matter, Mother? The fact that they *think* she's pregnant is as bad as it needs to be. Whether she ultimately is or isn't is kind of beside the point, don't you think?"

A valid argument. "Yes. I suppose it is."

The room suddenly felt too hot, too close. Libby stood and opened the window, glancing briefly at the twinkling homes perched across the way, their palm trees swaying in the ever-present breeze. She loved this rustic hillside on the cusp between Hollywood and the Valley below and was accustomed to the silence and serenity it offered, particularly since her other child, her second child, her much younger and far less irascible nineteen-year-old boy child, had settled into his freshman year of college a while back and a couple of hours away. With him soon home for the approaching summer, and Bridget now here for an undetermined spell, peace and serenity suddenly felt ephemeral.

In the pause, Bridget's mood calmed, and she took the opening to shift focus to her mother. Libby appeared tired, she thought, maybe a little heavier; older, at the moment, than her fifty-something years (she could never remember the exact number). Her dirty-blonde hair was pulled into a haphazard bun, her sweats faded and baggy; no attempt at vanity was evident. Libby had always been one of the cooler moms, but her current presentation hinted at middle-aged malaise. Bridget hadn't seen her mother in almost two years and couldn't remember if she'd noticed any of that before.

"I'm sorry for just dropping in on you," she said quietly. "I should have called first."

Libby sat back down, tenderness washing over her. "I'm happy you felt you could come home." A soft smile followed. "We just haven't talked in a while; I didn't know things were so dire. I wish I had. I wish you'd let me know so I could have picked you up at the airport." *So I had time to recalibrate and get used to the idea.* "It might have made things a little easier." *For me, for you.*

"I know. I have no excuse other than I lost my mind when I found out Candy was moving in."

Candy. Libby hated that name. Now she could hate an actual Candy. "I'm so sorry, sweetheart. That's a gut punch on every level."

"I thought it would take him longer to let go of me. And if she really is pregnant ... wow, not even a breath in between. And we'd just started talking about trying again ourselves."

A miscarriage a little over a year ago had shaken their already shaky marriage. Bridget had shared the event briefly with Libby at the time, but there'd been no follow-up conversations, and assumptions had been made that they'd recovered from the blow. Apparently not.

Tears welled as Bridget pulled back into a protective ball. "It's like I never existed."

Libby suddenly flashed on the moment she discovered herself pregnant with the very woman now curled in agony on the bed. She remembered panic mixed with an overwhelming sense of mystery, of something sacred and profound happening in her belly; the awareness that she was now fully responsible for another life. That reality had altered everything. New decisions emerged, jarring changes were made, all compelled by love for an evolving being who just suddenly *was*. And now ... was again.

She went over and sat on the side of the bed, instinctively stroking Bridget's back. "You existed. Your marriage existed. Now you just have to exist differently. It sucks, I know."

Bridget looked up at her mother. "I guess you do. But Daddy's girlfriend didn't get pregnant."

Even in this, a contest.

"No. So he had even less reason to leave but did anyway. And I learned to exist differently. You will too. But right now you get to grieve and mourn as much as you need to. You're entitled." She stood up. "Tell me, did you walk away with any money?"

"He gave me a very large check, said it was my half of our assets."

"Is it?"

"Probably not. But it's enough for now, at least until I figure things out. After that, I'll get whatever else I'm owed. I'm not that stupid."

"Good. You worked hard for those assets."

Tears rolled down Bridget's face as she burrowed deeper into her pillow.

"I'll leave you be," Libby said softly. "If you need anything, just holler."

Bridget reached out and grabbed her mother's hand in an awkward squeeze. "Thanks, Mom. I know this is a pain. I'll get it together, I promise."

"It's not a pain. It's just painful. And I know you will."

★ ★ ★

Libby sat at the top of the long rock stairway leading from the shabby 1920s Tudor (gifted by her parents when they fled to Houston) to the tiny cul-de-sac below. She leaned back and watched a helicopter skim the hills en route to downtown Los Angeles shimmering in the distance, trying to decide if 10:30 was too late to call Bart, Bridget's father, her ex, the man who once held her heart and was now a distant figure of late tuition checks and stilted conversation.

She didn't want to talk to him about this yet. Didn't want his questions when she had no answers. There would be discussion of getting them all together, something she had no desire to do but would because Bridget was, after all, his daughter too.

She gazed up at the stars and didn't call.

CHAPTER 2

Chloe's Attic was one of those eclectic gift shops with window designs of such panache passersby couldn't pass without stopping. It was an art form, those windows, a calling card. The sixty-nine-year-old proprietress, Chloe Falana, a second-generation Nigerian American whose hands created those vibrant works of art, realized early in her career that monetizing whimsy was good business. She and her husband, Martin, had recently negotiated for the space next door and were in the process of remodeling for a mid-July expansion. Business was that good.

The shop was on Franklin Avenue at the foot of the Hollywood Hills, set between a hipster pub on one side, and a small theater on the other; across from the ostentatious Celebrity Centre of Scientology notoriety, and just up the block from La Poubelle, the most enduring French restaurant in Hollywood. It fit the neighborhood perfectly.

Libby, who'd been the shop's bookkeeper since the early days of QuickBooks, managed both the record-keeping and basic accounting in a job she appreciated for its dependability but found uninspiring as a career. She was, however, happy to be ensconced in a place of such charming ambience. Originally just one of her many freelance clients, the Attic became full-time employment when her mothering duties lightened, and she'd been able to accompany Chloe on a number of buying trips. Learning the nuances of that end of the business offered some creative outlet, but it was the upping of her take-home pay that allowed the winnowing of clients to just the Attic. It was a lovely arrangement of more manageable hours and less freeway time.

Just as she was settling into her spare but sufficient office space surrounded by bamboo room dividers and multi-colored paper lanterns, Chloe buzzed.

"Good morning, Libby. Coffee on?"

"It is." She smiled; coffee was always Chloe's first question. "What's on the agenda today?"

"Actually, I'm wondering if you could come by my office in about half-an-hour; I want to discuss some new plans that happen to involve you."

A mild jolt shot down Libby's back. Her early years as a freelancer, with zero benefits and self-financed, very expensive, health insurance, had left her with a mild strain of work-related PTSD. She was exceedingly protective of the employee status she'd acquired over the last decade, particularly since her son, Rob, was also covered by the insurance that came with the promotion. There was nothing about plans that "happen to involve" her position that didn't stoke anxiety.

"Sure. Is everything okay?"

"Yes, yes, many exciting things happening; it's just time to bring you up to speed."

Chloe's natural ebullience served well as the store's face and name, but her exacting and efficient business acumen could intimidate at times. Libby could well remember a few tense sessions on the road as she learned the what, why, and how to buy for a store like the Attic. Chloe's need to bring her "up to speed" sent tremors to her stomach.

"Okay, let me wrap up a few things and I'll be in."

"Perfect. And if you wouldn't mind, bring me a cup of that coffee when you do—and don't forget, lots of cream, two sugars, no cookies."

Three things Libby had never forgotten.

★ ★ ★

After a long sip followed by a sigh of caffeinated satisfaction, Chloe, stunningly attired as always—today swaddled in brilliant layers of brown, pink, and white Ankara print—sat back and gave Libby a beaming smile.

"The contractor says he can expedite the remodel, and we may be able to open The Annex a week or two earlier than originally planned." The Annex was an amplification of the Attic, offering a wider selection of international and eclectic import items. Currently the design of Chloe's wildly decorated office hinted at what she envisioned for that space.

"That's good news, yes?" Libby asked. "Is that what you wanted to talk to me about, piecing together the buys for that room?"

"That is something we need to get methodical about now that we've got a more precise timeline, but no; what I want to discuss today has more to do with your other job."

"The bookkeeping?" Odd. Unsettling.

"Yes. Martin and I sat down with our financial adviser last week, and with the complexities of the expansion, particularly the widening array of import traffic, he believes it's time to get an official CPA on board to set us up a bit differently. Despite the fact that your job here has always involved basic accounting tasks, you're not a CPA, and there's no efficiency in *not* combining the positions for a business this size, which he advised us to do. That would mean phasing out your current job and replacing you, which is not my preference."

"Wow. Mine either." *Dear God.* A sheen of perspiration broke out on her forehead.

"So, what I want to present," Chloe, oblivious to the terror she'd just struck, continued, "is the option of you getting your certification and *becoming* that CPA for us. You do have your bachelor's degree, yes?"

In a fortuitous decision when Rob was young and there seemed wisdom in getting a teaching degree that would allow her potential work schedule to match his, Libby trudged through the requisites toward that goal. With the unexpected discovery that she had no desire to teach, she shifted her focus to accounting, finally accomplishing that objective on an elongated six-year trajectory. Getting CPA certified, however, would demand a whole other level of specialized education.

"Yes. I have my bachelor's."

"In accounting?"

"Yes."

"Excellent. That gives you the perfect launch pad. We would, of course, pay for the classes required, any certification fees, whatever is involved, but obviously, considering the rigor of the process, we'd like you to start as quickly as possible. What do you think? Are you interested?"

Given the choice, the answer should have been simple: *Yes. Wonderful opportunity. Thank you for thinking of me.* Instead, her most salient emotion was: *No, I'm not interested; in fact, I feel a tsunami of weariness just thinking about it.*

Bridget was two months into her home residency program with little progress and still no discernible plans, which remained a distraction. More immediately, Rob was arriving home in a week, something she very much looked forward to, having already spent time researching mutually-agreed-upon mother/son hiking ventures and day trips for the summer. Long hours in a florescent-lit community college classroom learning the arcane skills of the certified accountant sounded unequivocally dreadful.

"That is so generous of you, and certainly I'm, uh, interested, yes. But I would like to think about it for a minute. Would that be okay?"

Chloe's face registered surprise. "Well, yes, of course. But is there any reason you *wouldn't* want to take advantage of the opportunity? You are aware your salary would adjust commensurate with your advanced status, correct?"

She hadn't thought of that—a good argument "for"—still, she couldn't shake the sense that she'd just be digging deeper into an accidental career she didn't love. "Chloe, know that I'm honored and grateful on all counts, but you caught me at an odd moment. There's a lot going on with my family right now that's pulling my attention, and I'm just not sure how much time I can devote on top of my working hours. If you could allow me to think it over and sort through a few logistics, I'd be able to give you a more honest answer than I can right now." She pulled her navy cardigan closer, suddenly chilled.

"Of course, my dear. I guess I've thought about this long enough I forgot I did just dump it in your lap without warning!" Her laugh was boisterous. "So, yes, think about it for as long as necessary, but not too long. Progress is a mighty master."

CHAPTER 3

It was done. Bridget now had no impediment to officially start-ing her next chapter. After confirming weeks earlier that "the pregnancy test was positive," Seth Hart overnighted divorce papers that arrived yesterday morning, and by this afternoon, Bridget Conlin (she'd already removed "Hart" from her official identity) was standing in front of the South Coast College of Film & Media looking through the door, pondering entrance. In the two-plus months she'd been at her mother's house, amidst bouts of wretched grief and depression, clamorous phone calls, and the overriding sense that she was too old to start over, it had become patently clear she had no choice but to start over, age be damned.

"Weren't you interested in film during college?" Libby had asked. Bridget bristled, knee jerk reaction to any suggestion or question coming from her mother, but the truth was, she had been. Somewhat. More accurately, she'd dabbled. Taken a few classes at Cal State Northridge, made a few short films, won some accolades, then lost interest. She couldn't remember why, exactly, but suspected it had something to do with a certain counselor who'd emphasized the brutality of the film industry while baiting her with, "Do you have the spine for that kind of battle?" He likely meant to trigger her competitive spirit but suc-ceeded only in convincing her that her spine was questionable, and she didn't want it that badly. So instead, she took a waitress job at a high-end hotel on Sunset Strip where she made lots of money, learned the bar and restaurant trade; met Seth Hart, and a few short years later was handily seduced to the other side of the country and her tumultuous first chapter. Or second chapter. Whichever chapter it was. At thirty-five, it was hard to know when chapters began and ended.

Shaking her head, annoyed at her own reluctance, Bridget finally shoved through the doors and immediately took note of how young the milling attendees appeared. Most circumstances in her current life left her feeling callow and unformed, but here she was clearly one of the older crowd, which was disconcerting. She glanced around, wondering if she should proceed, where she would proceed if she chose to, and, really, what was the point of proceeding if—

"You look lost."

No truer words. Bridget turned to see the scruffy, smiling face of a tall, good-looking man with long dark hair, rumpled black clothes, and an air of locational confidence. His age—which she'd guess was close to hers—suggested he wasn't a student.

"I am, a little."

"Where do you want to go?"

And that was the question. "I'm thinking of signing up for some film classes, so I guess I'm looking for the admissions office."

"That's a great program. I run the recording studio here on campus and work with a lot of their students. Dean Park." He leaned in for a fist bump; she accommodated him.

"Bridget Conlin." Awkwardness kept her smile tight.

"Nice to meet you, Bridget. Yeah, it's a cool community, the Film Department. I'm sure you'll fit right in."

"Really?" Her incredulity was sharp. "I'd guess I'm a decade or so older than everyone I've seen here so far. With the exception of you." Her smile widened.

"That is true. But there are quite a few of us oldsters around. And we do look out for each other." His eyes had a charming twinkle. "Admissions is just to the left at the end of this hall, but let me walk you down there—"

"No, that's fine. I'm still just thinking about it, so I'll probably wander around a bit."

"Good idea. It's a nice little campus; take your time. If you do need any help, give me a call." He pulled a card from his T-shirt pocket and handed it to her. "Both my studio and cell numbers are there; call any time." Another smile and he was off.

She watched him traverse the lobby, appreciating the intervention. Still, and despite his pep talk, her legs didn't want to move in any of the suggested directions. She turned toward the parking lot and an Uber ride home.

CHAPTER 4

For God's sake, twenty dollars?

Libby was politically averse to exorbitant valet fees but knew parking anywhere near the restaurant would be unlikely.

"And this is why I hate going out," she mumbled to herself.

After some street trolling, she finally grabbed a spot several blocks down in a residential area and started walking, grateful she'd worn flats instead of her usual boots. This part of Hollywood's downtown was now so gentrified Libby barely recognized it. Gone were the seedy thrift shops she'd inhabited like a sartorial addict in her younger years. The shabby restaurants with good coffee and casual no-smoking enforcement had been replaced by multi-use developments that offered commerce and accommodations that were chic and impossibly expensive. Few of the scrubbier stores that once lent character to the neighborhood had survived. Still, there remained a handful of appreciated stalwarts: the old bookstore that sold the New Age tomes she'd devoured for years and now used to prop up crooked chairs and potted plants; the tiny clothing store whose handmade items once filled her colorful wardrobe; the gyro stand she patronized for her weekly Greek salad. Still standing. Still there. Though she rarely was these days.

Where she was today was Flâneur Café, a trendy bistro with an impressive bougainvillea arched over the doorway and an edgy, eclectic crowd tumbling around the bar into the patio. She'd agreed to meet her closest friend, Gwen Herrera, for an all-too-infrequent night out, and was now seated at an outside table only marginally quieter than the cacophonous main room. Libby nursed expensive sparkling water while Gwen threw back her second Wild Turkey, perusing the predominantly male crowd with appreciation. It appeared mutual.

"God, I love this place." Gwen grinned at Libby. "Something about Hollywood men just gets my libido."

"I didn't know your libido was locationally selective." Libby quipped.

"Come on, look at them. Young, quirky, ambitious, with great sunglasses and oozing urbanity. Downtown guys are so bland and buttoned up."

Gwen, appealingly curvy, brilliant, and very loud, was a successful wealth manager at one of the top downtown firms, a two-time divorcee, and an enduring friend of Libby's since their days at Fairfax High. Despite having never lived there, Gwen exuded a kind of sassy New York sensibility, even occasionally affecting the accent, something, she told Libby with sardonic glee, charmed certain clients, which Libby thought was pathological. She was always sharply dressed in the best of business wear, owned a stunning condo on Bunker Hill, and presented like she belonged on the cover of Forbes Magazine, where she'd once been featured.

Libby was suddenly struck by the fact that both the seminal women in her life—her boss and her best friend—made her feel pale. "Whatever you say. They just look like guys to me, but you're the one out here eating the world, not me."

Gwen sat back, gazing at Libby with squinted eyes. "And why is that?" she queried, her tone suddenly serious. "Why do weeks go by before we can manage a get-together? You work daytime hours, there are no small children; I know you dumped hot yoga. What's the hitch?"

Libby always cringed when Gwen started analyzing her life; there was a relentlessness to it she found exhausting. "Let's see, my chimney collapsed recently, apparently age-related erosion, which I can identify with; on top of that, my delightful but book-averse son failed his English lit requisite and will now need tutoring this summer. I'm saving money for all that mess."

"It doesn't take money to do the Venice Boardwalk, and you nixed that the last three times it was suggested. You love walking Venice, Lib; what's up with you?"

Libby sighed like weary teen. Which brought to mind her sighing, obdurate daughter who generally acted like a weary teen and was, in fact, one of the things that actually did impact Libby's socializing. Despite her emotional distancing, and the rare event of doing anything with her mother, Bridget demanded Libby's attention just by being present at the house.

There was also the covert embarrassment of her "post empty nest syndrome." Despite some dissipation since the initial inciting departure of nine months ago, the enduring pang of missing her son, Rob, seemed to have permanently altered her habits. Though, frankly, those habits had already been reshaped by Covid, which had them huddled inside long enough to normalize hibernation. Unlike so many others, she'd actually enjoyed that concentrated, insular time at home with her equally housebound son, with zero desire for previously desired outside activities. For him, of course, that was less the case but, unlike his sister, Rob tended to share his life with ease. He authentically enjoyed her company; made her laugh on a regular basis, and kept her busy with both essential and nonessential activities.

Then, as people found their way back into the light, Rob had the temerity to not only leave the house but leave for college—an exhilarating rite of passage for him; for her, it felt like the unanesthetized hacking of a limb, agony beyond what she'd have ever expected. Which she hated to admit because it embarrassed her. If she heard one more mewling mother (clearly less syndromed) say something like, "But don't you *want* him to fly?" she was going to punch someone. *Of course I want him to fly, you ass; I'm just suffering the loss of his presence.* It felt like a cliché, the depth of this thing. It was hard to explain to anyone; impossible to explain to Gwen, a woman who'd decided kids didn't fit into her life plan.

So Libby went with, "I don't find going out all that thrilling."

"You used to."

"I did, but things change. Netflix and popcorn are now my jam. Does that make me sound old?"

"As much as 'my jam' does," Gwen snorted. She took Libby in with real concern. "You're detaching from the world."

"I'm not detaching from anything, I'm just not that into—"

"Stop." Gwen raised her finger in shushing motion. "Just stop, Libby, I mean it. You *are* detaching from the world. We had an excuse for a while, but most of us have shucked our masks and rejoined humanity. You remain detached. If you don't stop soon, you're going to have dementia by the time we're sixty, and I'll be goddamned if I have to repeat my name every time I walk into a room. I don't want younger friends but if you persist on this premature aging project, I swear I'll find some."

Libby was a bit stunned by the onslaught, but Gwen's sincerity was clear. "You hate younger people." She had no other response.

"I do, so snap out of it."

Libby saluted her somberly. "Yes, ma'am." She wouldn't.

"Now, what's the latest with our prodigal daughter? New job, new boyfriend, something, anything, or does your malaise have something to do with hers?"

"No. That's all me. But no, nothing new. Lots of weeping and watching TV."

"It's great that you've given her a soft landing, certainly, but it's now been, what? Almost three months? Isn't some ass-kicking overdue?" Gwen considered herself Bridget's secular godmother and had no compunction about asserting any and all opinions on the topic.

"Probably. Clearly this is not a permanent solution and it's starting to wear thin."

"Rough between you two?" She'd been party to some of the more heated conflagrations between Bridget and her mother over the years and knew tensions between them could run deep.

"About what you'd expect. We've reverted to some old patterns. Sometimes she seems less thirty-five and more thirteen. Do not love that. But she's talking about using some of her settlement money for classes, maybe film or photography, I'm not sure. Obviously, she needs to find a job—"

The waiter suddenly approached with another round. "The gentlemen at the end of the bar sent these over with their compliments."

Gwen leaned forward with a wave and smile toward their grinning benefactors. "Please thank them for us," she instructed the waiter, "and—" she glanced at Libby, whose frown was fierce. "Let them know I'm here counseling my client about the murder of her husband, so we will not be joining them."

The waiter shot Libby a sympathetic glance then quickly departed.

"That was macabre." Libby laughed.

"Let's hope I haven't jinxed future husbands."

"There won't be any of those."

Before that topic could be further deconstructed, food arrived, and conversation gave way to eating. Briefly. Gwen couldn't stay quiet for long.

"Speaking of dating, you do know that upcoming is my third with Otto, yes?"

"I remain stunned that you date a guy named Otto."

"He transcends the name."

"What happened to your 'never date a guy from the office' rule?"

"I'm flouting it. And get this: when I told him I wanted to write a novel—"

Libby snickered; Gwen carried on.

"He offered the name of a writer friend who might be able to share some pointers. How sweet is that?"

"Sweet. Very, very sweet."

"Scoff all you want, but you had creative passions once. I hold out hope for their resurgence. Oh, speaking of dumb names, I ran into yours the other day."

Libby barely looked up. "Where did you see Bart? He never leaves Eagle Rock and God knows you wouldn't be caught dead there."

"Downtown farmer's market. Guess he was mixing it up."

"How'd he seem?"

"Fat. Ill-kempt."

"Nothing new there."

"Depressed."

"Probably why he's fat and ill-kempt. Did you talk to him?"

"Briefly. He seemed embarrassed. He must think you tell me everything. Late with the tuition check again?"

"That's what I get for marrying a freelance designer."

"That's what you get for divorcing one. You okay for money?"

"Sure." Didn't feel like opening that can of worms.

"Would you like me to see if Otto has a friend?"

The non-sequitur provoked an abrupt snap of Libby's head. "As much as I'd like to stick this fork in my eye."

Before either woman could say another word, Libby noticed the two gentlemen from the end of the bar moving their way.

"What part of 'murdered husband' do these guys not get?" Libby hissed, as she quickly stood and pulled her purse over her shoulder. She leaned in and gave Gwen a quick kiss. "Please pick up the check, I'll get the next one. I'm leaving you with these edgy Hollywood types to go home to my cranky daughter and the serenity of solitude."

Gwen's eyes lit up as she noticed the smiling approach of the two very handsome fellows. "Oh my, an embarrassment of riches. Libby, you've got to stay long enough to—"

She was already out the door.

CHAPTER 5

With its muted gray walls, sleek modern furniture, calendars, charts, and shelves of books, the admissions office at South Coast College of Film & Media made a smart impression while being reminiscent of every academic enclave Bridget had ever attended. There might even have been the old-school whiff of sharpened pencils, but that was probably sense memory.

She'd gotten herself there, again, after a long morning of juggling the pros and cons of this particular course of action (pros won, if temporarily), and was now in face-to-face discourse with Ellie Scamehorn, admissions director. With her intense eyes and sharp, direct patter, Ellie held the floor for the ten minutes required to discuss, "How best to get things started." Beyond her obvious expertise, everything about her, from the chic haircut to the stylish black suit, exuded "hip, young professional." Bridget, in jeans, a pullover sweater, dark, lanky hair in a messy bun, felt commensurately less so.

"Obviously, the salient question to ask, Bridget, is what experience are you looking for at SCC? You said you're interested in film studies; I'd love to know what your hopes and dreams are related to that field."

Hopes and dreams? Bridget had already told Ellie how her earlier college studies in film had been disrupted by a lack of career ambition, as well as her full-body immersion into the food service industry, but defining "hopes and dreams" demanded another language all together, one in which she wasn't particularly well-versed.

"I'm not sure. I've just always liked the medium. I was thinking about it earlier, and realized what I enjoyed most about running the wine bar with my ex was the creative stuff, you know? Shooting the promo videos for TikTok and Instagram, designing the photographs for the marketing materials, that sort of thing. My dad is a phenomenal graphic designer, so odds are good I got some of my creative talents from him." She stopped, hoping that would do.

"It's great to come from a creative family environment—"

"My parents are divorced; the creative stuff is just my father. My mom's an accountant."

"Well, wherever your creativity comes from, let's nurture it. Sound good?"

Bridget twitched in her seat. "My hesitance is partly because I can't afford to spend too much of my divorce settlement on college fees, especially for a career path I'm not sure makes sense at my age. I know I *need* a career path, but I can't dabble this time. Filmmaking, especially in this town, seems so delusional to me, you know? So pie-in-the-sky."

"If you presume you'll jump right from this program into an Academy Award, maybe. You might, I'm all for lofty goals, but there are lots of ways to utilize the skills you'll learn here without holding to that limited standard. Many of our former students run post-production houses, some make brilliant marketing films. One of my favorite alums took his degree and started a company that makes the most artistic, innovative wedding videos you've ever seen. He's now pulling six-figures, and his short documentaries are getting festival attention. There's lots of ways to parlay your talent, Bridget, not just Hollywood." She smiled warmly, clearly hoping to encourage enthusiasm.

Bridget nodded, if tentatively. "Thanks for the perspective. I hadn't thought of all that. I just know whatever I do at this point has to be the right thing. I can't afford to invest either my time or money unwisely."

"Keep in mind that loans and grants are also options. And our curriculum *is* designed for the adult student, which means we can accommodate work and family demands as they apply."

Work. An unfortunate reminder. "That's the other issue: I have to find a job. Plus, I'm still living at my mother's, which is awkward at this stage of my life. And beyond that, I'm older than almost everyone else here—"

"Bridget." Ellie gently interrupted. "You sound like you're trying to talk yourself out of this. Are you?"

A pause as she pondered the question. "I'm not. At least I don't think I am." She suddenly felt like the chair she was sitting on was too small, too constrained. *Why isn't a window opened somewhere?*

"Look, you're right to have these debates with yourself. It's important to get clear about any life-changing decisions you make. It *is* a rigorous program. I'd be doing you a disservice if I didn't push you to question just how much you want it, or how it might, or might not, fit into your current situation."

A flush of anger hit Bridget's bloodstream—*and here's another person suggesting I don't know what the hell I want for my life*—but logic intervened to remind her that she *didn't* know what the hell she wanted for her life.

"May I make a suggestion?" Ellie broke into the pause.

"Sure."

"One of the requirements for every applicant is to present a short piece that best exemplifies their voice, their artistic sensibilities. In your case, that could be a short film, a photographic collection, a marketing campaign mock-up, whatever you felt best presented your statement as an artist in the field you wish to pursue."

"Okay." She felt immediately overwhelmed.

Ellie, noting the shift, leaned forward. "Don't panic. What I'd like you to do while you're mulling your options is think about what you might present if you do apply. Explore what moves you, what stirs your imagination; what sort of presentation would speak in your voice. Meanwhile, this is something I like to give applicants who aren't sure what would best represent them. It's from an essay by one of our department heads and I think it captures the ethos of this place quite well. Can I read this one paragraph to you? It's short."

"Um, sure."

Ellie cleared her throat. "'What is our demand, our goal for being here? Must we all set the world on fire, make great discoveries, change the course of humanity? No, certainly not. But every opportunity we take to step towards individuality, every thought we have that leads to expressive freedom, every choice we make that shatters preconceived notions of who we are, what art is, how we define relationships; what age, race, orientation, or gender convey, is a minor rebellion. We are each capable of that worthy goal.'"

Ellie looked at Bridget with an open smile. "I love that. 'A minor rebellion.'"

"Yes, that's cool."

It was. She remained flummoxed.

★ ★ ★

Bridget was surprised to find Dean Park sitting on a bench across from the office as she opened the door. He leapt up when he saw her.

"I'm not stalking you; I promise," he said. "I just noticed you walk in earlier and was curious to see if you signed up."

She smiled, pleased. "Why are you so curious—it's Dean, right?"

"Yeah, Dean. I just figured you deserved a welcoming committee if you did. And, truth be told, I don't meet that many interesting, age-appropriate women on the job, so I was intrigued." He kept pace alongside her as she made her way to the door.

"I hate to disappoint you, but I didn't sign up."

"No?" His surprise registered.

"Not yet anyway." She abruptly stopped and turned to him. "I have no idea what I'm doing right now. My life is a mess, and I can't seem to make decisions. I'm newly divorced, living at my mother's, out of a job, and thinking about film school. How insane is all that?"

He continued following as she again charged toward the door. "You sound like a lot of people our age. Early midlife crisis. Nothing shameful about that. At least you're exploring your options, right?"

"That's a low bar."

"I don't think so." They reached the door. "Listen, why don't I buy you a cup of coffee, and we can discuss those options, see if anything jumps out?"

"Why would you waste your time doing that?" It was a sincere question.

"I don't know." He laughed. "I'm free right now, I need coffee, and mostly I'm interested."

She cocked her head, assessing the offer. It had been a long time since any man asked her to do anything that resembled something close to a date, and she wasn't sure she wanted to. Then Dean smiled again.

CHAPTER 6

Two weeks had passed since Chloe dropped the CPA bomb and Libby still hadn't delivered a response. Rob was scheduled home on Saturday, Bridget continued to flounder, and, quite honestly, she hadn't been able to stir up any desire at all to become a CPA. Not that being a CPA wasn't an admirable profession. It was the *becoming* that loomed large. Chloe alerted her at least twice in the interim that an answer would be needed by end of day Friday.

Just as that stressful thought receded, Chloe appeared at the entrance to her office. "Libby, you have a visitor." She escorted Bart Conlin, the ex, into the room, then mouthed *we need to talk,* as she graciously exited.

At fifty-seven, slumped, paunchier since even the last time she'd seen him, a worn baseball cap working hard to disguise his thinning pate, Bart was assembled like a guy who sits in afternoon bars eating stale peanuts and yelling at the TV. Libby's first thought when she saw him these days was "impossible to imagine." Imagine having been attracted to him, having sex with him, marrying him. Still, he was a decent enough fellow, the father of her children, therefore someone she would never be rid of. Given that, she made every effort to be civil, occasionally pleasant. On most days. Today wasn't one of those.

"Tell me you're delivering money." She couldn't even muster a smile.

He placed a crumpled white envelope on her desk. "And a good morning to you too. Look, I know this is late—"

"Three weeks late."

"Yes, which is why I wanted to drop it off." He looked around. "Wow, the store sure looks great. You guys do a nice job of—"

"Just tell me it's all there."

He plunked to the chair next to her desk with a dramatic sigh. "It's not, I'm sorry. It's been a bitch of a month."

The look she gave him could melt metal. "You mentioned that last time. Lots and lots of bitchy months, I guess."

"Libby, I'm doing the best I can—"

"Me too, Bart, me too. Yet his bills still have to be paid. This is not a good time to flake out on us. Rob is home in two days, which means all sorts of extra expenses, including groceries, which will double, triple, while he's here. His tutoring program is not cheap, his tuition for the Fall quarter is due, and I'm out of pocket on the last installment. With Bridget still at the house, it's—"

"I know, I know, I get it. Trust me, I'm not sitting around playing video games. I've taken on a new client, so things should pick up. I'm sorry, I really am; we're all struggling here."

Her teeth-clench was almost painful. "Some more than others, yet the buck always stops with me, doesn't it?"

"How could I forget?" he snapped. A pause, then. "Sorry. I'm just beat, and I feel like shit for not pulling my weight. This isn't my ideal scene either, Libby, but I'm doing everything I can to change it." The sincerity of his beleaguerment was clear.

She couldn't help but soften. The demands of Rob's existence, despite their unmitigated love for him, had long been a conundrum for them. His unplanned arrival in 2006, sixteen years after Bridget's, was both shocking and inconvenient, having interrupted a fractious time in their marriage that became terminal a few years later when Bart fell in love with a local sign-maker. He'd left the house shortly after Rob turned five, wanting to "give it a try" in a relationship that lasted only nine months, ending a week after Libby filed for divorce. Since then, they'd brawled, battled, and struggled to co-parent their beloved son, and clearly Bart was losing.

"I know it isn't intentional." She sighed, resigned to their roles in this recycling financial drama. "I just don't have a buffer to fill the gaps. After getting the chimney fixed and new tires on the car, I'm stretched as far as I can go. Please do what you can to get me the rest quickly. Or tell your son to eat less!" She attempted a wan smile.

He stood up, moving, she noticed, like a much older man. Funny how depression ages a guy. "I'll get him an In-N-Out card, that'll help. And I'll talk to him about finding a summer job. I know he's got this tutoring thing to deal with, but he can still do something part-time, contribute a little."

"Any help you can be on that front will be most appreciated."

"All right." He looked around as if reluctant to leave.

"Okay, Bart, thanks. I've got to get back to work."

"Yeah, of course. Again, sorry, Lib. I'll get the rest to you as soon as I can."

As he clumped out of the office, Libby opened the envelope. The number on the check did little to assuage her anxiety. She flung it into her mail basket, thoughts roiling, then stood and marched to Chloe's office. Her tap at the door brought an expectant gaze from her boss. She stepped in. "So, how do I sign up?"

CHAPTER 7

Charming was the word that kept popping into Bridget's head. Where her ex had been all dominant male energy and smoldering sexuality, Dean exuded a kind of quirky cool; smart and passionate about his craft with an easy take on life. She found him refreshing, liked his gentleness and simplicity. She wasn't sure she was attracted to him—there were none of the jolts and heart pounds of her first encounters with Seth—but she liked him, liked that he liked her.

After hearing her story, he filled her in on his own: father, Korean American, international banker; mother, a former Minnesota housewife; happily married and living in the Valley. One younger brother in Nevada, older sister, married with kids, in Sacramento. He confirmed he was thirty-four, never married, but recently ended a three-year relationship "that wasn't going anywhere." He wanted his own recording studio one day but was happy with his current arrangement; living in a new apartment not far from the school made logistics easy and that was appreciated.

After getting her agreement to brainstorm ideas for her potential application project, they met a few more times, always coffee or a food truck, nothing serious, nothing fancy. Nothing to imply it was anything more than two new friends sharing creative ideas. When Libby suggested dinner at the house, Bridget almost balked but didn't. He came up and it wasn't too arduous. Bridget thought Libby overdid the chirpiness but was grateful she didn't appear overly curious about the nature of their relationship. Which either meant she presumed it was more than it was or figured it wasn't.

Which was pretty much where Bridget stood on it.

CHAPTER 8

Rob wasn't coming home for the summer.

Sitting on the couch with her laptop open, Facetiming with her deeply missed son, Libby felt like she'd just been gut punched. Despite her plan to drive down to San Diego to pick him up the very next day, he announced that he'd just committed to a coveted summer job at the school's theater department. So instead of joining the newly configured family dynamic with Bridget in-house, he would spend the summer learning lighting design, a skill she had no prior knowledge was of any interest to him. Right now, and as much as she loved looking at his handsome, freckled face and the chaotic curls that framed it, she wished they were doing this without screens. She couldn't find a facial expression that hid her deep disappointment.

"That's a ... really big surprise. And you just found out about it today?"

Rob was lit up, excited and seemingly oblivious to his mother's letdown. "No, we've been talking about it for a couple of weeks, but a few things had to be worked out before it was for sure. I wanted to wait till everything was set before I told you."

Yes, before she filled the refrigerator with food specifically for him; before she hired the tutor to punch up his reading comprehension skills; before she cleaned every inch of the house and got new sheets for his bed.

"Uh huh, I see—"

"I know you're probably bummed—"

"I am—"

"But, Mom, you have to know, this is such a great opportunity. I'll even make a little money—"

"That's good, but—"

"—and it'll give me a real leg up in my career."

Again, not aware he had one of those. Or at least one related to theatrical lighting. "Oh, so you're looking to pursue a career in lighting design? For theaters?"

"I don't know if it's that specific, but I worked on the last production and really dug it. Seems like I have a talent for it, too, at least according to Hewitt."

"Hewitt?"

"The guy who runs the lighting department, Hewitt Taylor. They've got a couple of productions this summer, and when he asked if I wanted to stay on campus and be an assistant to the lighting team, I jumped on it. I'll be learning the design software *and* hardware, which, if I took classes for all that would be uber expensive, so I'm pretty stoked!"

He seemed stoked. Libby, less stoked.

"That's a good thing then. But what about your tutoring requirement? Obviously, that's a priority, and I already hired this woman—"

"I know, I know, Dad told me, and I'm real sorry about that, Mom. But getting that situation worked out was one of things I was waiting on before I called you guys. Turns out there's a TA here in the education program who tutors students staying on campus during the summer. I just arranged for her to work with me. And I don't have to pay anything; she gets school credit for the hours she tutors. I figured you'd appreciate that."

She did. She was also impressed that he'd taken responsibility to handle the matter. "I absolutely do; well done. But is what you'll be paid enough to cover the fees for the dorm? It all sounds great, but your dad and I don't have it in the budget to—"

"No worries on that either, Mom." He grinned like the proverbial Cheshire cat. "All handled. Hewitt worked out an arrangement with one of the dorms so his staff and interns can stay free-of-charge over the summer. I mean, we have to pay for our own food and laundry and stuff, but we'd be paying for all that no matter where I was, right? Anyway, I figure that pretty much makes this whole thing impossible to turn down." He was beaming.

She had no rebuttal. "Yes, it does. Sounds like you've got everything worked out. Though I should probably talk to Dad before—"

"We talked yesterday. He thinks it's a great idea."

"Does he?" The fact that she was second-in-line to hear about this major scheduling change contributed another kick. Strangely—or not so strangely, as he was often vigilant to the politics of his divorced parents—Rob picked up on her mood shift.

"And just so you know, Mom, I did call you first." His voice had softened. "Called yesterday, actually a couple of times, left two messages. But I had to give Hewitt an answer today, so when I didn't hear back, I finally checked with Dad. He said he couldn't imagine you'd have a problem with it."

Of course he'd say that. Of course she didn't.

At that critical juncture, Bridget and Dean clamored through the front door, and when she saw her brother's face on the computer screen, Bridget plunked down to join the conversation.

"Hey there, dork!"

"Hey back, dorkette!"

Libby was mutedly delighted they had jokes between them, suggesting they communicated with each other from time to time.

Bridget leaned into the screen. "I cannot believe, baby brother, that the first time I'm here in a hundred years I'm not going to see you."

Oh my God, Libby screamed internally. *Everyone* knew about this before she did?

"But then I got to thinking," Bridget teased. "Maybe it's a girl keeping you there, is that it? Have you got yourself a little girlfriend, or are you still planning to be a monk your entire life?"

"Perhaps it's my dating standards that bother you," Rob rejoined with a grin.

As they playfully bantered, Libby got up and checked her phone. He had, indeed, tried to reach her twice yesterday. Inexplicably there were messages, from him and others, she hadn't seen till now. She also noted her ringer was off. *Dammit.*

Returning to the living room, she saw that Dean had now jumped into the conversation, discussing the more technical, arcane aspects of Rob's new job, obviously comfortable taking a mentor role. "Sounds like you're already on top of things, Rob. Which is amazing, because that's a lot of hardcore stuff to figure out. But, hey, I'm learning that between you and Bridge this is one talented family."

"We can thank our dad for that." There was undisguised pride in Bridget's voice, which Libby caught. "We'll have to go over to his studio one of these days and look at some of his art and the ad campaigns he's done. He's an amazing designer, right, Rob?"

"Absolutely, but it's not just Dad." Rob grinned in Libby's direction. "He told me something the other day I'd never heard before. He said Mom was this amazing rock singer. Said she was the best 'chick singer' in L.A. when he met her; had a band and management and stuff, was really popular; he was the roadie for the lead guitarist—"

"Wait, *what*?" Bridget squealed, practically leaping off the couch. "Are you kidding me? Dad was a roadie? I cannot believe that. How cool must he have been?"

Maybe not as cool as being the lead singer, Libby internally snarked.

"Yeah, he said the band was amazing, and Mom was a stone-cold star. They recorded stuff, had all these industry people interested in them. It was wild to hear, Mom; I can't believe you guys never told us about it. It would've been awesome to know when I was younger and had friends to impress."

Bridget and Dean both turned to Libby, clearly interested in her response.

"Your father loves to wax on about that long-ago era of our lives. Yes, lots of fun, ancient history. But let's get back to you, Rob. Will you be home at all this summer, or is the idea that we'd—"

His phone suddenly pinged. "Oh shoot, sorry, Mom; I gotta go. There's a meeting happening right now, and it looks like I'm late."

"Okay, honey, but be sure to call Grandma and Grandpa like we discussed. They were hoping to see you this summer so they should probably know about your new plans, too."

He was up. "Sorry, Mom, gotta fly. Yeah, I'll call them tomorrow, promise. Good seeing you, Dean. And Bridge, be nice to Mom, okay?" And he was off.

As Libby disconnected the call, Bridget scowled in her direction. "What, did you tell him I *wasn't* being nice to you?"

"Absolutely not." Libby closed the laptop and headed to the kitchen. "But he does have a memory." She looked back and winked at Bridget. "You should call your grandparents too.

They both remarked last week that they haven't heard from you. Apparently, they were planning to send plane tickets to both you and Rob for a visit, which would be so fun, right?" Libby had to smile; she knew that both kids, while they loved her parents, didn't particularly enjoy Texas or the retirement village where they were currently ensconced.

"Ugh. Houston. But, yes, I'll call. Grandma actually cried when I told her I was getting divorced."

"I don't think she ever got over mine, so I can imagine. By the way, Dean, I noticed you and Rob seem to already have a rapport and I was curious when you'd met, so to speak."

"We Facetimed him last night," Dean answered. "Once we heard he wasn't coming home, Bridge wanted us to connect."

"That's really nice. Hopefully, he'll get home at least once or twice over the summer. Or we can all caravan down there; San Diego's not that far. Anyway, he's a great kid. I'm really going to miss him this summer." She turned away, unwilling to share her welling eyes.

"Yeah, I bet. But, hey, so wild about you singing in a band, Mrs. C. How long ago was that?"

"A long time ago. And please—*Libby*."

"Right, Libby. But what, like late '80s, something like that?"

She sat down at the kitchen desk, focused on a grocery list. "Something like that."

"And you've got tapes and everything?"

"I do, somewhere."

"Wow!" Dean, genuinely impressed, smiled like a kid. "Bridget never mentioned it—"

"Because *Libby* never mentioned it," Bridget retorted. "God forbid we should know anything about her life before we came along."

Libby turned to her. "Actually, I think I did tell you about it at some point during your childhood."

"Apparently before my undeveloped brain had the ability to retain information, because I have no memory of us discussing any of that, which, frankly, is really weird. And you talk about me not being forthcoming."

Libby looked at her sharply, ready to clap back, but Dean jumped in. "I'd really love to hear your music sometime. If you found the tapes, we could hook them up at SCC and—"

"SCC?"

"South Coast College of Film & Media—"

"Oh my God, Mom, the school I'm looking at," Bridget snapped, "where Dean works, which I've only mentioned to you about a thousand times."

The recurring snarl in her daughter's voice got Libby's jaw clenching. "The initials just threw me, Bridget."

Dean, noting the tension, persisted. "Honestly, if the tapes are something you'd like to share, just know I'm up for it. Got plenty of analogue machines to work with."

Bridget bounced up before Libby could further respond, heading toward the staircase. "Yes, thank you, Mother, for that fascinating glimpse of familial history, and I'm sure we'll all enjoy hearing your mysterious music when hell freezes or whatever it takes for that to happen, but right now I'm going to grab a few things, then we're off to Dean's studio for an evening soiree."

Dean shot her a look which, oddly, seem to curb her ire, something Libby immediately noticed. In fact, Bridget's general demeanor had lightened up in recent weeks, which, it now seemed possible, had something to do with him; his attention, perhaps; his helping hand, his ease. Whatever it was, Libby was grateful.

As Bridget bounded up the stairs, Libby turned to Dean. "Regarding my music, it's not all that mysterious, I promise you, it's just so long ago it's been easy to forget. Maybe one of these days I'll dig out some tapes and thrill you all."

"That would be very cool. I'd love to hear them."

Bridget returned with a jacket and bag in hand and headed for the door. "We should get going, Dean. You said the party started at six."

He looked at his phone. "Yep, we should hit it. Nice to see you again, Mrs. C, and let me know when you find those tapes."

"Okay, will do. You two have fun," Libby called out, not bothering to correct her name this time.

Bridget was gone without a goodbye.

As the door closed and the house grew quiet, Libby felt a slow wave of something close to grief settle over her. Gazing around the room with its high beamed ceiling and wrought iron chandeliers, its comfortable seating and gorgeous view; the open play area where children danced, balls were bounced, and dogs once chased little boys around a coffee table, Libby sank to the couch, as sad and lonely as she'd been in a very long time.

CHAPTER 9

The gathering at the school was brief, pleasant, and, for Bridget, an eye-opener. Ten other instructors came by Dean's studio for beer and pizza, lots of conversation about the summer schedule; everyone met Bridget and joined with Dean in sharing accolades about the school and the film program in particular. She enjoyed their enthusiasm—which succeeded in both exciting and intimidating her—and felt a sense of fitting fairly comfortably into the group. They ran the gamut from late twenties to early-fifties and seemed like people who might become friends.

Since most were obligated to get home to wives, husbands, families, and dates, everyone was gone by seven-thirty. After Bridget and Dean cleaned up the pizza boxes and empty cups strewn around the room, she grabbed her bag as if readying to leave, but he sat down at the mixing board; pulled up some tracks and started fiddling with them. She got the impression he wanted her to see him in action. Which was sweet. She didn't mind. She sat on the couch to listen.

The recording featured a female vocalist Bridget didn't find particularly appealing, but the band was good, the song engaging.

"Who's that?"

"Some sophomores from the CGI department. They're called The Graphics, which kinda makes sense." He grinned over his shoulder. "What do you think?"

"I'm not wild about her voice, but the song is good. Obviously, the recording is great." She smiled back. "Is it for a school project?"

"No, they're playing out, working some clubs around town; they want to post up some stuff, make a CD they can hand out at their gigs."

"Do you do a lot of outside work in here, too?"

"A fair amount. I have an arrangement with the school. For example, this group pays for studio time because it isn't a school project, but I can give them a killer deal." He looked up from the board. "Funny you don't like her voice; I think she's pretty good."

The comment piqued Bridget's curiosity. She wondered if his interest in the singer was purely professional. "Is she a friend of yours?"

"Sure, they're all friends. I've been to a couple of their gigs, but I don't know her outside of that. I agree her sound is a little odd, but the oddness is what I like. It's intriguing, I think." He went back to the mix. "Just give me a minute here."

Bridget watched him briefly, then picked up a magazine from the end table and fanned through. Put it down, pulled out her phone, scanned without purpose. She felt restless; wanted to get home. Maybe it was something about people having actual projects they were doing, art forms they liked, and voices that were deemed intriguing. Meanwhile, she was job hunting and watching TV.

He caught the mood shift and looked over. "You okay?"

"Just tired for some reason."

He spun his chair around. "Okay, I'm done. We can go." As she stood up, he gave her a serious look. "Hey, did all the cheerleading from everyone make you feel pressured about signing up?"

She liked that he'd picked up on that. "Maybe. I think I'm feeling a little inadequate these days."

"Don't. You'll get there. By the way, I wasn't sure we'd talk about this tonight, but I've got kind of a cool idea for your admissions project."

"Yeah?"

"Might be totally out there, but I figure it's worth a discussion. Want to hear it?"

Interested, she sat back down. "Sure."

He leaned forward. "I've been working with a band—not this one, another group that's been playing out for a while. They've got no label, no management; they gig constantly, post their stuff on Spotify, Insta, Tik Tok, Bandcamp, SoundCloud, everywhere and wherever; they do all the usual social media stuff, basically everything they can do on their own." He paused.

She was lost. "Okay."

He grinned. "Stay with me. They've sold over 2000 CDs at gigs, which is amazing, and have a shit-ton of downloads. Their YouTube channel is exploding, TikTok is wild, and now they're getting heat from some label. They've been in here for the last month doing another record. Which got me to thinking about your mom."

The non sequitur was so jarring, Bridget couldn't hide her headshake. "Whoa. How does even a speck of that have anything to do with my mom?"

"I guess I didn't exactly set that up right." He laughed, his excitement palpable. "First off, I think it's awesome that she was this '80s rocker."

Bridget cocked her head. "It's mildly exotic for a frumpy middle-aged housewife."

"Is her stuff any good?"

"I wasn't kidding when I said I don't know. I honestly forgot she even sang until Rob brought up today. I have a vague memory of hearing some of it when I was really little, but I don't think I've heard her mention it for the last thirty-some years, so it clearly wasn't a big deal to her. But what's the connection with all this?"

"That era is still really trendy, probably always will be. Bands in here are mixing '80s sounds into their tracks every day—that's what these guys I've been telling you about are doing. So, how cool would it be to take tracks that are authentically *from* that time and post them up, with new packaging and a cool name, and see how they fly?"

Bridget looked at him with a mix of confusion and fascination. "How *what* flies?"

"Okay, here's the whole idea—I help you put the music tracks together, do whatever it takes to get them digitized, cleaned up if need be. You film a mini-doc, maybe interview your mom about that era in music, compare it to now, maybe talk to some of the groups I have in here; we post it up as an experiment to see if we can make her music translate in the current marketplace."

"That's so random."

"Is it?"

"Kind of. I mean, who would be interested in some old singer no one's ever heard of? It could be embarrassing."

"For her or for you?"

"Both?"

"Okay, so we don't reveal who she is or her age, we leave her out of it for now. We just get some background stuff from her for context, then package it anonymously, don't say anything about when it was recorded, and let the music take the lead, see what happens. See if people like it. It all depends on the music."

"Which I don't remember."

"Can you get any of her tapes?"

"I don't know. She made it sound like they'd be hard to find, but she keeps all her old stuff in the attic, so they're probably up there somewhere."

He stood and started shutting down the mixing board. "I don't know, maybe it's a lame idea. The music could also be crappy garage band junk we couldn't clean up enough anyway. Lots of that going around in those days. But if nothing else I think it's an original idea, don't you?"

"It's definitely original," Bridget snorted.

He stopped and turned to her. "You think it's too lame?"

She so rarely thought about her mother, certainly about her mother's life prior to her arrival, that she didn't know what to think. "I don't know. Maybe. Maybe not."

"Fair enough." He continued flipping switches and closing boxes, shuffling papers and folders, silent long enough that she noticed the pause.

"I'm not trying to negate your idea, I just—"

"No, no, it's cool." He dropped to his seat and swung around to look at her. "And maybe it is too random, or just not the right fit. I notice things get pretty stressed between you two, so I get that it might not be comfortable involving her in anything you're doing."

Bridget felt a jolt of chagrin, embarrassed that her churlish behavior had been so transparent. It was such a baked-in, knee-jerk response, and had been for so many years, its obviousness eluded her most days. Which, in this moment, was mortifying.

"Yeah, sorry about that. It's just what happens between us. It's always been that way, for as long as I can remember. I get twitchy around her for some reason, so many things she does or says irritate me. I don't know why, and I'm not saying it's fair or even her fault. I'm probably being overly critical. But it's what happens."

Her face flushed in the confession, but his response was empathetic. "Hey, I get it. As someone who's not her kid, she seems pretty great to me, but I know how it can be with families. My sister's always at odds with my mom, but me and my brother get along with her just fine. It's chemistry, different personalities. But you know what? Let's shelve this idea for now and see what else we can come up with, okay?"

Bridget stood up, walked across the room, and gazed at a bulletin board as if pondering the posts, stretching her shoulders; exhibiting the traits of someone uncomfortable in the moment. She finally blurted, "I'm not saying that."

He looked up from the console. "What?"

"I'm not saying we should abandon the idea completely. It just hit me a little weird at first. But I'll think about it. Maybe it is clever."

"Yeah?"

She turned to him with an abashed smile. "Yeah. Maybe."

He flushed with a grin. "Fantastic. Main thing will be the music, seeing if it's good enough to even pursue the idea. If you can grab one or two of her tapes, that'd be key. We'll give them a listen and go from there. Want to at least try?"

"Yeah, sure." She came back to the couch, picked up her bag again, and found herself inexplicably shy around him. She wasn't sure why, but his entreaty about the project felt touching somehow. That he thought of her mother that way. When even she didn't.

Dean suddenly stood and wrapped his arms around her, leaned in for kiss, clumsy and tender. Bridget's immediate reaction was to pull away; he almost leapt back in response.

"Sorry, sorry. Went with an impulse, sorry. Completely off-base? Too soon?" Now he was blushing.

It was. Yet she also felt something she hadn't experienced in a long time: the rush of desire. The thrill of being wanted. By a kind, sweet man. She arched up on her tiptoes and planted a brief kiss on his cheek, then turned and headed toward the door, smiling.

CHAPTER 10

After an exhausting day for Libby and continuing bouts of introspection for Bridget, their evening at home was one in which peaceful coexistence had been achieved, however temporary. A night when energies were mild, talk was easy, and the warmly lit house felt homey and comfortable. They'd just finished Facetiming Rob, making his presence felt and tangible. Bridget was cleaning up after dinner, earbuds vibrating loudly enough to be heard across the room. Libby sat hunched at the kitchen desk going through an online banking journal with ripples of financial dread.

It could have been 2008.

Shutting down the offending spreadsheet, and with Rob's good cheer still suffusing her mood, Libby sat back and noted how the cycling waves of pleasure and sadness she felt permeated in equal measure. These moments of nostalgia were happening more often these days. Maybe it was having Bridget home; maybe it was missing Rob's physical presence. She could close her eyes and pretend there were still two children here, two children who still needed her; wanted her involvement and contribution in their lives; still made plans with her permission, coveted her approval, looked forward to favorite dinners by her hand. She could push past the distance and divorce, the fracturing of their family life, the separate tracks they each now traveled, and feel as though they were once again an entity, cohered and connected.

Libby suddenly caught Bridget gazing her way, a strangely wistful expression on her face. "What?"

Bridget pulled out her ear pods. "Do you ever wonder why we don't talk to each other about much, I mean, that matters?"

"I do." This wasn't Bridget's usual approach, so it felt surprising. Fragile. "Why do you think that is?"

Bridget paused. She'd given some thought to the question since Dean's comments of the other night. His awareness of the tension between her and her mother had embarrassed her. No one outside her family had ever called her on the behavior, ever brought it to her attention. It was a bad habit of such tenure it had simply become part of her personality, which was likely why she'd been unaware of how obvious and jarring it could be to outside parties. There was shame in that. She'd decided to make an effort to change it.

"I don't know exactly why, Mom," she said, full-frontal candor still a struggle. "Why do you think it is?"

"I've always gotten the impression you don't enjoy having deep, meaningful conversations with me, sometimes *any* conversations with me, so I've let you call the shots in that arena. Which is probably some form of parental abdication. Maybe I should've pushed harder, tried to connect more. I'd actually love to know more about your life, what you're thinking at any given moment."

"Okay. So let's talk."

"Right now?" Libby again wondered if Dean was responsible for her daughter's sudden interest. Whatever it was, she'd take it. "Yeah, why not?"

"Okay. What would you like to talk about?"

"How about why you never told me about your singing, about that part of your life, at least that I can remember."

Not what Libby was expecting. "Is your father still carrying on about that?"

"No. It's just something I'd like to know more about. But speaking of Dad, why didn't *he* ever talk to us about your music either, at least not until the other day? He was involved in it too, so it seems like he should have. It was how you guys met; it's a pivotal family story. I don't get the mystery of it."

"I don't think either of us meant to *not* talk about it." Libby remarked. "It's just one part of our past, our childhoods, really so long ago, with so much life in between, it hasn't been much of a topic of conversation for either of us."

"Dean finds it fascinating."

"Does he?"

"Music is his business; it's not so strange he'd be fascinated."

"But you're not?" Libby teased.

"Hey, I'm the one who wanted to talk about it." Her eyes flashed, but she quickly resisted the snark impulse. "If it was a part of your life that meant something, I'd think you'd want to share it with us. Unless it's some kind of deep, dark secret."

Libby took a breath. "It did mean something to me. It meant a lot, actually. It was an amazing era of my life. It was just—it was just a long time ago."

"You already said that."

"Well, it was!"

"At your age, everything was a long time ago." Her smirk softened the blow.

"Finish the dishes, demon seed." Libby laughed in response.

Bridget went back to the sink, muttering, "So I guess we'll just keep this topic a great big mystery."

An inscrutable look flitted across Libby's face. "Honey, it's not a mystery. I just tend to let go of my past, which I think is healthy. I learned a long time ago that holding onto youthful imaginings isn't always a productive use of one's time."

Bridget's knitted eyebrows made clear she wasn't buying the feint. "I get that in a general self-help kind of way, but if you were the 'best chick singer in L.A.,' like Dad says, with lots of people interested in you and your band, it had to have been a pretty big deal. So if it's *not* a mystery, tell me what happened, why you stopped. I'm interested."

Libby got up and started collecting papers from the desk. "Lots of reasons. Mostly I just grew up and had to get on with things. But let me see if I can find some souvenirs from that time, okay? I'll be happy to share them with you." Her cell buzzed, welcomed distraction from the conversation. She looked at it, let it go to voicemail. "It's Gwen. I'll have to call her back. There was a third date so she's no doubt got something urgent to impart."

"Everything okay with her?"

"She's dating a guy named Otto; how okay could it be?" Libby grinned.

Bridget had known Gwen her whole life, and even from a young age had been regaled with the hilarity of her dating antics. "Well, enjoy that colorful event. I'm going over to Dean's studio. All right to take your car?"

"Sure, but wow, you two are sure spending a lot of time together. That's really nice."

"Mom." Bridget winced. "Please don't. He's a friend. If I do apply to SCC, he's going to help me with the admissions project, that's all."

Libby didn't need the admonition: She was already berating herself for being a cliché. "I'm sorry, that was a dumb way of putting it. I like Dean, and I'm glad you've got a friend helping you out. That's all." She grabbed the keys; tossed them to

Bridget. "Have fun, drive safely. I don't care if you are thirty-five; you're living with me at the moment, so I worry."

Bridget found that oddly touching. "By the way, Mother, we are going to finish this conversation."

Libby looked at her wryly. "Wasn't it done?"

Bridget rolled her eyes.

"Okay, daughter. We will soon sit down and deconstruct my teenage dreams."

"I'd like that."

Which surprised Libby; that she seemed honestly interested. She smiled as she turned toward her bedroom. Breadcrumbs from Bridget. She'd take them.

CHAPTER 11

Libby tucked under the comforter, gazing around her room, her sanctuary. With beveled windows that opened to the gorgeous hillside, dark green walls cluttered with paintings and photographs she loved, stacks of books tilting on every capable surface, she felt warmed by everything in the room that was so *her*.

Then she reluctantly thought about returning Gwen's call.

She adored her friend but was less enamored of what would surely be an overly detailed replay of her date with a man Libby had met only once and of whom she had no opinion. *But this is what we do*, she reminded herself, *this is my role right now*— even if the favor was never returned because Libby never had dates to discuss. Which got her to thinking about Gwen's earlier lecture and the undeniable aloneness (she rejected the word *loneliness*) of her life.

She and Bart had been divorced long enough that natural evolution would normally have ushered in a new man by now. It hadn't. Not that she didn't meet men—Gwen couldn't stop dragging "hopefuls" to her table for introduction and interaction—she just couldn't stoke up the interest. Mostly because the particular men Gwen dragged up didn't interest her, but also because the whole complicated endeavor of dating held little appeal.

She liked men in general. She remembered liking sex. She appreciated feeling attractive and coveted. But, almost without noticing, some essential lifeforce had dissipated in the protracted transition from full-time mother and alpha-wife to a barely-there parent and forever divorcee of a man who'd cheated on her in that most banal of ways: with a younger, prettier, less burdened women with great arms and lots of money. Though that lovely young woman didn't last long, the detritus of Libby's imploding life had. She couldn't shake it. And now it was like a chronic injury that no antidote could ameliorate.

But a phone call was waiting.

★ ★ ★

In her gorgeously appointed, very glamourous, condo in the sparkling downtown Libby could see from her window, Gwen perched on a king-sized Duxiana, casual in silk pajamas, manicured hand wrapped around a large glass of wine, and proceeded to debrief with enthusiasm. The date had been, as Libby expected, a wonderful, if largely uneventful, undertaking, meaning, and without need for explicit mention, no sex. But, Gwen insisted, "The chemistry is definitely there; we're just being prudent, given work-related proximity and mutual slews of previously rushed disasters."

Then followed a far-too-long soliloquy about Otto's life (something Libby had even less interest in than the timing of their eventual sex), and how his life choices were influencing her own. Somewhere in the conversation, Libby realized she'd drifted. "Wait, so you didn't go back to his condo?" she whisper-talked.

"No. I just said that. Are you sleeping?" Gwen snapped. "And why are you whispering?"

"I'm not sleeping, though I'd like to be. And I'm whispering because Bridget hasn't left yet, and grown children tend to be nosy and lacking in discretion."

"This is not classified information, for God's sake."

"I just don't want—"

"Though my love life *is* racier than yours."

"So is my grandmother's."

"The dead one?"

"Exactly."

Gwen guffawed. Her laugh could only be described as a guffaw. Loud and concussive. Libby often wondered if men exposed to it thought it inelegant, but given Gwen's frequent and sustaining attention from men, clearly not.

"On that topic—" Gwen continued.

"We're not on that topic."

"I've made an executive decision about something I know you'll hissy fit over, but I want you to listen without prejudice."

Libby slunk lower into her pillow. "Already sounds hideous."

"It could be. It could also be the first day of the rest of your life."

"Kumbaya, sister." Libby eyerolled. "What?"

"You have a date with a guy named Jeff," Gwen announced brightly.

Libby abruptly sat up. "*No.* I do not." No brightness was evident in her tone.

"You do. One, it's a perfectly acceptable name; two, I met him, he's good-looking, funny, pleasant; and three, Otto says he's a stand-up guy. And it's just coffee, so no arguing."

Libby sprang from her bed, feeling immediate and, perhaps, disproportionate annoyance. "Why do you do that, Gwen?" Real anger framed the question. "I get that you find something humorous about my solitary state of life, but I don't appreciate you pimping me out to your new boyfriend's boyfriend because *you* can't tolerate my willingness to keep my own company."

There was a weighted pause.

"Wow," was all Gwen could manage. "*Pimping* you out?"

Libby slumped back down. "Too much?"

"A little."

"Gwen, my darling best girlfriend, I know what you're trying to do and I—"

"What am I trying to do, Libby? What?" Now she was spinning some vexation.

"You're trying to make my life seem happier *to you*."

"Huh. That's an odd way of putting it, painting me as the narcissist you clearly think I am."

"Maybe not a *clinical* narcissist, but I do think—"

"So tell me, is your life so happy for *you*?"

Dammit. "Here's the better question," Libby offered. "Would dating some guy *make* my life happier? Not necessarily. Likely not. The truth is, Gwen, my life is fine, it's good. It really is. I've got my daughter here, which makes me feel somewhat useful. I have a son I adore who'll get me down to sunny San Diego, a place I enjoy. I'm going to be a CPA and make tons more money. I like where I work, I love where I live, I have you. I have other peripheral friends—"

"What peripheral friends? I'm not aware of these people."

Libby felt cornered. But there *were* other women, friends she'd made during Rob's school years, PTA moms who'd made the transition from school culture to the occasional 'let's grab lunch or walk Bronson Canyon.' Gwen didn't know them; during the pandemic they stuck to phone calls, and, more recently, Libby got together with them less and less often, but still, they were there. Peripherally.

"You don't know everyone in my life."

"Since when?"

"Since I had children and, therefore, many, many opportunities to spend time with other parents who occasionally like to get together and do things you wouldn't enjoy, like hiking and yoga."

Gwen huffed as though this were irrelevant and ridiculous. "Okay, whatever."

"All I'm trying to say is, I quite possibly have a fuller life than you give me credit for." She didn't. "But either way, my life is okay enough, and for now I can live with that. Apparently, you can't."

There was a pause, then Gwen burst into one of her louder guffaws. "Oh, my God, Lib, you're right. I *am* a narcissistic bitch. I keep thinking that because your life would drive me fucking nuts it should be more like mine."

"Flattering," Libby commented dryly.

"You know what I mean."

"I do."

"If you're okay, I'm okay."

"Please find more contemporary clichés."

"But, hey," Gwen continued, putting down her wine glass and pulling her laptop open. "I'm going to email you his picture anyway."

CHAPTER 12

While the phone chatter continued in Libby's bedroom, and with plans to head directly to the studio, Bridget realized this was an opportune moment for clandestine measures.

Upstairs was a shabby loft area that was poorly lit and just as poorly decorated, haphazardly fitted with a pullout futon and small dresser that had designated it the guest room in earlier days. Given its uninviting décor, as well as the dearth of visiting guests, it was never a place anyone spent much time; now it was just a throw-away room. A hobbit-sized door at the far end of the loft led to an undeveloped space under the pitched roof which stood-in as an attic. No one spent any time in there either. At least, not anymore.

During her middle school years, Bridget did attempt to carve out a little spot behind that door, not too far into the drafty, slightly creepy, space, just somewhere for her to escape when family life rubbed raw. She'd fashioned a tent out of quilts and old boxes, decorated it with discarded camping lights and whatever living room castoffs could be found, and called it "Bridget's Den." It served a purpose, but, ultimately, the generalized gloom of the place, along with the thumps and scratches of roof-roaming wildlife (usually racoons) drove her off. It had been years since she'd been up here, and as she pushed the diminutive door open to look inside, it appeared smaller and creepier than remembered.

A bare bulb hung from the overhead beam, swinging in the draft that wafted through the century-old roofing shingles.

Bridget pulled the worn string to avail its dreary illumination, and as she stepped into the shadows, dust skittered with every move. Her eyes trailed past boxes of old clothes and photo albums, worn furniture being inexplicably saved, and various mounds of various things. There was no evidence of her make-shift hideaway, but as she slowly made her way through the maze of salvage, stepping around unidentifiable heaps of random items, she unexpectedly came upon her quest: Dusty stacks of half-concealed analogue tapes.

A couple of ratty quilts were thrown over an impressive pile of boxes in two different sizes. Even the way they were being "preserved" indicated her mother's disregard for their survival. Bridget gingerly lifted off a quilt, sending up enough dust to trigger a cough. Stifling it quickly for the sake of stealth, she pulled out one of the larger boxes, examining it as if it were an anthropological find. She opened the top flap to reveal thick two-inch tape with a sheet of paper, a chart of sorts, atop. It was marked: *Liberty/Final Masters, Juniper Studios, 2/1/88, Tape 1, Track Sheet.*

She pulled out another similarly marked box. Opened it. Its track sheet fluttered out. She picked it up and read: *Track 1—kick, Track 2—snare*; her fingers traced to Libby's name in the box marked *lead vocals*. It was surprising, the surge of emotion that hit her in that moment. It was real; this made it real. Her mother had been a singer, a singer who recorded in a place that wrote her name in the box designated for "lead vocals." Bridget stood, trying to picture it. She couldn't. It was impossible, but it left her feeling strangely anxious.

With a confused sigh, she grabbed a couple of the smaller boxes, the reel-to-reels as instructed earlier by Dean, tucked them into a canvas tote she'd brought up with her, and slipped out of the dusty mausoleum of her mother's life.

CHAPTER 13

The lobby of SCC was empty and well lit. Bridget stood outside, having texted Dean, waiting for him to come and open the door, their first encounter since the chaste kiss of the other night. Her pulse quickened as he approached, smiling at her as if no one made him happier, and she felt—instead of delight—a rush of panic. *What am I doing? I'm barely divorced. This is stupid.*

But Dean exhibited no such reticence. He pulled her into an enveloping embrace, which she returned with, perhaps, a little less exuberance. He didn't appear to notice.

"You look nice," he said, remarking for the first time on her sartorial presentation. He brushed the top of her head with his lips.

She had, in fact, taken longer than usual to put herself together, clear evidence of the evolving nature of their relationship. She blushed at his compliment. "Thank you."

Walking to the studio, his arm around her, he remarked with excitement. "So you found the tapes. Amazing."

"Right here. I brought two." She pulled a box from her bag. "The reel-to-reels, right?"

"Yep. Those'll have completed mixes on them. If we end up wanting to finesse anything, that's when we'd need the two-inch masters. No point worrying about that yet."

As they entered his studio, she noted that though there were a few discarded coffee cups and an empty fast-food bag or two, it seemed Dean consistently kept his space neat, which, from Bridget's perspective, was a point in his favor. She flashed on how sloppy her ex had been and appreciated Dean's attempt at order. She also realized she was now observing and comparing him as if compiling a dossier. *Stop it.*

He threaded the quarter-inch tape through a large recorder, clicking everything into place like the pro he was. Looking over the sheet included in the box, he turned the machine on. A whirring sound filled the speakers. "There are four songs on here. The first one is called 'What Can I Do.' Ever heard it?"

"If I have, I don't remember."

He pressed the play button. They both sat at the console, Dean expectant, Bridget anxious.

There was the familiar hiss of rolling analogue tape. Suddenly, the punch of a keyboard; drums, bass, and guitar crashed in around it, driving the track with the jangly, sparkling edge of '80s production sensibilities. The groove was infectious, the quality of the recording, stellar. Bridget felt a clutch of anticipation, waiting for Libby's vocals to kick in.

Then they did.

She leaned back in her chair as if struck. The voice ringing from the speakers was nothing she could have imagined emanating from her mother. Not only was it clear, powerful, and quite brilliant, but it conveyed a soulful emotionality that made the hair on her arms stand up. She felt hot tears rush to her eyes and she didn't even know why.

"Holy fuck!" Dean exclaimed; his face lit with amazement. When the first song finished, he paused the tape, turning to Bridget, wide-eyed. "Fucking hell. She's insane. *Insane.* You don't remember hearing this?"

"No," Bridget said so softly he barely heard her.

"No?"

"No. I honestly think I would have remembered this." She got up and moved away from the deck, flustered and disoriented.

"I am completely blown away," he continued, oblivious to her state. "I figured it might be okay, but this is hit record stuff. Star quality. Great production, great song, solid band, and, damn, kick-ass vocals. Your mother so fucking rocked. I can't believe she isn't famous." He looked at the sheet in his hand. "Okay, next one is 'He Used to Know Me.' Let's keep going."

He punched the button, and another infectious, raucous tune poured out. Libby's voice was at turns soft and sexy, then wild and filled with rage. It was an inspired performance.

While Dean stood at the console nodding to the beat of the music, Bridget slid down to the couch. There was no way to identify the tsunami of emotions that swamped her. It was as if, in this singular moment, she realized the woman she tangled with, loved, hated, defied, adored, ran away from, and came back to, was—or at least *had* been—a completely different person than the woman she knew now, the one she'd known her entire life. She didn't know *this* person on these tapes. She couldn't reconcile this person with the woman she'd had a pleasant chicken dinner with earlier tonight. This person was an explosion, a revelation, an exciting young voice, someone who'd obviously had reasons for her dreams, for seeking something, for *reaching* for something.

The woman she knew was none of those things. Where did it all go? Where did *she* go? Bridget had no idea. Which shook her, to know so little about her own mother, this part of her mother's life, a part that had clearly been an essential and driving force.

Dean finally turned and saw her clear anguish. "Oh man, Bridget, I'm sorry. Am I being insensitive? Are you okay?"

"You're being fine," she said, quickly readjusting her demeanor. "I'm just so, so really, really surprised, that's all." It was an understatement but all she could get out.

He clicked off the recording and joined her on the couch, gently put his arm around her. "Yeah, it's got to be weird if you've never heard any of this before, to suddenly realize your mother was truly gifted. And at something she never shared with you guys."

She leaned into him. "It's definitely weird. And confusing. I feel like I don't know who she is anymore."

"I can understand that."

They sat quietly for a moment, then she wiggled out of his embrace and stood again, went to the little refrigerator, and grabbed a water bottle. "You want one?"

"No, I'm fine." He looked at her, unsure of how to proceed. "You okay?"

"I'm all right."

"Do you want to listen to the rest of them?"

She hesitated. Then: "Yes." She pulled the second tape out of her bag and handed it to him. "Let's listen to them all."

He smiled and stood up, moved to the console with undisguised enthusiasm. "Well, whatever else we've got here, I do believe you've got the makings of a very interesting admissions project."

She could only give him a tentative smile.

CHAPTER 14

Annoyed that her black jeans, a favorite item she'd avoided for months, would not zip up, Libby decided she looked like packed sausage in them anyway and went for a wiser choice. Vanity had been an inactive impulse in her life for far too long and clearly she was now paying the price for that neglect.

She examined herself in the mirror, slowly, closely. Given how infrequently she did that with any real candor, she was honestly surprised at how tired, ragged, and chunky she appeared. She wasn't sure how fifty-four was supposed to look, her own mother having been a very different sort of buttoned up matron at that age, but whatever she'd specifically made of the number was not the apex of appealing physicality. By any metric.

I love and appreciate my body. It was an affirmation Gwen insisted she verbalize daily. She didn't, she hadn't, and this, apparently, was the result.

Fifty-four. How did that happen? It had been difficult embracing the decade right from the get-go. Fifty. *Fifty.* When it happened four years ago, entering a decade that officially (optimistically) relegated her to mid-life, she found it impossible to believe she was an age others legitimately considered "old." Though she did, in fact, *feel* old. Certain body parts presented as old. It was as if arriving at that number, fifty, swung open the door to a club she didn't wish to but was forced to join. Though, "consider the alternative," was surely a valid argument. So she did; she considered it and agreed that feeling old was better, at the moment, than being dead.

Still, there was some distant, wistful part of her that remembered feeling young, *being* young, and she was convinced the mindset could be rehabilitated, which was partially why she'd agreed to this inexplicable interview today.

Libby was unclear why her mercurial daughter had taken such sudden interest in her "view of the '80s music scene," but ever since Rob had brought it up, Bridget seemed progressively more intrigued. Likely something to do with Dean's interest. But whatever it was, and in a fit of good-sportsmanship, Libby had agreed to chat with the two of them on the topic, which, apparently, would contribute in some way to Bridget's admissions project.

And though it made no particular sense, she felt obligated to look as much the part of "chick singer" as she could muster. She realized it was an audio interview, in her kitchen, with her kid and the guy her kid was hanging out with, so it didn't matter what she wore, how well it fit, or really, what her hair was doing. But for the sake of her daughter's pride (and some niggling of her own) she was compelled to make the effort to present as trendily as she could despite her status as a chubby, middle-aged, soon-to-be-CPA bookkeeper.

Fleeing from the unforgiving mirror, she grabbed a pair of more recent jeans in a bigger size, laid down on the bed, sucked her stomach in as far as it would go, tugged the zipper, and remarkably, achieved the goal. She rose carefully, not wanting to challenge the strain she'd just inflicted, flung a striped scarf over her black tunic top, fluffed her hair and applied enough spray to keep it where she'd put it.

It was going to have to do.

★ ★ ★

The dining room table was set with a vase of perky sunflowers, courtesy of the interviewers, with an iPhone placed strategically in front of Libby's designated seat. Bridget and Dean sat across, she with a notepad, he, a list of questions, and both appeared awkward.

It felt too formal, Bridget thought, too staid and artificial. Which was silly, really. This was, essentially, her home. The interviewee was her mother. And though she and Dean discussed the intent of the conversation, it still felt like a clumsy, amateurish attempt to trick Libby into revealing what she clearly hadn't chosen to reveal over the past many decades. Beyond that, having never talked to her mother about those pre-family years in music, at least in the detail she hoped to today, Bridget had historical disadvantage, which left her feeling graceless.

The plates had shifted since the night they listened to the tapes. Bridget found herself discombobulated, distracted, as if the foundational narrative of her family life, her childhood, her relationship with her mother, had been upended. It would have been one thing if the tapes were awful, mediocre even. She could have dismissed Libby's silence on the topic as logical. But to hear what they heard, to realize what a bona fide talent her mother had been yet chosen to abandon—bury away, in fact—was inexplicable. It both angered and saddened her, that Libby would hide the most interesting aspect of her life. But sitting here now, waiting to do this interview, demanded that Bridget put those confusions aside to, hopefully, excavate some deeper truths.

Libby finally swooped in with a folder in her hands, more makeup than usual, and what was clearly an attempt at dressing up. Bridget felt a flash of tenderness as her mother sat down.

"Thanks for doing this, Mom. I promise it won't take long."

"I am always delighted to spend time with you, and though I don't know what, exactly, I can provide that's of any value, I will do my best." Libby put the folder on the table, clasped her hands together, then sat back and looked at them expectantly. "Fire away."

"You don't mind if we record this, do you?" Dean asked, his finger poised over the record button on the phone.

Libby laughed. "As long as you don't blackmail me if I say anything stupid!"

"I doubt that'll happen." Dean smiled, pressing the button.

"Don't be so sure. It's been a long time since I've been interviewed."

"Oh, but you did interviews during your band years?" Bridget picked up the implication.

Libby looked almost startled. "I, uh, yes, from time to time. Nothing too exciting."

"Then you know the drill; we'd just like to hear your thoughts on your band years back in the day," Dean responded.

"And why, again?" Libby continued to be flummoxed about her role in this endeavor. "I appreciate the interest, but I'm not sure what about my past life is relevant to your admissions project."

"Okay, let me explain it a bit more clearly," Bridget said patiently. "You know that photography and film are where my interests lie, right?"

"Yes, of course. And you're very good at both, as I recall."

Bridget looked surprised by the compliment. "Thanks, Mom. Anyway, Dean and I brainstormed some ideas and decided that putting a short film together was the most obvious medium for me to use. And since I have access to Dean's interactions with contemporary musicians, as well as a mother who was active in the '80s, we thought it might be interesting to explore the similarities and differences between the music world now and then." Bridget quickly shot Dean a *Did I get that right?* look. He nodded approvingly.

"I guess I can see how that might be interesting, even if I'm not the most exciting example of *then*," Libby demurred.

"Let us be the judge of that." Dean smiled again. Clearly he was hoping to charm her into candor. "Maybe you could start with how it all began for you."

"Okay." Libby couldn't seem to relax her face; her mouth was tight, eyebrows flexed. She took a deep breath and began. "I obviously don't know anything about the music business today, but if I think about that time, what we were all doing and listening to, I guess I'd say things started to change in a big way when MTV came around, I think that was 1981. It was a wild, crazy evolution for every single aspect of the music world. What used to be all about sound suddenly got visual, too; it wasn't just the songs anymore, and that's when—"

"So sorry to interrupt," Dean nonetheless interrupted, albeit gently. "But before you get too far down that track, which I would like to hear about later on, it would be great if you could focus this first interview more on your specific experiences with your own band, like, how you got started, how you got in the band, how the band developed, that angle. Would that be okay?"

"Yes, yes, of course." Libby took another breath. "But I'm not sure how typical our experience was, and if you want the *era*—"

"Dean's right, Mom," Bridget jumped in. "Seeing it through your personal experience would be more interesting than just general stuff about the time. We can get that anywhere. I'd really love to hear your story."

The look that crossed Libby's face was inscrutable, bearing flashes of both wistfulness and panic. She opened the folder in front of her and took out three 8x10 photographs, spread them in front of Dean and Bridget. One was a studio shot of a band in full '80s regalia, including a very young Libby, hair sprayed high and wild, dressed in a tiny black and white skirt loaded with studded belts, and a biker jacket thrown over a sequined camisole. Another was a live shot: the band on stage under red, blue, and amber lights, young Libby in a fierce pose in front of the microphone, arms outstretched, mouth wide in a wail; a band of wildly attired, incredibly good-looking musicians huddled around her in classic rock star poses. The last was her singing directly to a group of clearly enamored fans leaning toward the edge of the stage reaching out for her. In each, the clothes, the hair, the makeup were extreme and completely of the time. And Libby was strikingly beautiful.

Bridget looked through them with stark awe. "Mom. Wow. I have never seen these before. I cannot believe you never showed them to me; I would've devoured them. I would've wanted to dress just like you when I was little, oh my God, for Halloween? And the band looks amazing. *You* look amazing. Is your hair really blue there? On the sides, where it's shaved?"

"It was pink once too, but yeah, I think that time it was blue." Libby chuckled.

"You know everyone's doing that with their hair now, right? Dyeing it all shades of the rainbow. You didn't even know you were ahead of your time."

"Oh, baby, we *were* the time; current kids are just borrowing." She winked, thrilled that her daughter was fascinated by the show-and-tell.

Dean was equally impressed. "These are awesome, Mrs. C."

"*Libby*, please."

"Right, Libby. Really awesome."

"Anyway, that's what we looked like. Very typical for the day."

"And the band was called Liberty; that was cool," Dean remarked.

"Band names are always tricky, but the guys liked my full name so that's what we went with."

"How did all this start, Mom, you singing in bands? I mean, did you always sing?" Bridget, still awkward with the interview process, struggled to find a question provocative enough to keep Libby talking.

"Yes, I always loved singing. Your grandma used to say I woke up singing and didn't stop till I sang myself to sleep. I remember riding my bike down the street belting out songs as loud as I could, the neighbors applauding from their porches as I flew by." She smiled at the memory. "When I got to high school and could start dreaming about my actual future, all I wanted to do was sing and write songs. I met Gwen our freshman year, and she introduced me to a classmate named Leroy Larson— I'll never forget his name—who played guitar. We put a duo together and did all the talent shows, sang at campus events and parties. Which was great fun, but I had much bigger dreams. Unbeknownst to your grandparents, Gwen and I started sneaking into clubs our sophomore year—things were a little lax with IDs in those days—and that's when I met Nick Jackson. He's the tall one right there." She pointed to one of the two guitar players in the photographs, a good-looking guy affecting a dreamy expression as he leaned back with his guitar.

Bridget grinned. "He's a hottie."

"He was. Though who knows what he looks like these days; rock stars don't always hold up well. Anyway, he was playing with a Van Halen copy band around town, and we'd seen them a couple of times. I developed a serious crush on him, and a bunch of us started hanging out with their crowd when his band played. He was going with the girl who did their hair and stage makeup, and clearly just saw me as some starry-eyed kid who was sort of a PG-rated groupie, but when I told him I wanted to sing in a band someday, he seemed to take that seriously. There was one night when Gwen and I and some of our other friends were sitting around the dressing room after one of their gigs; Nick was fiddling with his guitar, and asked if I would sing for him. I was terrified, but we found a song we both knew and, shaky as I was at first, I finally got into it and really let go. Got big applause from everyone, and he seemed impressed with my voice. In fact, I can remember exactly what he said: 'You just kill me.' Which pretty much made my head explode."

Bridget's eyes gleamed. "Amazing that you remember that detail."

"Oh, it was a *serious* crush." Libby grinned. "Actually, it kind of surprised me, his response."

"Why, though?" Bridget asked. "You must have known you were a good singer by then."

"The stuff I did at school was acoustic, and even though we always got compliments, and Leroy thought I was the next Pat Benatar, having this older, really cool, very talented guitarist and all his bandmates, even his girlfriend, tell me I was good, well, that was life-changing for me. It took the dream I had tucked away and pulled it right into the light, said it wasn't just whimsy. Kind of woke me right up."

Bridget looked back through the photographs as if picturing Libby's story in the context of these young men gathered around her.

Dean jumped back in. "So, that was the spark to it all?"

"It was. A few nights later he called, said he'd been wanting to put an original project together, asked if I'd be interested in giving it a shot as the lead singer, and of course I was. He kept one of the guys from the copy band, the drummer, then reached out to a few other players he knew from around town, all great musicians, all great guys; we got together and started rehearsing.

I had to keep it quiet so Grandma and Grandpa didn't stymy the whole thing—they thought I was rehearsing with Leroy every time I got together with the band, and I *was* only sixteen at the time. But Gwen was an expert at running interference with them, which saved my ass in many a circumstance, and when everything with the guys clicked into place, it was magic, really. The rest, as they say, is history."

Libby got up and started making a pot of coffee. Bridget and Dean looked at each other, uncertain of whether or how to continue. He nodded, and she perked up in response: "That must have been so amazing, Mom, I can actually picture it." She rolled her eyes at Dean, but he just smiled.

"It was." Libby came back to the table. "Of course, once they found out, Grandma and Grandpa went ballistic. They said I was too young to be spending time in Sunset Strip clubs, traveling around with a bunch of 'rock & roll hooligans,' as my dad put it, worried about what was happening with my schoolwork and all that, but I was undeterred. Because it turned out we were really, really good, and lots of people thought so. We wrote some great songs together, especially Nicky and I, and after not even a year of playing out we had a huge following, with financial backers and a manager; we recorded our stuff, played every club in town, ultimately did some road tours, opened for some big-name bands, built a lot of momentum ... what can I say, it was a stellar experience."

"Did you ever go for a record deal?" Dean asked.

Libby got up to check the coffee. "Of course. Everyone did. It was like the wild west back then, this crazy new wave era, MTV, like I was saying earlier. There was so much going on, it was a very fun time to be involved in the music business. It just never panned out for us in terms of a deal."

"How come?" Bridget asked. "I mean, as good as you were, and obviously you all looked the part, so—"

"Anyone want coffee?" Libby asked, pouring herself a cup.

"No, thanks," Dean chirped.

Bridget sank a little, aware that her mother had clipped her question.

Libby saw the shift and sat back down, put her hand on her daughter's arm. "Honey, it was just the way it went for us, you know? There were so many great bands and solo artists all vying for the big prize, not everyone was going to get picked."

"That's it? You just didn't get picked?"

"Pretty much. We couldn't make it happen, one of many bands who couldn't, and some of the guys got twitchy about that and, well, things just stopped working."

There was a pause as Libby meticulously attended to her coffee, sweetener, cream, lots of stirring. Bridget glanced at Dean.

"Um, here's another question, and not to get all dark," he interjected, "but given the time and general craziness of rock and roll life, did drug issues or anything like that have an impact?"

Bridget shot Dean a fierce look, stunned that he went there.

Libby, sipping her coffee, appeared unfazed.

"Sorry if that's too personal," he backtracked, face flushing. "I just wondered because I know a few vets from that time who saw their own bands blow up because of drugs and related bad behaviors. Pretty rampant in the day; still is, unfortunately." He was truly fumbling at this point.

"No, it's a fair question. Sure, some of the guys liked to party. It *was* the '80s, after all, and cocaine was known to be present and available at various moments and events. I never got into it myself. Felt like I was already walking a fine line with my parents just being in the band; the last thing I needed was to get caught up in that scene. But it wasn't a big thing for the guys, at least not that I was aware of. No, our problem wasn't drugs;

our problem was that things got in the way that we couldn't overcome."

"Like what?" Bridget asked.

"Personnel issues, conflicts within the team, that sort of stuff."

"And that broke the band up?"

"That was the gist of it, yeah. While we were trying to make a deal happen, things got ... well, let's just say the momentum and focus shifted. Some of the guys started moonlighting with other groups hoping one of them might break sooner. Nick was spending lots of time on the road with a group opening for Journey, and it became impossible to keep our band functioning. Your dad was roadying for Nick when he was in town, which is how I met him, and he and I eventually got together. When I found out I was pregnant with you, Bridge, and with all the chaos going on with the band, other things ultimately became more important to me." Libby slipped the photographs back in the folder, then looked up with an expression that signaled she was done.

Bridget, however, appeared stricken. "Wait. So you basically quit because of *me*? *I'm* why you stopped singing?"

Stunned, Libby shook her head. "No, not *because* of you. Life just changed. Things got difficult, and it was like the universe was telling me the moment had passed."

"The *moment*? You were nineteen when I was born. Surely you could have—"

"Circumstances changed, Bridget, life evolved. To be honest, at some point I wasn't as driven by the pursuit, the chasing, anymore. It's a tough business and—"

"How could you not be as interested? You said it was all you ever dreamed of." Bridget's voice was edgy, her face tense.

"It was, and I did get back to singing for a while after you were born, tried to see if I could crank it up again. There was a cool little R & B group I worked with for a couple of months, but it never took off. I kept looking for the right fit, the right chemistry, and never found it again. So, you move on, Bridget. You adjust to changing circumstances. Your life becomes about other things."

"Like what? Bookkeeping and babies?" Bridget knew that was cruel, but she suddenly felt angry. No wonder she'd never heard these particulars of her mother's life; her arrival had been the unhappy turning point.

"That's a pretty reductive way to frame my life, dear daughter."

Libby and Bridget were almost squared off at this point, though neither was sure what the other meant or was thinking. Dean, struggling to keep things on track, attempted intercession.

"Actually, Libby, I'd still love to hear about the labels that were around at that specific time, how they found bands and built them up, because now things are—"

"You know what, Dean ..." Libby got up from her chair, the folder of photos in her hand. "Given how things ended for us, I don't think I could offer much on that particular angle, sorry. But I hope I helped a little." She smiled at him, squeezed Bridget's shoulder. "Thanks, guys. Always fun to trip down memory lane." Though she didn't much look it, exiting out the door without a glance back.

Bridget reached over and clicked off the phone recorder.

CHAPTER 15

Peeling off her jeans to return to sweats and a tank top, Libby dropped to the bed and stared at the wall. She couldn't shake the sense that she'd unwisely cracked open a box that was best left closed. She'd felt the heat coming off her daughter. She felt her own potent mix of emotions. It was all too much; she flung herself flat and closed her eyes.

What she told Bridget the other day was true; she *didn't* tend to think about the past. It was a choice, an active decision, and she was good at it, having worked hard to exorcise the youthful angst involved in letting go of that damn dream. Why had her ex-husband suddenly exhumed her history in front of the kids, both now curious enough to ask questions? She appreciated their interest—to a point—but didn't see value in dredging up old memories, old feelings, old longings and regrets. As her father used to say, "Best let the past be past." She'd operated on that maxim for the last thirty-five years; why now was she being forced to flout it?

She could sense she'd let Bridget down and didn't much like the feeling. Because it was true; they typically didn't talk to each other about much of importance. There'd been a lifetime of too many glib, facile conversations, and here in this rare moment when real interest was being extended, Libby couldn't go deep. She had her reasons, but why hadn't she been more gracious, more generous in sharing facts and perspective? What might it have done to change that tired pattern between them? *A lost opportunity, dammit.*

She sat up just as Bridget appeared in the doorway, her tentative, unsmiling expression evidence of Libby's concerns. "You two taking off?" she asked a little too cheerfully.

"Yeah, in a bit." There was a pause.

Libby sighed. "I'm sorry, Bridge. Clearly that wasn't very helpful. I just, I don't—"

"I'm the one who should apologize. That 'bookkeeping and babies' line was a shitty thing to say."

Libby reached out her hand; Bridget walked over and took it. "It was. But it was also sort of true." She smiled ruefully. "For whatever it's worth, I wish my life *had* ended up as glamorous and exciting as I'd imagined it. That would have been a much better story to tell. And certainly you would be more impressed with me."

"Mom, I—"

"But what I did end up with—you, Robbie, Gwen, the happy years with your dad—it's been an amazing life and, I promise you, I wouldn't have traded it for world."

"But it seems like you shouldn't have had to—trade it, I mean. You should've had your dreams too; you didn't need to give anything up. But what do I know? I've finally reached an age where I get to find out how disappointing life can be."

Libby got up and pulled her daughter into her arms. "Yes, you've been painfully initiated into the life-can-suck club, that is true. And just as you're learning how to survive it, so did I. We're strong women, we Conlin girls."

★ ★ ★

Later, as Bridget and Dean trudged down the hillside steps to his car, she noted his atypical reserve. "Why are you so quiet?"

"That was awkward."

"It was."

"Do you think I pissed her off, asking about the drug thing?" His concern was sincere. "I felt like it was something to at least touch on, considering the time and the business we were talking about. Didn't want to just ignore the topic."

"I don't think you pissed her off; I think *I* did. But I apologized before we left, and she seemed fine. I'm just not sure we've got all that much to work with. Especially since we can't use those really cool photos."

At the bottom of the cul de sac, they climbed into his car; Bridget stared out the window.

Dean looked over. "Now you're being quiet."

"That *was* weird though, wasn't it?"

"Which part, specifically?"

"Finding out she basically quit because of me."

"That's not what she said."

"Maybe not, but that would at least make sense. Otherwise, it seems like she gave it up for no good reason, which is worse. Maybe that's what she's embarrassed about. She always told us to be tough and follow through on our dreams, but if she couldn't do that for herself it's a strange message to run on us all these years."

"I think you're being a little rough on her. I get the feeling there's more to it, stuff she doesn't want to talk about. Maybe she couldn't handle the rejection. The music business is brutal; I keep saying that because it's true. I noticed she got emotional talking about it, so I don't think it was just a matter of not following through."

"Maybe, I don't know." As he pulled away from the house, Bridget leaned back, her eyes misting. "It's strange, though, thinking about her being young and wanting things. It's hard for me to picture. She seems so settled now, so stuck; boring, even. I know this sounds mean, but it's like everything interesting about her has already happened. Which is just sad."

Dean reached over and squeezed her hand. "Are you still up for doing this? I don't want it to stir up a bunch of stuff for either of you. I'm not sure we got much from this interview either, but her music *is* fucking incredible. And I have no doubt you could come up with a script based on the whole 'then and now' narrative that would be interesting. I'm still on board if that matters."

She turned to him and finally smiled. "Of course that matters. I couldn't do this without you, at least not the music part. Plus, I've already sent the proposal to Scamehorn, so I'm committed." She took a pause. "And I think her music is fucking incredible too."

"Good. Then let's get practical: we need funds. Converting the analogue tapes to digital is going to take studio time. I get reduced rates for my own projects, but we still have to pay the school some for the time, the tapes. Plus, if we're going to run some CDs for giveaways, we need money for that too; covers, artwork, replication. It'll add up."

Bridget thought for a moment then pulled out her phone. "I've got an idea."

CHAPTER 16

Libby traipsed down the hill to the coffee shop on Gower Street, a familiar route she knew well but traversed more often these days from the confines of her car. Hard to remember when she daily marched through these same streets determined to get her steps in, powering up the various (and steep) stairways strewn throughout the hillside neighborhood, music pounding in her ears and, in earlier days, her dog in tow. Now her only exercise was managing the many steps to and from her front door. Given how breathless those left her lately, it was clear more activity was required. She'd have to do something about that.

She missed having a dog. She didn't want another one but missed the one she'd had. Beanie was a feisty mid-sized husky who made her laugh with his melodious howling and forced her to exercise with his panting need to get out and about. She had to put him down three years ago and though the finality of it broke her heart, the ease of life since, particularly as she took on more hours with buying trips, became exponentially easier. Still. Beanie had been a delight.

As she turned the corner at the block where the Great & Grounded Coffee Shop beaconed, Libby felt a tremor of anxiety. She'd been talked into it. Coaxed. Coerced. Browbeaten. Into a blind date with Otto's pal.

As reluctant as she'd been, Libby had to acknowledge there was a modicum of curiosity about what kind of guy Gwen, and Gwen's new love, thought would be a good match for her in these current times. Her last date had been so long ago that any assessment on the point could only be speculation, but her best friend was the indefatigable sort when it came to the potential of true love. Or at least the "sparkage of romantic interest," as she so hopefully put it.

So Libby was there. Walking through the door of the neighborhood coffee shop, a quiet place with fresh flowers on the tables, paintings and photographs of creative locals propped and hung with artful clutter, and dangerously delicious baked goods. She ordered a latte and maple scone and grabbed a table in the corner to wait for Jeff Morley, a purportedly good guy with excellent hair and a commendable sense of humor.

Within minutes, a tall man dressed far too nattily for a late afternoon coffee date set the doorbell tinkling as he entered and immediately glanced her way. Photos had been exchanged so there was no awkward scrambling to certify the who's who of the encounter; they knew exactly who was who. He smiled brightly then motioned that he'd be grabbing something from the counter. When he sat down across from her with his black coffee and homemade angel food cake, a specialty of Great & Grounded, she surmised that his awareness of the confection signaled familiarity with the place, which he immediately confirmed.

"My son and I used to come here after his Little League games back in the day, so this is a real treat for me. Love this cake!"

She smiled, and they commenced with the standard niceties, paying particular note to discussions of Gwen and Otto, and how they both knew the besotted couple; the two men had shared a dorm room in college. They then exchanged banal chatter about favorite writers, current TV shows, and whether or not Netflix had forever changed the course of viewing history; got back to sipping and nibbling, proffered a refill for each, and before long Libby was mentally scrolling through her litany of departure lines. It wasn't that she didn't find him likable; it just seemed the event had reached its natural obsolescence, evidenced by her picking her napkin apart and him tapping a beat with his spoon. Just as she was about to commence with, "I need to get home for a scheduled Facetime with my son," Jeff cleared his throat.

"Are you as uncomfortable at this moment as I am?" he asked with a crooked smile.

She grinned, appreciating his situational awareness. "Pretty sure."

"I don't usually do this blind dating thing, but when Otto introduced me to Gwen, I figured it couldn't be too painful."

"Gwen's the most painful thing about me, so odds are good it'll be uphill from here."

They laughed. Awkwardly. A beat of silence. Finally:

"Okay, so how about I tell you a little bit about myself; does that seem appropriate?" Jeff asked.

"Good plan. We'll share mini-bios and see where that gets us."

"Okay. Let's see ..." He gazed off as if pondering his resume. "Divorced four years, one son, Michael, the aforementioned Little Leaguer; he's currently doing a master's program abroad. My ex and I are friendly but not in each other's pockets. I own a well-established dental practice in Beverly Hills, a home in Benedict Canyon, and am financially comfortable. I like good food and baseball, vote independent; I believe in God though not sure what that means. I don't want more kids of my own. I hate pierced tongues and bad cosmetic surgery; bigots, liars, and fascists stir my outrage, and people attached to cellphones are my pet peeve. I'm okay being single but would love to find a woman who's wise, funny, enjoys the great outdoors, and still looks good in a pair of jeans." He stopped and looked up at her, his face charmingly flushed. "Too much? Enough for a start?"

"Wow. Did you rehearse that?"

He laughed out loud. "Not exactly. Though I did give it some thought on the way here. I was determined not to make too big a fool of myself when we got to this part."

"Well done. I'm impressed."

"Excellent. That was my goal. So, how about you?"

She took a sip of her latte, stalling for time. "To be completely honest, I *didn't* think about it on the way over. I was too focused on making my feet walk in the direction of this coffee shop."

"You walked? Does that mean you live nearby?"

"Yes. Up near the top of Beachwood Canyon."

"Nice."

"It's a shabby old Tudor my parents gifted me when they moved to a shiny new condo in Houston, so I get to live in locational splendor while the walls come tumbling down."

"Seriously?"

"No. Well, yes, a little. We sustain a few cracks with every new earthquake, and for some reason my chimney decided to partially crumble a few months ago, all of which I've minimally repaired, but it's a hard house to keep up with. Like you, I'm divorced, fourteen years for me, but since then, given that he's a freelance graphic artist and I do bookkeeping, Tudor repairs get persistently backburnered. I've got a nineteen-year-old son who just finished his first year at San Diego State, where he flunked his lit course and is getting tutored while working a summer job at the school's theater. My daughter is thirty-five, recently divorced herself, returned to hearth and home after the fireworks, and has been trying to figure out what she wants to do when she grows up. She and her ex had a successful wine bar in Georgetown, so she's got some money but no solid plans, though she is exploring a nearby arts school. I was touched that she chose to come home, but we're not the best of roommates, which has been the case since she was, well, since she was born."

He grinned. "Come on, there had to have been at least some easy preschool years!"

"You'd think, but we've been head-butting the whole time. I love her to death, but I think we're better from afar."

"Then I hope she figures it out sooner as opposed to later, for both your sakes."

"Me too. As for me, I'm starting a CPA certification course at the behest of my place of business, a gorgeous gift shop down on Franklin owned by a brilliant woman who thinks the world of me. And though it's something I need to do, and have agreed to do, I'm not remotely excited about it. And that's me. Given all that, it seems everyone in my family is in the process of reinvention." She stopped, smiled, then reached for her latte.

He leaned back in his chair, taking her in with a thoughtful expression. "That's a lot. You're dealing with a lot. I admire you; for being there for your kids, for taking new steps. It's hard, I know. After my wife left, and particularly when my son went overseas, I felt seriously abandoned. Couldn't make myself do anything outside of my practice and a workout or two. But we adapt, don't we? I adapted, you're adapting, even your kids are adapting. That's life, isn't it?"

She liked his take. "Exactly. I said something similar to my daughter just the other day." She slid her chair back. "And speaking of life and one of those kids, I've got a Facetime call scheduled with my son, so I should start heading home."

"Understood."

Jeff stood, she stood, and it went immediately back to awkward.

"Can I drive you?" he asked. "You said you walked and if you need to—"

"No, I factored in time to walk back, thanks. There's not enough exercise in my current schedule, so I grab every chance I can get."

As they pushed through the doors and stood mid-sidewalk, he reached out his hand.

"It was very nice to meet you, Libby."

"Very nice to meet you, Jeff."

They shook, both grinning. As she turned in the direction of home, he blurted, "I have no idea what the next step might be here but is there any interest in taking another one? Step, that is?" His hands were in his pockets, affecting a nonchalance he clearly didn't feel.

She cocked her head. "Yes. As long as it's slow, whatever those steps are."

"Fine with me."

"Do you know where Lake Hollywood is?"

"Yes, up near the Hollywood sign, right?"

"Well, sort of. There's a nice walk around the reservoir. I'm busy this coming Sunday, but if you'd like to meet me at the North Gate Sunday after next, we could both get in a bit more exercise. Though you're probably back to daily workouts by now."

"Hah. Hardly. But either way, I'd love to join you. It's been a long time since I've been up there so that would be fun."

"Great. I'll text a few days before and we'll set a time."

"Perfect. Until then, take care, Libby."

"You too, Jeff."

The walk back felt longer, often the case with walks, and as she trudged up the hill, slightly ashamed that she'd played the "I've got to get home" card when Rob wouldn't be calling until later, she took some pride in the fact that she'd accomplished the date at all. It hadn't been horrible. As advertised, he was nice, and yes, good-looking. There was nothing offensive about him in any way, at least as far as she could tell.

Strange, though, thinking about a man, any man, moving into the orbit of her life. After the debacle of her divorce, the possibility of someone getting close enough for impact had been anathema to her. Bart had been such a pivotal presence for so long, in ways good and bad, that the thought of another person in any version of that role strained incredulity.

Still, he was nice.

Her vibrating phone signaled the latest of four breathless texts from Gwen wondering, *"How's it going?!!"* Libby almost responded, then decided that walking up the hill during the golden hour, admiring the many and beautiful homes along the way while listening to the symphony of ever-present birds, was too lovely an activity to disrupt with chatter. Debriefs could wait.

CHAPTER 17

Gwen's office was on the twenty-seventh floor of a downtown Los Angeles high-rise, every inch of it the classic presentation of "tony financial establishment," from the slick architecture and designer interior to the expensive suits and elegant attire of every person buzzing through the softly lit hallways. Gwen fit right in. Her current visitors did not.

One shaggy recording engineer and her best friend's daughter were awkwardly seated in plush Jonathan Adler chairs, both appearing nervous yet determined. They had delivered their pitch; she'd listened attentively and was now mulling her answer as prudently as if advising clients on IRAs or the value of bitcoin. Gwen tended to take even the smallest of financial matters seriously.

"Essential question, Bridge: Does your mom know what you're up to?"

"Not the part about her music," Bridget responded. "We want to keep that secret until we have it put together enough to decide if the mini-doc is even worth sharing. It might not be, but if it is, we'd rather present it to her as a finished product."

"Okay, I get that." Gwen stood up and began pacing.

There was a quiet knock at the opened door as a tall man in a well-tailored suit and the shiniest bald pate Bridget had ever seen leaned into the room. Gwen smiled coyly in his direction.

"Sorry to interrupt," said the bald man. "Gwen, you wanted me to alert you when I heard back; I heard back, apparently it went well. Feel free to let me know about the, um, client on your end."

"I certainly will." She turned to her guests. "Bridget, Dean, this is Otto, a good friend of mine. Otto, Bridget is my friend Libby's daughter; she and Dean are here pitching a very interesting project."

Otto beamed his very engaging smile; Bridget decided he was actually quite attractive once she got past the Vin Diesel presentation.

"Very nice to meet you both," Otto said, "and I'll let you get back to it. Gwen, shoot me a text when you've got the information."

"Will do." Gwen couldn't hide a smile as he slipped out. "Sorry about that, kids." She closed the door and sat back down, face flushed. "Okay, as to your project: here's the first obstacle that hits me. It's not the money; the money's easy. What, you're looking for ... what?"

"I think we could do it all for fifteen hundred, max," Dean replied.

"Pocket change. No, the problem from where I sit is Libby. She is a very, very private person—I think you know that, Bridgie—particularly about that part of her life. I'm just not convinced she'd want her music used for something, anything, without her having a say in the matter."

"Yeah." Bridget slumped. "I thought about that too. Considering how secretive she's been about it for basically our whole lives, I do kind of doubt she'd get all generous now. But why is that, Gwen? She did give us some of the history when we talked to her the other day, but it seemed like we could only go so far before she got twitchy, which I don't get."

Gwen sat back, considering her response. "You know, sweetheart, all I can tell you is this: it was a very intense time of her life. She put every single thing she had into it, even *before*

she met Nick and the band started. Even her high school performances got people talking. There was so much potential, so
many people who believed in her, and later in her band, that
there was no doubt she was going to be one of the ones to suc-
ceed. Then circumstances changed, certain people changed;
momentum changed, and the wave they were riding crashed to
shore. She tried, but she couldn't get past the tumble to get back
up, you know what I'm saying?"

"No. I don't. I wish I did. She insists that having me was not
the reason she quit, so, okay. What was, then? It makes no sense
to me."

There was a freighted pause as Gwen pondered the comment. "I understand why you feel that way, sweetheart. It's hard
to explain. And not mine *to* explain. There were things that hurt
her, enough that she doesn't want to talk about them. So you
might just have to leave it there, and trust she made the right
decision for herself at the time."

Before Bridget could respond, Dean interrupted. "Well, how
about this? What if we finish the project as we envision it, but
before Bridget submits it to the school, or we show it to anyone,
we run it by you first, see what you think? Odds are good, as
her closest friend, you'll know if it's something she'd find upset-
ting. Though I'm convinced when she sees what we plan to put
together and hears her music all buffed up and sparkling for the
first time in three decades, she'll be really pleased. How does
that hit you?"

Gwen considered that for a moment, then nodded. "Okay.
You bring it to me when you're ready. I'll see how it strikes me,
and we'll go from there. But let me tell you, if I think it's something that'll break her heart, or piss her off, or make her want to
hit me, it's a big no-go, got it?"

They nodded.

"Now, who do I make this check out to?"

CHAPTER 18

Sitting in a classroom on the second floor of an academic building at Santa Monica College surrounded by attendees of varying ages, most, like her, older than the average college student, Libby felt she both fit right in and was egregiously out of place. It was a lovely city campus near enough the ocean to catch breezes off the water. Palm trees swayed over the attractive walkway, there was gorgeous landscaping and smart architecture, and on this beautiful Saturday when most people were out enjoying the beach, the sunny parks and palisades of the city, Libby was inside learning how to CPA.

Though not part of the school's regular academic curriculum, the CPA prep course was offered to any paying student looking to gain their credentials and, as the perky woman who signed her up make zestfully clear, "You couldn't pick a nicer part of the city to buckle down and crunch numbers." She couldn't. It was that nice an area. Still.

Having an accounting degree was, indeed, a boon to the process, as were the significant number of hours she'd accrued over the years doing work specific to the arena, but the many steps involved in attesting to those accrued hours were ponderous, and the course stretched out over an eight-week schedule of Saturdays, obliterating any free time she had for the duration. Sundays were now the only days relegated for such things as housekeeping, laundry, and progeny maintenance. How she would squeeze in social activities like dating a certain dentist was, once again, a challenge.

The droning lecture by a teacher who was clearly adept at numbers but not a particularly vibrant orator—and vaguely resembled Jonah Hill—almost put her to sleep as she drifted through thoughts of her recent get-together with Jeff Morley. After their first, somewhat brief, coffee, life had been distracting enough that she hadn't thought all that much about him, not exactly a harbinger of romantic zeal. But the various discussions with Gwen over ensuing days, absolutely demanded by the "event organizer," as Gwen had deigned herself, rehabilitated her interest a bit. As did Gwen's comment, "He told Otto you were a gem."

A gem. That was nice. Though right now she felt more like a sloth languishing at a desk trying not to droop into slumber. When Jonah Hill pointed to her with a question, she was quick to perk up and answered appropriately, which elicited a surprised nod and sent him off to harass someone else. At that moment, her phone buzzed with a text. Jeff. As if her daydreaming had conjured him up:

Just got some new cross-trainers. Ready for our hike around the lake. Let me know what time to be there. I'm looking forward to it. JM

Clearly, it had been a while since he'd been to the lake, as it wasn't exactly a hike, more a very level, and therefore unchallenging, three-point-five-mile looping meander, but she appreciated the enthusiasm. After texting, *Let's say noon,* activity which provoked a frowning reminder from Jonah Hill that, "students are required to turn off their phones," she settled into the unavoidable task of paying attention, though not without another petulant sigh.

How did this become my life? ... her last thought before buckling down.

CHAPTER 19

Being the social media manager for a small but popular catering company was not what Bridget had in mind for her next adventure, but after sending thirty-seven resumes, filling out twelve applications, and meeting in-person with five different potential employers, the position at Heart To Table Kitchen was at least a job. With its mix of remote and on-site work hours, decent pay with some benefits, and seemingly amenable bosses—two very creative lesbians in their forties—she decided it was good enough for now. At least until she came up with a more career-oriented plan while considering the possibility of going to school, which seemed slightly insane at this unsettled post-divorce moment of her life.

The "okay for now" job was, however, in the charming downtown area of Tarzana, a good twenty miles from the house and, with predictable traffic, often an hour-long drive, which made getting a car essential. They'd discussed it the previous night, Bridget and her mother, with a plan to get out to a few dealerships over some upcoming weekend to see what was available at a price she wanted to pay, which wasn't much. Until then, with Uber grossly expensive at that distance, Libby arranged with Chloe to come in a bit later, allowing her to be the driver designated to get the less-than-excited new employee to her first day of work.

"Now tell me, what is this job again? You've had so many interviews I've lost track." Libby's perky attempt to break the silence was met with a sullen response.

"Social media manager." Bridget continued staring out the passenger window.

"What exactly does that entail? I obviously understand the process of social media promotion, I do a lot of it for Chloe, but is that all you'll be doing, or are there other tasks involved?"

"I don't know yet." Bridget finally turned to her with a touch of exasperation. "Mom, could we talk about this later? I didn't sleep well last night, and I just want to focus on getting there."

"All right." A beat of silence. "Okay, different subject, if you can stand it: How's the project going?"

"Fine."

"Yeah?" She looked over hopefully. No returned glance. "Good. I know my interview wasn't exactly a standout so I couldn't help but wonder what else you might have to work with." She smiled in Bridget's direction, committed to lightening the morning's gloom.

"We're still in the process of putting the pieces together."

"Ah, okay." Libby went back to driving in silence.

Bridget squirmed in her seat, reluctantly recalling the conversations of weeks earlier about being more open with each other. Sitting here now, being chauffeured to her first day on a new job, anxious and grumpy, she couldn't help but acknowledge that this was an obvious opportunity to act on that intention. She took a deep breath. "So, how was your date with Gwen's friend?"

Libby kept her eyes on the road, but the ghost of a smile flitted across her lips. Bridget asked a question. "Okay, I think. Hard to tell after only one forty-minute coffee break. His name is Jeff, he seems like a nice guy; he's a dentist, so there's good teeth. We're going to walk around Lake Hollywood next Sunday, so I guess 'okay' is apt."

"Wow. Another date. That's some bold, daring stuff for you."

"I figured it was better than inviting him to the house for dinner and sending you scrambling to your corner." She smiled benignly.

Bridget looked at her mother as if to snap a retort, then turned back to the window. "Whatever." *Dammit, it slipped out anyway.*

"Really? *Whatever?*" Libby shook her head, weary of the continuing trend. "Didn't we get past this? Seemed like we did for a minute. Please don't revert to being a teenager, Bridget. We already did that bit, and we're both too old for a replay."

"I know. Sorry." She meant it.

Traffic started to loosen up; Libby checked the time and GPS, determined to get her daughter where she needed to be without further comment.

Bridget again relaxed her shoulders. "So, you like him?"

"I don't know." Libby replied. She looked at her daughter with a raised eyebrow and grin, grateful for the conversational olive branch. "Ask me after Lake Hollywood."

CHAPTER 20

Sex.

Bridget had almost forgotten about it. The way it felt, the urge to have it; the mechanics of the act, etcetera. Her last year with Seth Hart had included little of the stuff, and what there was usually proved perfunctory and uninspired. Despite being at the age defined as a "woman's sexual prime," she'd stopped thinking about any of it. Sex. Primes. Seth. Etcetera.

But after a long day of discomfort, anxiety, and overwhelm related to the first day on a new job, Bridget did something she hadn't done in a very long time. She ignored prudence and self-consciousness. Abandoned caution. Embraced need and want and desire and ... had sex.

It wasn't planned. It had barely been thought of in all the time they'd spent together. But when Dean texted asking if she needed a ride home, she was so delighted to accept and thereby pre-empt the onslaught of Libby's chirpy interest the entire drive from Tarzana to Hollywood, she let her delight sprout into something else, something new; something less platonic. She considered the prospect of sex.

She liked him. She was definite on that. Though, as already noted, he didn't inspire tremors or make her nerves jangle when in close proximity, Dean intrigued her. He was different—smart, sweet, kind, and considerate. Good-looking in his own unique way. The affection she felt for him was clearly mutual, and that, too, had impact. It was erotic somehow, his liking her without exhibiting the typical, compulsive need to make it into something more, the libidinous trajectory she'd experienced with most men. She did wonder if the slow percolation of her own feelings meant it *was* more platonic than romantic, but, as she'd so recently discovered, considerations of quality and character had, in the past, been ignored when lust led the way, as it had with Seth. No, she decided; her nascent ability to appreciate traits beyond generic hotness and growling sexuality were evidence of personal growth. And it was now time for continued evolution.

When she hopped in the car and Dean said, "You want to grab some dinner?" she turned and gave him a look that signaled something he hadn't expected and wouldn't, couldn't, ignore. They drove straight to his apartment and proceeded to have the tenderest, most wonderfully unburdened sex she'd, quite possibly, ever had. It was almost transformational in its disparity from every other kind she'd previously experienced, and that, she decided, signaled a new era in her sexual life.

In the quiet afterglow, wrapped in sheets and sweaty limbs, they looked at each other with amazement, bursting into laughter. It felt transcendent, laughing after sex, as if the goal of enjoyment and mutual pleasure had not only been achieved but could be openly celebrated.

"That was incredible." He was the first to make the point.

"*You* are incredible." She felt coy and girlish, two things rarely felt. Something about his warmth and protectiveness triggered the softening.

"I don't know about incredible. I do know I've wanted to do that for a long time but didn't really expect it to happen. I'm very glad it did, though. I hope you are too."

"I am."

A pause, then: "You really are so beautiful, you know that?" He said this with such gravity it had impact.

Her face got warm, and she felt like ducking under the covers.

But he continued. "I don't think I've ever mentioned that before, and while, obviously, who you are, what you're about, is far more important than how you look, I do think you're amazingly beautiful and always enjoy looking at you."

His compliment was so sweetly sincere she could barely find a commensurate response. "Thank you." She snuggled her face into his neck. "I think you're beautiful too."

He pulled her closer, and they held that way for a long, quiet moment.

When they relaxed back on the bed, their arms still linked, she looked around, taking in his apartment for the first time since walking in. It was small, with the generic appeal of new and functional, nothing worn or in need of repair. Neat configurations of sound equipment were tucked in various corners standing in as end tables and bookshelves, with enough color thrown around, and well-placed band posters hung, to qualify the place as cool. It fit him.

"I like your place."

"Thanks. It's basic, but it's close to work, and the landlord is nice. I've learned to appreciate those things." He grinned.

"I look forward to appreciating those things, too."

"Still tough at your mom's?"

"Not too bad—if she leaves me alone. Which she occasionally does. Enough, I guess. I'm trying to be better with her when I'm there. I don't know that I'm quite succeeding yet. I still get regressive around her for some reason. But the whole thing *is* weird, isn't it? I mean, how perverse; a thirty-five-year-old divorcee sleeping in her childhood bedroom with her mother making sandwiches for her work lunchbox."

"I don't know." He leaned up on one elbow. "Sounds kind of nice to me. Having someone take care of you, look out for you, especially after a crazy thing like a divorce; it has to be at least a little comforting. If it were me, I'd try to enjoy it while it lasts."

She curled back into his side. "You're probably right. I guess I really *am* a crappy roommate, as my parents used to say in earlier years."

"Well, now you've got a chance to rewrite your history."

"God, are you always this positive?" she asked with a frown and honest curiosity.

Taken aback, he turned to her. "Why, is that a bad thing?"

"No, I've just never met anyone so authentically optimistic pretty much all the time. I come from grumpy stock; that's going to take some getting used to."

He laughed out loud. "Okay, I'll try to tamp it down."

"No, no, don't tamp it down. It's one of your best traits; I mean it." She did. She also meant it would take some getting used to.

"I have faith we'll find the balance. As for your roommate situation, I hope, now that you've been here, you'll find your way back as often as possible. Give yourself a break from the homestead whenever needed, and, well, you know, have hot, crazy sex from time to time with the cool guy who lives here."

She kissed his shoulder. "I will look forward to taking you up on that."

Consensus achieved, last kisses administered, they got up, took showers, and went to a local pizza joint for a large Italian meal. In the car on the way back to the house on the hill, hands occasionally reaching out to touch a shoulder, a leg, a cheek, Dean veered to discussion of the project.

"By the way, very cool about Gwen throwing in. I thought you handled all that really well."

"It was easy. She thinks of herself as my godmother, so I knew she'd be up for it. She's a little crazy, but she's always been someone I could count on. By the way, my dad said he's looking forward to meeting you."

"Yeah, me too. Why don't you set something up for this week to show him our ideas for the artwork? Since we don't have a band to photograph, he's going to have to get creative."

"Oh, he will. That's his forte. I've also created some cool photo composites he can use." She looked over at him again.

He caught her glance. "What?"

"You okay working with all these people from my life? We're not overwhelming you with the Conlin-ness of it all?"

"No, I'm enjoying it. I think we all make a pretty good team. I've got the music stuff covered; you're the artist, and we've got people for the rest. It'll be fun working with your dad."

"Oh, he said we need to send him our fake band's name as soon as possible so he can start working with it."

They'd reached the house; he pulled into the cul de sac and put the car in park. "I did have an idea."

"Yeah?"

"Minor Rebellion."

She frowned. "I don't get it."

"From the manifesto Scamehorn gave you after your first meeting with her, the essay? When I was thinking about names, that line, 'minor rebellion,' popped into my head."

Bridget laughed. "How on earth did you even remember that detail?"

"Are you kidding? I've heard Scamehorn read that essay at assemblies about a thousand times, so I guess the phrase stuck. And think about it, the concept of it: a minor rebellion—being bold, breaking pre-conceived ideas. Kind of fits the mission of this project, don't you think?"

"I can't remember much about it, to be honest, but I have it here." She picked up her phone; tapped the screen and took a minute to read through the essay. "I'd forgotten about this, but yeah, you're right. It does fit the mission. Okay, we've got a name. Minor Rebellion."

They looked at each other and smiled. Progress.

By the time Bridget walked up the steps to the door of her mother's house, she felt like a different person than the one who'd reluctantly left that morning.

CHAPTER 21

Libby kept expecting him to call with an excuse, a reason to postpone, even cancel, the proposed walk around Lake Hollywood. While that might have been, in various and obvious ways, ego-shaking, part of her hoped for it. Not pursuing this relationship would be far easier than trying to figure it out.

Gwen had called several times in the days between the coffee event and the scheduled hike, demanding Libby continue to discuss her thoughts and feelings about Jeff Morley. It was clear Gwen suspected she might blow things up, which Libby had certainly considered, still struggling with her baked-in resistance to social engagement or anything resembling obligation. Despite that urge, she agreed to stay amenable.

So, on this day, Sunday, the one day of the week she had to herself until CPA hell was over, she was going to walk around Lake Hollywood with a nice man she had just met. A walk, that was it; nothing else. She could manage that and still have time for tasks requiring her attention before the day was done.

As she made her way up the pitted road to the even more pitted parking lot that adjoined the reservoir walking path, there he was, already at the entrance, a big smile on his face. Climbing out of the car, Libby again noted that he was, indeed, very good-looking. Track pants and a form-fitting T-shirt made clear he was in good shape, and, in the bright sunlight of the day, his remarkably abundant hair (for a fifty-something guy) practically glowed. Even his shades were hip. Another shiny person in her life.

The best she'd managed was a clean pair of cranberry colored yoga pants—which, at least, had no stains or snags—and a blousy safari shirt long enough to cover her ass (always the goal these days), with enough pockets to forego a purse. It was all about cloaking and convenience, not appeal, though she hoped her lack of fashion flair didn't make her appear slovenly. His big smile dispelled her concerns; he was clearly a forgiving fellow.

As they walked, they conversed about their kids, the scenery; the Hollywood sign in the distance. They dipped gently into politics, enough to ensure that, though he tilted more conservative than she'd originally thought, he wasn't a flaming right winger, even agreeing to attend the next Women's March together (which she was fairly certain wasn't a pander). They wandered through families of origin, schools attended, and "how I ended up here" (she was born and raised; he moved to Los Angeles from Ohio for dental school). There was much expressed appreciation for the natural beauty they were ambling through, which included countless birds, a glorious vista of trees framing the curve of the reservoir, and the vintage architecture of the Mulholland Dam. It was a good walk, a good, meaty conversation, and by the time they'd traversed back to the parking lot, having circled the entire lake, she was not only sweaty, but grudgingly certain he'd passed another level of muster.

Whatever that meant.

To him it meant continuing the day. "Want to grab some lunch?"

She *was* hungry. She was also convinced they'd exhausted the natural list of topics typically covered on a second get-together. Deciding it would be wise to preempt the potential of awkward conversational lulls over BLTs and iced tea, she begged off.

"I'd love to but with Sunday being my only free day at the moment, I've got a list of errands in front of me that would crush a lesser person. I think I've got to dive in." She smiled warmly, hoping to convey a vibe of *I'm not* not *interested, I just want to keep this to short increments for now.*

He appeared to translate it as intended. "Totally understand." They'd made it to her car by that point. "This was fun." His smile was warm, which seemed his default setting. "Let's do it again. I know a great hike—another easy one, I promise." He laughed. "It's close to my neighborhood, so we could stop by my house afterwards. How about we try that next time?"

Libby appreciated that he saw her as someone who hiked. Made her seem robust and outdoorsy, traits that had never once specifically applied to her. She also hoped his definition of "easy hike" was close to her own. Where he lived in Benedict Canyon, an affluent area north of Beverly Hills, had some very hilly areas, so "easy" could not presumed. But still, she was now curious about his environs, which seemed to augur future potential. "That'd be great. Let me check my schedule and we can trade texts till we find a time."

He laughed. "We're so modern, aren't we? I may just surprise you and call. I'm old school that way."

When she smiled back, he leaned toward her and, to her shock and awe, appeared to be heading in for a kiss. In the split-second given to respond, her mind raced through myriad options, landing on one that involved tilting her head slightly so that he landed on her cheek. Which he gently kissed as if that was exactly where he'd intended to land.

"You feel very natural to me, Libby. I like that."

"I need to take this slow. Really slow."

He took her chin in his hand and turned her face to his. This time a very slow, very soft kiss on the lips ensued. "Slow enough?"

Despite not wanting to, she felt a sudden rush. "Yes, thank you. But I'm serious."

"Libby, there's no timetable here. I think you're great and I'd like to see you again, okay?"

"Okay. I just don't know what I'm up for at this point in my life. I wouldn't want to disappoint you."

"I'm not that fragile." He brushed her cheek with his hand and walked to his car, hollering back, "I'll call."

She stood watching him drive away, flushed with a strange mix of confusion and titillation.

CHAPTER 22

Bridget and Dean were having their first fight. Or something closely resembling one. He thought she should videotape herself giving a short introduction to the project; she wanted the introduction to be voice-over. He felt seeing her in person would offer more personality and immediacy—advantageous, he said, considering the purpose of the exercise. She felt it was unnecessary and distracting. She was also deeply self-conscious about putting, and seeing, herself on film, which was clearly the crux of the problem.

This kerfuffle took place in her father's studio, where they'd come to introduce the men to each other, discuss concepts, and move the project forward. Currently Bart was at his desk sketching ideas for the marketing materials and CD cover, pretending to ignore what was uncharacteristic terseness from Dean and all too characteristic snark from Bridget. It was a brief snit and concluded when Bart finally looked up and said, "Bridget, I think Dean's right," after which she flounced out of the room and slammed the door behind her, leaving the two men to look at each other in commiseration.

"She's a tough one," Bart remarked with a sigh. "Always has been." He went back to his sketching.

"Yeah." Dean dropped to a chair. "She's mentioned that."

"Hah!" Bart shot him a sly look. "I'm surprised she'd admit it. Never met a kid more willing to battle over anything and everything, just to be contentious and usually for no good reason. I think she literally drove her mother crazy, though Libby seems to have recovered well since those early days of mayhem."

"Libby is very cool. And, man, those pipes! Bridget and I were both blown away when we heard her tapes. It must have been amazing to be part of all that when it was happening in real time."

Bart shifted in his seat. "It was. A wild few years, I'll say that. And, yeah, she was a knockout."

"'Best chick singer in LA,' is how Rob said you put it." Dean grinned, clearly hoping to entice further conversation on the topic.

"Oh, that was just some goofy quote a promoter put on a band poster thinking it would bring guys into the club. None of us would have had the balls to call Libby a 'chick singer.' A chick *anything*. But it did bring in the guys." He grinned in response. "She was the best. No doubt about it."

"Which makes it easy to understand why Bridget finds it weird," Dean commented.

Bart looked up at him. "Finds what weird?"

"She's confused about why Libby walked away from it back then, considering how good she was and how much traction it seemed the band was getting. We talked about it when we interviewed her, but she was vague on the topic, which seems to be a sticking point with Bridget. The *why*. I think she's caught up in thinking it was because of her, which doesn't sit well. Any thoughts on that?" Dean was determined to fill in the blanks.

Bart, his focus directed toward the computer screen, took a beat before answering. "Whatever Libby said about it is what it was. It's her story to tell. I didn't mean to stir up anything, talking about it with Rob, but it seems I did." He sighed, leaning back in his chair. "Basically when Libby's done with something, she's done. She's always been like that. Believe me, I know." He snorted. "I just think when the deal fell apart, she—"

"Wait, so there *was* a deal?"

Bart looked up sharply. "There was *talk* of a deal. It ultimately didn't pan out, and that was the impetus for the band breaking up."

"But why didn't she just find other musicians, given that she was the voice, the lead singer, the most identifiable part of the band. I would've thought—"

"Frankly, I don't remember all the logistics and details, but odds are good she probably did try that—in fact, I'm pretty sure she did—and it didn't gel for some reason. Plus, she was pregnant, so we naturally shifted our focus to that situation. I think taking a break at that point was almost a relief for her. But, like I said, it's her story to tell. Or not tell. I'll leave it there."

As if on cue, Bridget pushed through the door with a stack of papers in hand, now wearing a smart jacket over well-cut jeans, her face expertly made up and hair doing everything it was supposed to do. Camera-ready.

"Okay," she announced. "If you two think I should jabber on camera, I'll jabber on camera. I've got my intro notes here, I'm all shined up, ready to go." She looked at them expectantly as they stared at her, speechless. "What?"

Dean leapt up. "Nothing. You look amazing. So yeah, let's do this. You're the director; tell me what you want."

"Okay." With that, Bridget rattled off a list of instructions, Dean hustled through the necessary steps, and Bart just smiled and went back to his computer.

CHAPTER 23

Libby had to cancel the next scheduled hike with Jeff. It was the second time. The first was due to an unexpected request from Chloe to accompany her on a very exclusive trade conference trip, an invitation she could not turn down; the second was the delightful event of Rob's visit.

He'd called to say he had an open Sunday and, "would we all be able to get together for dinner or something if I borrowed a car and drove up?" She assured him they would, made a reservation at his favorite Lebanese restaurant, got Bart and Bridget on board, with a thumbs-up to her request to include Dean, and, buzzing with excitement she diplomatically tamped down, she called to break the date with Jeff.

He took it well. Made a wistful comment about looking forward to meeting her family at some point in "the hopefully not-too-distant future," but said he completely understood. She realized that, as excited as she was to have her son home for a visit, she was genuinely tugged by the sense that she was already disappointing this very nice man and said so.

"You were candid about the demands of your life," he somewhat somberly reminded her, "and I accepted the situation with open eyes. It would be very ungracious of me if I got disappointed the first time or two those circumstances kicked in."

"That's very kind, and to be honest, *I'm* a little disappointed. I really do want to get another hike in, so I hope we can put it back on the books soon."

"How about next Sunday?"

She was taken aback by his immediate response. "Um, yeah, I think that would be okay. I just need to—"

"Let's both put it on our calendars and, barring any unexpected events, I have faith we can make it happen. Will that work?"

She could see that nothing was booked for next Sunday but still felt a little pushed. "It looks like it will."

"Good, I'll look forward to that. Have a really great time with your family, Libby. Frankly, I'm jealous; I haven't seen my son in a while, so I'll take some vicarious pleasure in your visit." He was genuine enough that Libby felt a rush of warmth for him.

★ ★ ★

Later, seated around a table of favorite dishes in a welcoming place they'd patronized many times together as a family, with Rob next to her, attentive and funny, Bart more present and lighthearted than usual, Bridget and Dean keeping the conversation bright and intense, Libby felt a powerful wave of love and gratitude. She couldn't stop finding reasons to squeeze Rob's shoulder, brush hair out of his eyes; drink in every aspect of this child she so loved and missed. She looked around and wondered if it really was possible to find some version of her family that could work, that cohered, that offered warmth and love in predictable doses. It was the best night she'd had in a very long time, and she looked forward to reporting back to Gwen that she was, indeed, exceedingly happy with her life.

CHAPTER 24

Cohesion was brief.

The following Friday morning, Libby and Bridget lit into a conflagration that was as heated and hurtful as any they'd ever had. It started innocuously enough; Bridget wanted to discuss the logistics of Libby getting her to a few dealerships to look for a car. Apparently, Dean was locked into a schedule that had him occupied all weekend, and Bart was out of town on a job. This request led to Libby explaining, once again, the timing of her Saturday class, as well as the hiking date she'd booked with Jeff for that Sunday, which sparked a snarl from Bridget that, "I'd think helping your daughter get situated in her new life would be prioritized over a pointless date with a man you barely know and don't seem that excited about, but *whatever, Mother!*"

It was the *"whatever"* that tipped Libby's patience.

What followed, despite all prior agreements to be more congenial with each other, was an exhaustive volley of criticisms and accusations of stunning variety (that was Bridget), teeth-gritting suggestions to "grow the fuck up" (Libby), the volatile kinetics of several heaved couch pillows (both), concluding with a dramatic exit inclusive of the very loud slamming of the front door (Bridget). Which was pointless, as Libby still had to drive her to work, a tense, silent affair buttoned with a final demand (Libby) that Bridget arrange an Uber for her weekend plans.

Later that night, dispirited and weary after the rough beginning of what evolved into a stressful day with Chloe out at meetings and Libby left to run both the front and back of the store, Gwen swept in bringing good cheer in the form of pumpkin bread from the local monastery and some of Libby's favorite Huckleberry Pepper jam. Seated at the patio table slathering butter and said jam on a rather large and perfectly warmed slice, Gwen watched as Libby huffed around the patio sweeping leaves.

"Excuse me, but why doesn't the rapturous smell of my delivered confection inspire you to join me in this unparalleled evening nosh? How many leaves do you plan to assault with that broom?"

Libby gave her some fierce side-eye and kept sweeping, long enough that Gwen finally snapped.

"Sit the hell down, Liberty, and eat some of this damn pumpkin bread. It was the last loaf they had, and I had to fight off some damn Karen with unchristian intentions just to get it, so *sit.*"

Libby sat. Following artful attendance to her bread and the deep satisfaction of devouring much too large a bite, she launched into a retelling of her "mane horribilis."

"I honestly hate my daughter sometimes. I don't know how I could have been so bad a parent that she grew up to be this rude, entitled, narcissistic brat. I'd blame Bart but he wasn't around enough to bear that weight. Do you think she was born with it, or was I just the worst?" Her angst was clear, and Gwen leaned back with a raised eyebrow.

"Bridgie's a tough one. That is a fact. And since you *were* a good mother—well, for the most part—I'd guess this is just her soul-of-origin blueprint, albeit a fairly obnoxious one. But let's be honest, Lib; she's not that hideous all the time, right? The few times I've been around her lately she's seemed a lot more settled, more mature even."

Libby turned to her with surprise. "When have you been around her, other than that one lunch we had months ago?"

Gwen, realizing the slip, quickly adjusted. "Well, *then*, then. She seemed more mature then, didn't you think?"

"I don't know. Clearly not enough to convince me of its sustainability." Libby sliced another hunk of bread, gazing off as she slowly chewed. "Sometimes when I'm feeling existential and digging deep into my own hand in all this, I wonder if I transferred some of my confusion and resentment to her in vitro. I was so young when I had her, so fucked up, and overwhelmed. Maybe she subconsciously absorbed some of that and it stuck, psychically infecting her, forming her into a confused, resentful person. It would make sense, given how contentious things have been between us since, well, since always." She turned to Gwen. "Any merit to the thesis?"

Gwen stood up and started clearing the table. "I think blaming your overwhelmed nineteen-year-old self for Bridget's chronic cantankerousness is self-flagellating and unhelpful. Even if some tiny modicum of that new-age meandering could be true, she's a grown woman now and responsible for her own behavior. She gets no breaks from me. Set some damn boundaries. Let her know what you won't tolerate. Then kick her out if it happens again."

"I wish you were raising her."

Later that night, after a fit of parental guilt compelled her to, once again, cancel the hike with Jeff so she could trundle her daughter around to car dealerships, Libby got a text:

I'm sorry. I'm an asshole. I don't know why I get so shitty with you. I could give you excuses about being impatient with getting my life in order, but I know there is no excuse. I'll figure it out. Again, sorry, Mom. I'll get an Uber to a few places this weekend.

When Libby texted back to say she'd already rearranged her plans and was available to drive if Bridget still her wanted to, her phone rang.

"Now I feel horrible."

"You should," Libby replied, meaning it.

"Just go on your hike. I'll get it handled or we can wait until you have another free Sunday. I'll just feel guilty if we go now."

There was a pause.

"Bridget. I will take you on Sunday. We will enjoy the day together. You'll get a car; you'll also buy me lunch, and after that we won't ever have to have this argument again."

Bridget finally relented. "Okay, deal."

"But Bridge?"

"Yes?"

"I don't want you to talk to me like that ever again on any topic. I'm dead serious."

"Wow."

"And please don't get snarky now and twist this into some kind of battle. I just want us to have a respectful relationship with each other, as we've already discussed. We're both grown women with the ability to control our behavior. So let's do that with each other, okay? Both of us."

"Got it. You're right."

"Okay. Good. You staying at Dean's this weekend?"

"Yes."

"Give him my best. I'll text you when I'm heading out on Sunday; you can shoot me his address."

"Okay. 'Night."

"Good night, sweetheart."

There was a pause. "I do love you, Mom."

Libby felt her heart catch.

CHAPTER 25

Libby Conlin libbyconlin@gmail.com
To: Gwen Herrera gwenherrera@BKRWealthManagement.com
Subject: I'll apologize now

Gwennie: I wanted to give you the heads up in case Jeff says something to Otto and he says something to you, which he no doubt will, and then you'll implode into small pieces, and I'll feel responsible for your disintegration.

About Jeff: I like the guy, he's great, but it can't go anywhere right now. I've had to cancel our last three dates for unavoidable reasons. I have only one day a week that's not obligated to someone or someplace else, and I need that day for the many overwhelming demands on my time. I can't expect any man to deal with that.

Bringing a new person into my life at this moment is not an act of charity, so I'm going to very nicely tell him this just isn't the right time, but maybe some other time will be, and we can pick it up again.

Don't hate me. You did good choosing this one, I just can't do it right now. xo L

132 | LORRAINE DEVON WILKE

Libby Conlin libbyconlin@gmail.com
To: Gwen Herrera gwenherrera@BKRWealthManagement.com
Subject: One more thing

Oh, and I emailed instead of called because I know you'll yell at me, and I can't handle another ornery female in my life at this particular time. 🙂

Gwen Herrera gwenherrera@BKRWealthManagement.com
To: Libby Conlin libbyconlin@gmail.com
Subject: You're a stupid idiot

You're right. I would've yelled.

Honestly, Liberty, it seems you have a robust self-punitive streak I was not heretofore aware of.

FFS, if your weekends suck, why can't you grab a night during the week to nurture a relationship with a really great guy in a world where really great guys do not come along all that often? Do you have some moratorium on having a meal together on, say, a Wednesday?? Get creative, girlfriend.

Grrrrr.

Libby Conlin libbyconlin@gmail.com
To: Gwen Herrera gwenherrera@BKRWealthManagement.com
Subject: No, you are!

Clearly, you're not aware of my hideous work/life lack of balance. Sometimes I don't leave the Attic until 8:00, 9:00, or I'm off with Chloe to various meetings. The nights I'm not, I try to get in a walk to prevent my aging bones from calcifying. Other nights I'm dog-tired and just need sweats and TV.

On top of that, I have homework, *homework*, for this fucking CPA class. If you don't get all that you're the stupid idiot.

If Jeff and I are "meant to be," as the romance novels you like to read often say, we'll connect again later. Shut up. xo L

Gwen Herrera gwenherrera@BKRWealthManagement.com
To: Libby Conlin libbyconlin@gmail.com
Subject: Spinsters can be fun...

Fine. I will transcend my natural impulse to browbeat you into bringing sex back into your life (It keeps you young! You could do fewer walks and still have good bones!!), but I do get it. I'm sorry you can't work it out now. He really is a great guy.

At least get some new sweats. I hear beige is big with spinsters.

CHAPTER 26

Jeff was at a five-day dental conference in Milwaukee, leaving Libby to delay the inevitable "I can't do this right now" conversation until they could speak unencumbered. After she cancelled the last hike for the sake of Bridget's vehicle search by way of text, he'd called and left a message asking her to join him for dinner the following Saturday night, which seemed as good a time as any to lower the boom. Then Chloe once again preempted this plan by requesting her participation that same Saturday evening at an important buyers' gathering in Pasadena, requiring her to leave immediately from CPA class to hit the freeway east, always a logistical clusterfuck. It also meant she had to cancel the dinner date with Jeff, the fourth date she'd canceled on him in as many weeks, triggering guilt that actually made her feel queasy.

He had a professional banquet to attend Friday night, so she waited until Saturday morning to alert him of this latest scheduling snafu but was only able to leave a message. At that point, it seemed cruel not to at least allude to the looming break-up plan, which she reluctantly did, telling him she simply didn't have the time or headspace to be a good girlfriend, a word she didn't say specifically, as she would certainly *not* refer to herself as a *girlfriend*, but it was what she was thinking. Being a good girlfriend required dedication, time, dependability, etc., and she could offer none of those. She ended the message by apologizing and suggesting they talk sometime on Sunday to wrap things up.

He chose not to wait.

She was sitting at her computer terminal in the Saturday classroom, Jonah Hill droning through some explanation of something that was no doubt essential to what she was supposed to learn, when her phone suddenly sprang to life with its rattling ring tone. So few people called her these days, texting being the preferred mode of almost everyone she knew, she'd forgotten to set it on vibrate, a major faux pas that not only disrupted the class but tendered the ire of her teacher, now glaring at her from across the room.

"Ms. Conlin, I do believe I've made myself abundantly clear that turning off your phone is a non-negotiable requirement of the class."

"I am so sorry," she mumbled as she quickly silenced the ringer. Glancing at the screen she could almost feel Jeff's pique oozing from his caller ID. "And, to apologize again, this is an emergency I must respond to. I will do so out in the hall."

He shot her some wicked side-eye, but she skulked out of the classroom anyway, determined to get this unpleasant task done and over with.

"I want you to know I am now on the shit list of my teacher, which doesn't bode well for my passing grade." She said this lightly, humorously, hoping to set a light and humorous tone.

"I'm sorry about that, but I just got your message and felt it required a call." He sounded less humorous. Or light.

Libby, appropriately chastised, launched into her explanation. "I know I should have waited to talk about this with you in person, but the idea was to pre-empt ruining your *entire* weekend, especially after you'd been away all week. It wasn't a matter of avoidance; I was hoping to give you the opportunity to make other plans more conveniently."

"I see. Well, considering I don't really want to make other plans, also considering this is the fourth date you've now cancelled on me, which has to be a record in my dating history—"

"I know, I'm sorry—"

"Don't apologize, things happen, you're busy, I get it. But besides being a little hurt by the rejection, I've got be honest; I feel like I'm missing something, Libby. It seemed like we were enjoying the time together; there's no pressure for any more than you can give me right now, and I thought we both agreed we'd keep it simple and easy for as long as it needs to be simple and easy. No one's pushing you beyond that, so explain to me why you're essentially breaking up with me instead of just rebooking our dinner date."

She dropped to a metal folding chair tucked under the hallway window. "I know, it must seem abrupt. But too many things are piling up for me right now, Jeff. This class still has many more weeks of commitment, plus my boss has needed more of my time lately with her business expanding, so my life is too complicated for anything else that demands time and attention."

"I haven't demanded anything."

"I know, that was clumsily put. But I am tapped to the limit, and I've never been a carefree dater. I can't imagine dating you would be any different since we seem to—"

"What? Like each other?"

"I'm just too crowded right now to navigate all this."

"I'll take a number."

"Too glib. Too easy."

"It's not that hard, Libby."

Suddenly, she was annoyed. He reminded her of Gwen in that moment, presuming he could determine what she could or couldn't do, what she should or shouldn't find hard. It didn't sit well. "But you can't really say that for *my* life, can you?"

He heard the edge in her voice and took a breath. "No, I can't, you're right. I'm being a little clumsy here too. But take it as a compliment; I don't want to give up that easily. A dinner here and there must be doable, yes? You need to eat; can't you just consider me part of your meal plan?"

Libby had to laugh. "Ah, the blush of romance."

"Hey, we take what we can get."

She smiled at his persistence. "Okay, let's do this. I'll get in touch when I can carve out some time, and if that coincides with time you've got, we'll meet for a meal. That's the best I can do right now."

"Works for me. Now, get back to class before he sends you to detention."

Which she did, smiling, despite Jonah Hill's fiercely directed frown as she sat back down.

CHAPTER 27

A n "assessment meeting" was set for Saturday morning at Gwen's office. With Bridget now working a full-time schedule, carving out time to get all the pieces of the project put together had become more challenging, but they were finally at the place where Gwen's thumbs up, the next crucial step, was needed. Delighted to be able to pick up Dean in her new/old Hyundai Sonata, Bridget grabbed some baked goods on the way downtown, determined to make this gathering more of a celebration than a test.

Over muffins and good coffee, Gwen perused the artwork, then watched the opening segment of interviews with various contemporary musicians juxtaposed against Bridget's narration of Libby's (anonymous) commentary. When they played all four remastered songs for her, Gwen's face lit up as the music flung itself into every corner of her office. They watched her expression shift from delight to introspection, as if each song conjured up specific memories that neither Dean nor Bridget was privy to.

As the last song faded on a raucous vamp-out, Gwen sat back in her chair, head shaking as she looked at the two eager faces before her. "Wow. Unbelievable to hear those songs again. They sound amazing. She sounds amazing. Excellent work digitizing and remastering everything, Dean."

"Thanks."

"Clearly the video's not done—"

"No, we have to wait to see what happens after we post everything online," Bridget jumped in. "Once we see what kind of traction we get, I'll write up a concluding statement, maybe cut in a few other short interviews, then decide how to wrap it all up."

"We have to give it some time for the songs to get out there," Dean added.

"Yeah." Bridget agreed. "Not sure how much yet—" She looked at Dean.

"Maybe a month or so," he suggested. "That's probably enough to see if anything happens, if we get any downloads, any listeners."

"Curious: how do you plan to promote this?" Gwen was making notes. "Obviously, that's needed if you expect anyone to find the songs."

Bridget walked around the desk with her iPad, pulled up some web pages to show Gwen. "I set up a really basic website and social media pages in all the usual spots using the band's name, some of my dad's art, and some generic photos I put together with musical instruments, faces in shadow, that sort of cryptic stuff; anything to suggest a band without actually *having* a band. I'll stay on the social media, keep it really active, and with all that, the songs should get out there."

"Very clever," Gwen mused, as she scrolled through the various pages and portals. "This is good, professional stuff. Well done, Bridgie."

Bridget beamed as she sat back down. "We're using a dedicated number at Dean's studio in case anyone calls, and I created a Gmail address with the band's name. Not that we expect that kind of response, but we needed contact info to set the media stuff up. Anyway, I think it all works. Now we're wondering what you think."

They waited for the verdict, which, oddly, was not immediate.

Gwen leaned back for a moment, then asked, "What did your dad say about this, Bridget?"

"He was sort of non-committal. Said we did a good job putting it together, that it's a cool idea, but when I asked him to keep it to himself for now, he said that he thought we should clear it with Mom before we post anything. I think he's worried she might get weird or something."

"See, that's where I go too." Gwen sighed. "I hesitate to sign off on this only because I know how she can get about that period of her life."

"I think she'll be really pleased to hear the tracks polished up and sounding so damn incredible," Dean said hopefully.

"Yeah, I do too," Gwen agreed, "but the girl can get ornery when she's feeling ambushed."

Bridget's face fell. "This would be an ambush? That's what you think?"

Gwen looked at her, surprised. "Oh no, honey, not at all. I totally get the homage here, the honoring of her artistry. I'm just a little unsure how it'll strike her."

All three sat for a moment, pondering. Dean finally perked up.

"Okay, how about this? We post everything and see what happens. It's quite possible nothing will, which would suck for Bridget's project, but it might be pointless to get too concerned about Libby's reaction when that's an actual possibility. But, if we do get traction, we'll use that data for the concluding statement, and when it's all done, we'll take the songs down. They won't be out in public for that long. And we can have a private screening of the presentation for Libby when it's wrapped. Once she knows it was only for the school admissions team, no one else, I have a feeling she'd be okay with it." He looked expectantly at Gwen. "Right?"

Nodding, she stood up and moved toward the door. "That's a very smart way to frame it, Dean; you've convinced me. Okay, I'm going to make an executive decision and say go ahead, do what you're going to do. I think it's a clever idea, I love that you're using your mom's music, Bridget, and, ultimately, I think she will too. Odds are good she'll be touched once she gets over the shock, but I'll take the heat if there ends up being any. Now get out of here; I got a client who wants to give me her money."

CHAPTER 28

After several stimulating phone conversations and just as many thwarted attempts at scheduling, they finally found a Sunday with enough time to accomplish a hike in Jeff's neighborhood. Trekking the hills of Fryman Canyon Park, Libby was grateful the trail was less exhausting than expected, there was the occasional bench to sink into, and the views were worth the exertion required.

They talked about picnicking somewhere in the park afterwards, or grabbing some lunch back down the hill, but as they headed toward their cars, Jeff added the option to "pop over" to his house where fixings for lunch were in ample supply.

"Besides," he added with a wry smile, "I'd love for you to see my place."

She was immediately hesitant, but ultimately decided her curiosity merited the detour.

A short drive got them there, and the neighborhood, high above the city with dramatic views of the surrounding hills lush with trees and desert flowers, was impressive. As was the house, a stunning modern thing of wood and glass that completely fit the surrounds and was just one of many gorgeous homes on the street. As Jeff led Libby into the foyer, with its dark hardwood floors and contemporary copper chandelier, her reaction was not unlike the standard HGTV "reveal"; she almost gasped as they made their way into the living room.

Gazing around the impeccably neat, gorgeously designed room, with its luxurious modern furniture and artwork that looked important and original, Libby was authentically impressed. "I hate to sound all Daisy Dukes, but I don't think I've seen a house this pretty that wasn't on TV."

Jeff, clearly pleased, laughed. "The wonders of good decorators and no one around to mess things up. Sit down, get comfortable."

She sat at the couch, perching on the edge as if afraid to muss the sumptuous velvet corduroy in deep rusted brown. Noting the white flokati pillows and ornate coffee table of distressed copper, she suddenly felt sweaty, plebian, and completely out of place. "It's all so, wow, so exquisite, Jeff. Really. I'm speechless. And concerned I'll get trail dust on something."

Jeff joined her on the couch. "Go ahead; mess it up. It could use some character." He stretched his arm behind her, cupping her shoulder, pulling her gently toward him. "I'm glad you like it. I hope you'll enjoy spending some of your elusive free time here."

She leaned into his shoulder. "I don't know, I'm used to crumbling chimneys and clothes piled on the couch. All this fancy makes me nervous."

"It's only fancy because I'm alone here most of the time. Throw in some family folk and a dinner party now and then, and you'll be surprised how lived-in it can get. Want the tour?"

She did.

Much like perusing an art museum, she discovered that every room, every inch of it, was beautiful, artful, and perfect. Libby was glad he hadn't been to her house yet. It would be a locational comedown.

Still, she enjoyed the poshness of the place. There was something almost titillating about being around a man of means, a circumstance she was not accustomed to. Most (all) of her years with Bart were relentless scrambles to get bills paid, afford school costs; determine which repair was more urgent than the next, which never allowed her to even imagine the kind of abundance she saw here. The idea of having enough—of having more than enough—was both foreign and self-consciously appealing.

Suddenly they were at the master suite, another stunning room with dramatic lighting and each item of furniture and art in complete, balanced harmony.

"And this is the master bedroom," Jeff intoned in a mock narrator's voice. "I promise it was not saved for last for any particular reason."

"Whatever." She feigned nonchalance with a grin. "Just another dazzling room in a dazzling house with not a thing out of place, big whoop." In reality, the only thing remotely out of place was a closet door left ajar. She couldn't help but peek inside, first noticing the sheer size of it. "This would qualify as a bedroom in my house!" She laughed. Next to be noticed was the almost military precision of its contents. Closet art. Sport coats, each sheathed in plastic, hung so that blues followed blacks, followed plaids, followed casual. Dress shirts were categorized with similar exactitude. A glance at the floor revealed each pair of shoes with its own tree, all spit-shined and color arranged.

She stepped back. "Wow. I don't think I've ever seen a more meticulously arranged closet. I am honestly in awe."

Jeff walked up and quietly shut the door. "Guess I like things neat," he responded with a tinge of defensiveness. "That's not a bad thing, Libby, is it?"

"No, no, not at all. I'm impressed. All the men I've ever known in my life, of every age, were bona fide slobs. This has recalibrated my opinion of men." She laughed and looked over at him. "I didn't mean to embarrass you—"

"I'm not embarrassed." He was. And working to hide it.

"It's just wonderfully unique."

"Hey, I'm a unique guy." Recovery quick, he sat on the bed and patted the spot next to him. "Come here."

His voice was gentle and, she hated to admit, alluring. Still, she hesitated.

"Come on, I'm not going to pounce. As organized as my closet is, you shouldn't worry about me having impulse control issues."

Libby laughed and sat next to him, side-by-side, shoulders touching, without words. Then, in a moment of quite considered impulse, he turned and kissed her, a long, passionate kiss. As they fell back on the bed, contact escalated until Libby sat up, flustered.

Her heart pounded, her skin tingled; her insides roiled with that forgotten sensation of yearning, lust; pelvic heat. She didn't know what to say, what to do. It had been so long, so damn long, she'd lost the script, unclear if she should banish caution and melt into this lovely man or keep walls up for the sake of safety and security.

Jeff sat up and gently took her hand. "Libby, I think we both know something good is happening between us. I think we both feel it. At least that's what I've gotten out of our conversations, our time together. I hope so because I want you so bad it hurts. But I'll take whatever time you need. You just let me know."

She felt like a teenager wrestling with which rules applied and which could be flouted. She also felt like an old woman who was worried about what she'd look like naked and how appealing or unappealing that might be to this very fit, very handsome man. It was a strange conundrum to balance in this pivotal moment of decision. "I promise I'm not trying to be coy, and I realize many women would have typically leapt by this point, I just—"

"I know, I understand, you need to take is slow. But you control the pace of things here, I promise. Just know I think you're the hottest girl around and, neat though I may be, I'd like to rend your garments and ravage you like a Viking."

Libby couldn't help but smile. He bordered on geeky but was so sweet and sincere she'd grown to not only feel, but appreciate, maybe even *need*, his clear affection for her. It brightened her stressful existence and gave her something to look forward to. She wanted to stay cautious, to keep her distance, but the pull toward him, the longing she felt right now, was visceral, and she was suddenly tired of the constraints with which she so relentlessly held herself.

She got up, dimmed the overhead light, then returned to the bed.

Pushing him onto his back, she straddled his hips, pressing into his obvious arousal, pinned his arms overhead and planted an exquisitely drawn-out kiss on his willing mouth. Brushing her hair out of her eyes, she gave him a seductive smile. "Have at it, Einar."

CHAPTER 29

Wrapping up work for the day, texting back and forth with Dean to find out when he'd be done at the studio and if they could meet for dinner, Bridget was surprised to see a message from Ellie Scamehorn, the admissions director at SCC.

Hi, Bridget. Checking in to see how you're progressing on your project. If you want to talk about your idea, or if you're ready to schedule your presentation, please give me a call. The next deadline is coming up fast, and I don't want you to miss it if you're ready. Hope all is well.

She felt an immediate rush of anxiety. It had now been a month since they posted everything, and while managing the social media accounts of her employers, she'd squeezed in plenty of activity for Minor Rebellion. At first there'd been little interaction, but she'd noticed a spike of late—people commenting on various posts, some asking who the players were and "where's the band's picture?" but very little commentary on the music itself. She could tell people had clicked the song links, but the last time she checked there'd only been a minimal amount of downloading. She began to wonder if they were going to get any useable data before too much time passed to keep the project viable.

Bridget thought about calling Dean to discuss the situation, but his last text said he had to work late. When she sent back a sad emoji, he suggested she meet him at the studio, and they could "grab dinner somewhere in the neighborhood." She felt less than enthusiastic about that option, having hoped they could meet at his apartment, order in, and discuss all that needed discussion after some vigorous and mutually satisfying sex, but that was not to be. She tapped back a "thumbs up" and hit the freeway.

Later, ambling with him through a trendy shopping district just blocks from the school, Bridget found herself irked in a general way, but certainly by the cacophony of sound that surrounded them: the squeals of passing cars, the clashing choruses of muzak bleating from store to store as they wandered by; horns honking, voices yelling, noise, noise, *noise*, and suddenly she just wanted to go home and curl up with a book. She emitted a deep sigh.

Dean noticed. "Are you okay? You seem, I dunno, something."

"Just my usual stuff. The slow pace of the project. Still at my mom's. Still in a state of waiting. I like my job for the most part, but it's not enough money to make any real changes in my situation. The women are nice, happy with what I'm doing; they make *great* food—"

"But?"

"I made the decision to get out of the food industry after the debacle with my ex and this is still a food industry gig, even if I don't deal with the food and customers myself. If I was actually on a path toward getting a degree that would ultimately lead to a real career job, I might feel a little bit better about my life at the moment."

"Wait." Dean cocked his head, bemused. "Isn't that exactly what we're doing here—working on your admissions project so you *can* get into the school to get that degree that ultimately leads to a real career job?"

She laughed out loud. "Yes, it is, I know. I'm just being cranky. I guess because I'm not seeing much action on the music end of things and that's depressing. There are a fair number of responses when I post content, but I'm not sure the music is getting to actual ears or having any kind of impact. And that was the whole point of the experiment, to see if it would. If nobody's interested in the songs, I won't have much of a point to make."

Dean stuck his hands in his pockets. "Yeah, that's true." He spotted a taco truck on the corner. "You want to just grab some stuff here and go back to the studio, keep talking about it?"

"Sure."

After getting their order, Bridget continued her vent. "And just so you know, I'm not giving up, not yet. But even my dad says the odds of anything happening are pretty remote. These are almost forty-year-old songs, there's no actual band attached, and without hot, young musicians for the influencers to get behind, stirring up movement is probably unlikely."

"I like your dad, but he's a bit of an Eeyore," Dean remarked. "Plus, he doesn't know much about the current music scene or how music gets delivered, how people consume it. I still think the songs are strong enough to break through. When was the last time you checked the download stats?"

"A couple of days ago. I force myself to wait a few days in between or I'd be checking by the hour."

"Well, who knows, maybe there's been more action since then. We'll just keep promoting and see what happens."

"Scamehorn texted today; wants to know if I'm ready to book my presentation."

They pushed through the doors of the school lobby, which was lit up and filled with a gaggle of twenty-something students sitting in a circle chattering and laughing, takeout containers and coffee cups everywhere, music blaring from someone's iPad. Dean nodded to them in passing, inspiring lots of waves and, "Hey, Mr. Park!" callouts. Just as he and Bridget got to the studio door, and almost inaudible in the chaos of conversation bouncing off the walls, a familiar strain pushed through.

Both froze.

Suddenly, unmistakably, "What Can I Do" was booming around the room. Dean looked at Bridget, whose eyes had turned to saucers. "Oh my God. That's our song!" she yelped.

They quickly reapproached the group of students, one of whom looked up at Dean with curiosity. "What's up, Mr. Park?"

"Sorry to interrupt, Sophie—it's Sophie, right?"

"Yeah. I took your Pro-Tools class last year. Are we being too loud? We had a screening earlier, and we're just hanging out. Is that cool?"

"Yeah, yeah, that's very cool, Sophie. No, I just wanted to ask about the song you're listening to right now."

She looked at her iPad. "Oh, I just downloaded it today. A friend of mine shared it with me yesterday, and I loved it."

Bridget felt a bolt of electricity shoot down her arms. "That's so amazing. That's our song."

All the kids suddenly looked up at her and Dean. Sophie, with an expression somewhere between awe and confusion, turned the music up louder. "This? *This* is your song?"

Dean jumped in. "Well, a band we, uh, manage."

"Wow." Sophie grinned. "That is so awesome. It's a great song. Got a really cool vibe, sorta '80s but modern. A bunch of my friends have shared it in the last few days, so you should know it's going kinda viral. That's gotta make you guys happy, right?"

Dean laughed. "Oh, yeah. Makes us very happy."

"Well, cool, Mr. Park, congratulations!"

Bridget was suddenly struck by a thought. She pulled out her phone. "Hey, Sophie, would you mind letting me film you saying all that again? We're making a little doc for the band, and it would be great for them to hear some positive feedback from real-life fans."

"Absolutely!" Sophie grinned and stood up, fluffing her hair, and straightening her clothes. "I'm building my own influencer network so if you wouldn't mind sending me a copy, I'd love to."

"Of course," Bridget beamed. "Influence away!"

While Dean stood with steaming bags of tacos, and a group of young students watched with fascination as "What Can I Do?" soundtracked the moment, Sophie repeated her gushing accolades, and Bridget, relieved and excited, shot the concluding tag of her admissions project.

CHAPTER 30

Seated in Chloe's office, having her first meeting with the company's financial adviser while the boss was out to lunch, Libby surprised herself by being moderately fascinated by the arcane mathematical data being conveyed about the Attic's fiscal set-up. She listened and jotted notes in her laptop files, fairly certain they would be useful at a later date. She was just weeks away from taking the first two parts the four-part CPA exam, which the dour man sitting next to her (whose name was Thor Chapman) claimed was, "one of the most challenging professional exams on the planet," watching to see if she blanched at the description. She didn't.

Despite reluctance and general resentment at having to spend her Saturdays in a dull classroom with Jonah Hill and a cadre of deeply focused students bent over computers, her aptitude for mathematics held her in good stead, and for that reason alone it came fairly easily. There was some of that same "putting order into chaos" satisfaction she gleaned from ironing shirts or weeding the garden, two things she did as infrequently as possible. And though she wasn't sure where this streak of left-brain competence came from, her gratitude was immense, especially since the current version of the exam would take her a long sixteen hours to complete.

As she and Thor Chapman concluded their meeting, the door flew open, and Chloe entered in a rush of color and energy. After hellos were chirped all around, and she and Thor stepped outside to briefly chat, Libby gathered her various accoutrement to head back to her office. When Chloe re-entered, she cocked her head, perusing Libby with interest.

"What?" Libby was immediately self-conscious.

"Thor thinks you're very smart. I told him I already knew that."

"How nice." Libby rolled her eyes playfully. "Kind of him to deign me as such."

Chloe laughed, following with, "And you're wearing red."

"Thor mentioned that, too?" Libby, incredulous.

"No, for heaven's sake, I am!"

Libby had scored a brilliant red tunic at a formerly favorite thrift shop in Hollywood and had enjoyed it frequently in recent days. This was the first time she'd worn it to work.

"You never wear colors." Chloe was examining her as if she were a potential buy. "I have never seen you in anything but black, navy, or muted earth tones. This is a remarkable change."

Libby blushed. "It was just a good find at one of my favorite stores. Why is that remarkable? Do I look odd in colors?"

"Oh no, my dear, you look fabulous. Vibrant, beautiful, alive."

Now Libby cocked her head. "And you're saying I look none of those things in blacks, browns, and earth tones?"

Chloe came over and wrapped her arms around Libby, delivering a hearty hug. "Not at all." She sat down behind her desk, motioning for Libby to sit as well. "It's just a wonderful addition. In fact, I've noted a slight uptick in your general joy energy lately as well, wondered if there was a specific reason for it. Say, the new man in your life?" Her eyes sparkled.

Libby hated that a slight uptick in her joy energy (*such a Chloe phrase*) was being attributed to the new man in her life. Hated that Chloe made the guess. It felt so regressively cliched and unliberated. It was also, inarguably, the accurate reason for that "uptick." In fact, Libby was convinced her skin had taken a different tone, her muscles had strengthened; her heart had warmed, and somewhere in all that the desire to wear red had emerged.

"I approve wholeheartedly, my dear. He sounds like a very special man." Chloe remarked after Libby admitted to the influence of said man.

"He is. We're taking it slow, but so far it's been a nice change of circumstances for me. I'm enjoying it."

"As you should. It's been a long time a'comin', especially after being in the trenches all these years with Bart."

Chloe, who liked everyone, wasn't fond of Bart, who, she once said, was "a loafer who takes your generosity far too much for granted." Libby always appreciated her vicarious outrage, but knew it was her own vents about Bart's repeated failings that had helped formed those opinions. Perhaps she could soften the view at some point for the sake of goodwill and charity.

"I'd like to meet your Jeff when we can; perhaps a dinner with the four of us. Until we can work that out, I hope you continue to find—with your new love and this new, more abundant chapter of your career here—a better life/work balance, as you've put it. I very much want that for you, Libby."

"I think I will; I have. Thank you for your patience. And the invitation. I'm sure Jeff would love to get together with you and Martin, so let me know when you've got time."

"I will. Now off with you. I've got phone calls to make!" With a wave and her bright smile, Chloe sent Libby to the door. "And, by the way, you should wear red frequently; it's quite a wonderful color on you."

Libby thought so too.

CHAPTER 31

Curled on the couch in the studio, her iPad open to the panoply of social media sites set up for Minor Rebellion, Bridget gazed at Dean, who was bent over the console mixing a school project, headphones on, focus intense. She smiled softly to herself, enjoying the quiet, easy intimacy that had developed between them, taking pleasure in knowing he was someone worthy of her emotional investment. In her slow transition from ex-wife to new girlfriend, she realized that Dean's innate goodness, his warmth and dependability, never seemed to wane, and were, in fact, elements of him she'd grown to very much count on.

He caught her smiling in his direction and blushed. "What?"

"Nothing. Just admiring you at work."

He leaned down and gave her a kiss. "I like being admired by you."

The jangle of the studio phone disrupted their moment. It was the second line, the one dedicated to the project. He didn't move to answer it.

"You don't think you should answer that?" she queried.

"Nah. I've gotten a ton of messages on that line, and they've all been sales stuff."

"Like, from who?"

"Spammers. Lots of vinyl and CD replication places, some publicity companies, promotional companies, that sort of thing. Nothing of value to what we're doing."

"Okay. But do you check the messages every day?"

"Not every day. I think the last time I checked was Monday."
It was Thursday.

She got up and went toward the phone. "Do you mind if I
check? I need a break from my 'influencing' anyway, and I can
clear the messages for you."

"Sure." He gave her the voicemail code and went back to
work.

She sat down and dialed the number, listened without reaction for a few minutes, then her eyes widened. She abruptly
stood. He looked over.

"What?"

"You are not going to believe this. Oh, my God. Let me put
it on speaker." She fumbled with the phone console until she
found the speaker button. "Just listen. This came in yesterday."

*"Hello, I'm calling for Dean Park, got this number off
your YouTube page. Dean, this is Aaron Leifer at Delgany
Records. I'm not sure if you're familiar with the company,
but we're a subsidiary of Warner Music Group, and I'm head
of A&R over here. We're a small but well-financed label
always looking for what's new, what's viral, and I keep an
ear open for interesting bands bubbling under the surface
of some of the bigger acts out there. Your band's name has
come up with more than one of my street teams lately, so I
listened to the tunes you've got posted online. Really excellent. I also noticed you're getting some active hits on social
media, which always impresses me. I'm a little surprised
there isn't any info about the band itself, the singer—who is
amazing, by the way—no pictures or names, so I wanted to
reach out for a little more information, maybe talk to you
about setting up a meet."*

He then left his number and the invitation to call.

Bridget's face had blanched in the relisten. Dean reached over and shut down the song he was working on, sinking to his seat. They both looked at each other, incredulity dominating the moment.

After a beat, Dean stated the obvious. "*That* was not an expected call."

"Nope, not at all." Bridget's expression suddenly bordered on terror. "What do we do with this?" she practically hissed. "We're a front, a fake. We're impersonating a band that doesn't exist, using music we don't even have permission to use, and now some real record company guy wants to talk to us? What the hell, Dean? We could get in trouble for this!"

"Get in trouble for what, Bridget? First of all, we don't even have to respond to the guy if we don't want to. But there's nothing to get in trouble for anyway. If we did want to talk to him, we could just tell him what we're doing, and he'd probably think we were geniuses."

"Oh, I think it's more likely he'd think we were assholes." She was now pacing. "I'd also guess he wouldn't appreciate wasting his valuable time on a phantom project."

"What time has he wasted? He listened to some songs, looked at some websites, made one call. Come on, Bridge—" Suddenly he was grinning. "Don't you see? This is so fucking cool! You basically just proved the thesis of your project, which is that old music *can* translate in a new market if you set it up right. What a perfect way to conclude the presentation—with his message."

She plunked down to the couch, her mood shifting to curiosity. "I guess that would be cool, wouldn't it?"

"Absolutely."

"But what do we do about this guy?"

Dean joined her on the couch. "I'm not sure. But I think I *gotta* call him back, right? I mean, it's Delgany Records. They're one of the best indie labels around. I know people who'd cut off an arm to get a call from their head of A&R."

"But what do we say? 'Hi, Mr. Big-Time Record Man, we've got a school admissions project going here with my mom's old music. She's a fifty-something CPA, and the band doesn't exist, but, hey, thanks for your interest.' He'll think we're insane."

"Maybe." He sat back. "Or, how about this? I call him back and you film the conversation. That way if there's anything we can use for the doc, we've got it, if not, no big deal."

"When do you want to do this?"

"Right now."

"Now? It's seven o'clock."

"Hey, it's the music biz; people work late. And if he's not there, I'll leave a message. At least I'll be showing some respect by returning a call to an interested party from a cool label."

"Okay, but what are you going to say?"

"I don't know. I'm going to wing it."

"Is that wise?"

"Probably not, but let's do it before I lose my nerve."

"You're definitely braver than me," she said, setting her phone up to videotape.

Dean listened to the message again, then dialed the number, keeping it on speaker.

The line picked up. "Aaron Leifer, what's up?"

Stunned that a receptionist hadn't answered, more stunned that the guy was actually there, Dean immediately stumbled. "Uh, hi, Aaron, yeah, uh, this is Dean Park. You called the other day about Minor Rebellion?"

Bridget looked like she was going to throw up.

"Oh, hey Dean, how's it going?"

"Pretty good, pretty good. What can I do for you?"

"As I laid out in my message, I listened to your stuff up on YouTube, thought it sounded really great. Wondered what you guys were up to at the moment."

Bridget and Dean looked at each other. He hesitated. She shook her head furiously, no idea how to respond.

"Well, the band is basically, uh, writing new material and keeping a low profile."

"Oh, yeah? Why the low profile?"

"Well, they've been, um, on the road for a couple of months, doing small gigs around the country, and they were ready to take a break."

"Gotcha. Well, listen, I'd love to check out the new stuff when it's ready."

"Yeah, that'd be great—"

"Is there a time when I could meet the band, maybe sit in on a rehearsal or at the studio?"

Again, they looked at each other with barely contained panic.

"Well, we haven't been recording."

"Okay." Aaron sounded a little confused. "Look, I've got people up here looking for the next big thing, and your music has got them interested; seems like a good time to jump on this. If they're not doing any gigs at the moment, maybe we could set up a showcase, something to get a feel for them live."

Dean rolled his eyes at the camera; Bridget just shook her head.

"Yeah, yeah, that would be cool. Ah, let me run that by the band and see what we can do. Obviously, I'm thrilled by your interest, and I'll get back to you as soon as I can."

"Great. In the meantime, could you pop me a picture of the group? I didn't see any on your media, and I'd like to get an idea of their look, their image."

"Of course, yeah, that makes sense." He stared at Bridget, suppressing the bubbling urge to laugh.

"Okay, Dean, thanks for calling. Be in touch."

"You got it." Dean hung up the phone and turned to Bridget, who was now lying flat on the couch as if she couldn't sit up any longer. When he finally burst into laughter, she looked at him like he was insane.

"*What* is funny about this?"

"You don't realize it yet," he hooted, "but your project just went seriously off the hook!"

CHAPTER 32

San Diego had always been a favorite destination of hers, and as they pulled up to a theater sparkling with Edison lights, the marquee lit up and lively, Libby was glad she'd ignored her post-class weariness to accept Jeff's offer to drive down together. They were attending the eight o'clock showing of the first summer musical (written by junior year students) for which Rob would be working the lights. Or, at least, part of the crew working the lights.

He'd been thrilled to get the call from his mother about their trip down, and they met for dinner at a place he recommended (excellent Korean barbeque). Libby noted his hair was longer, his frame thinner, his face maturing past pimples and soft curves toward the sculpted, handsome adult he was becoming. Conversation was easy, and he appeared to find Jeff perfectly acceptable, whispering in his mother's ear: "I like the guy!" She hadn't realized, until her shoulders relaxed, how important that was to her.

The play, however, was tedious—too much youthful pontificating with a slight strain of "high school musical"—but the lighting shined. At the after-party at his mentor's house, they met Hewitt Taylor, a short, fiery-eyed man of about forty-five, who regaled them with accolades of his newest mentee, claiming, "Robert has a real future in the craft should he choose to pursue it!" Clearly "Robert" had made an impression.

He also introduced them to another member of the lighting team, a handsome young man named Dustin, who seemed delighted to make their acquaintance and was, Libby suspected, delighted to know Rob. While nothing outright had ever been stated, she'd always held suspicion that her son might be gay, occasionally opening the door wide enough for him to talk about it with her, but up till now it had been unspoken. It remained unspoken, but still, there was Dustin, smiling at Robbie as if the sun shone behind his eyes and she knew that, given enough time, he would eventually share his true self with his family. She could wait.

There was discussion of meeting for breakfast the following morning, but with a late night assured (when Libby and Jeff exited at midnight the party was still in full swing), and an early matinee call on Sunday, Robbie begged off and they said their goodbyes before leaving Hewitt's, which was fine with Libby; she felt they'd had ample conversation and accomplished the mission of introducing her new boyfriend to her son. Perhaps the next time he'd be comfortable enough to introduce his own.

With Jeff out Sunday morning being far more ambitious than she by getting in an early run, she lay in the sumptuous bed at the U.S. Grant Hotel downtown, curled under the unfathomably cozy down comforter, musing on life—her life specifically—at this specific moment of time.

As much as she'd resisted the assignation, once the sexual divide had been crossed she fully immersed herself in the role of "Jeff's girlfriend." Given her schedule, they still weren't able to get together as much as he'd like, but she was satisfied with their impromptu dinners and Sunday day trips; the seductive nights at his "mansion," as she teasingly called it, and the frequent late-night phone conversations. They were easing into ease with each other, and it felt good, right; she was comfortable with its pace.

Which got her to thinking about Bridget, who seemed to be existing in a parallel universe with her own evolving relationship. The two women saw less and less of each other, as Bridget spent most of her free time at the studio and her nights at Dean's apartment. When they were in the house together, despite earlier discussions on the topic, their conversations stubbornly remained largely light and inconsequential. Though she clearly preferred this to snark and disrespect, Libby worried that she was wasting an opportunity to deepen her relationship with her daughter during what would surely be a relatively short-lived interval of house-sharing.

But when she'd ask, "What's going on with you these days?" Bridget offered only casual reportage: an assessment of her job, the admissions project, maybe a comment or two along the lines of, "Dean and I are having lots of fun." She did ask Libby about developments with Jeff, who she'd met weeks earlier, slightly amused that they both seemed to have entered similar phases in their social lives, but other than echoing Rob's, "I like the guy," she had little curiosity about her mother's thoughts or feelings on the topic.

It left Libby dispirited at times, how they seemed to come together for a brief spell, then pull apart again. But try though she might to change the chemistry of their relationship, it remained true that whatever existed between them was almost always on Bridget's terms. At least she was occupied, and from what Libby could glean from their occasional conversations, happy about her burgeoning connection with Dean. All else would have to be presumed.

Jeff. *Let me think about Jeff,* she mused, leaning toward the room service table to grab a glass of orange juice. She could tell her body was responding to his attentions by relinquishing some of its surplus (her black jeans fit again). Happily, their own conversations were always meaningful and balanced. He seemed commendably well-adjusted on practically every level and topic, though she still did find his pathological neatness worthy of merciless teasing. That he took her jokes with good humor was in his favor.

In fact, we're doing this just right, she acknowledged with pleasure. She was relieved that they'd actually found a workable rhythm—not only in terms of schedules, but the pace of their emotional evolution. Though at one point the previous night she sensed he was edging perilously close to blurting something like, "I love you," so she'd steered away from that percolating development for the sake of avoiding awkwardness.

Because she wouldn't have been able to return the sentiment. Not yet. Ever? She didn't know, couldn't tell. But *now* would have been too soon, too fast; faster than she wanted things to go. But she liked him too much to make any more noise about "slowing things down." Things seemed to be progressing on their own timetable and, as Gwen suggested, she should just "go with the flow." She'd never been a "go with the flow" kind of person, but maybe it was time to become a different kind of person. Right now, liking him, looking forward to him, was good enough. And the sex ... that had become an occupier of her thoughts.

Sex had always held a confusing place in her life. Having been sheltered and regulated by parents terrified that she'd get pregnant and "have to get married" at far too young an age, she'd gone off and done exactly that, preempting any youthful eras of randy promiscuity. Her immediate foray into motherhood and its many demands distracted her from exploring sex to any extent even within her marriage, so much so that she'd come to see herself as not a particularly sexual person. She liked sex; sex with Bart had been generally sweet and satisfying, at least in their early days, but it was never a driving force. It didn't keep her up nights, make her body tingle, dampen her parts, or compel her to make stupid, passion-driven decisions. It was just a nice thing they did once in a while.

There was one guy, shortly after the divorce, one of Gwen's many hopeful introductions, who was charming and unthreatening enough to land in her bed for a brief interlude, but it petered out (one of Gwen's punning ways of putting it), and since then, nothing. Until now.

Laying back on the pillow, she stared up at the ceiling, excavating deeper on the topic. Men. Sex. Attraction. Which led to remembering the one time in her life when undeniable chemistry had been felt in the presence of another person— her old guitar player, Nick Jackson. Her first youthful foray into titillation and sexual curiosity. Though it was always the music, the band, that bound them together, she couldn't deny that she'd been stirred by a powerful attraction, a sense of wanting his attention, his touch, at a time when she was so young and he was ensconced in a significant relationship. Though there was a moment when they teetered toward the divide in the latter era of the band; that one time backstage when they were standing close, the lights down, and he leaned in for a kiss. The shock of sensation and heat had shaken her to the core, but it was a brief encounter and never happened again. Because there was his Mercy. And then there was Bart.

And now there was Jeff.

With no demands on her time or attention, she lay in the luxurious cocoon of the amazing bed, closed her eyes and pictured him touching her. Her hand slid under the covers, down her belly, between her legs. She smiled at her own rare and wonderful lasciviousness, enjoying the slow, tactile sensation of her fingers, picturing his body above hers, strong and sensual. She let her hands do what his would do, and it was exquisite.

The door suddenly opened and the man himself, flushed and sweating, hair tousled in very attractive post-run fashion, stepped into the room. She blushed but didn't stop what she was doing. Taking immediate notice of her hand's location and movement, he kicked off his shoes, pulled off his T-shirt and shorts, and happily joined her.

CHAPTER 33

It had been decided: they were going to put a band together, however temporary, however cobbled, however bizarre, to fully play out the possibilities with Aaron Leifer, head of A&R at Delgany Records.

Dean was "pumped" by the idea.

Gwen practically swooned with excitement.

Bridget thought it was madness.

They'd set up an evening Zoom from Dean's apartment to inform Gwen of the unexpected development of Leifer's call, presuming she'd advise them to come clean with Mr. A&R and use the mere fact of his interest as the conclusion of their thesis. But Gwen being Gwen did no such thing. Instead, she screamed out loud—literally screamed—announcing that this was "the most exciting thing to happen to Libby's music in thirty-some years."

They reminded her that Libby was blithely unaware of the rapidly shifting circumstances with which they were dealing, something she herself had insisted upon, but Gwen remained galvanized by those very circumstances.

"But it's so fabulous! What's the worst that could happen? You audition a bunch of hot, talented young musicians, find a killer vocalist, put the thing together and play nice for the guy. If he bites, the band will love you, your mom's songs will see the light of day; if he doesn't, you'll still have a killer ending, and no harm done."

"Seriously?" Bridget queried; very real anxiety splayed across her face. "It feels to me like it's getting completely out of control."

"In what way, sweetie?" Gwen appeared honestly confused.

Bridget shot her a look of incredulity. "You really need to ask? For starters, we're going to put a fake band together? To take a few pictures and set up a fake showcase for this very real record company guy? In what real world would any bona fide musician want to do that?"

"How about because you pay them to take those pictures and do that fake showcase?"

"We don't have money for that."

"Okay, what do you need?"

Bridget looked at Dean, unclear. "I have no idea."

"We could probably do the auditions at the studio if it doesn't take too long to find what we're looking for; that'll save some money," Dean answered. "We'd also need some professional photos taken—"

"Well, *I* can do that," Bridget remarked.

Dean looked at her with a grin. "Of course; what am I thinking?"

"Look at us; we're already saving money, and we just got started." Gwen chortled.

"Factoring in the time we'd need, I figure two rehearsals and then the showcase." Dean continued. "If we go up to S.I.R. the rooms are expensive, four-hour minimum at four hundred. I can look around to see if we can find a cheaper place for the rehearsals, maybe somewhere on campus, but for the actual showcase, S.I.R. is the place to go."

"Okay." Gwen was making notes. "What about the players?"

"Fifty dollars a rehearsal and a hundred for the gig is standard. But with six of them, that gets expensive."

"Let's see ..." Gwen began working her calculator. "That's three hundred per rehearsal, six for the gig; total, twelve hundred. Plus four hundred for the showcase room—will you need food and drinks for the event?" She looked up at them.

Bridget appeared to gulp. "I guess?"

"I think for the quick 'sit in on a rehearsal' kind of thing he mentioned, we don't we need to get into that." Even Dean was getting twitchy at this point. "Seems like it's getting a lot more expensive than we originally thought, so maybe we should just—"

"If you can find a cheap room for the rehearsals, I'm happy to throw in another couple grand for the rest. It's all for a good cause and, honest to God, we'll have so much fun putting this together—"

"Gwen," Bridget interrupted, "that is really, that is so generous, but—"

"Anything for my godchild, child."

"No, no, wait, listen to me: what if, *what if*, the guy actually likes them and wants to sign them? What then?"

Gwen cocked her head. "And that would be bad because, why? And, I don't know 'what then.' What then, Dean?"

"I've done a bunch of showcases with bands over the years, and most of the time they don't lead to anyone getting signed. In our case, given the fact that there's no public record of the band, no reviews, no actual gigs, it's pretty unlikely some big label is actually going to jump on it. Odds are good Aaron will come, he'll listen, he'll tell us to stay in touch, let him know when we're playing out next or have new songs, and that'll be it."

"Then why bother?" Bridget remained unconvinced about the whole scenario.

Gwen almost jumped from her chair. "Because it'll be fun! Damn, you're such an old woman."

Bridget's eyes rolled. "Thanks. That helps."

"You know I love you, sweetheart, but I think some of your mama's drudgies have rubbed off on you. Just think of it as an experiment, okay? A chance to shoot some interesting stuff that'll take your project to a whole other level. I mean, come on; getting footage of a real live A&R guy listening to your fake band has got to be way more interesting than middling interviews with a bunch of wide-eyed college kids."

Bridget had to crack a smile. "You might have a point there."

"And we'd get to dress up. It's been decades since I've hung out with musicians and felt all cool and hip and stuff. I'll drag out my old rocker-chick jackets I used to wear to your mom's gigs and pretend I'm at a 'Behind the Music' shoot. Come on, let's get this going; I'm ready to rock and roll!"

"Wait, you want to be involved in the auditions?" An incredulous look crossed Bridget's face. "You're absolutely welcome, of course, but it'll be a slog trying to find the right people, and—"

"I don't think it'll be that hard," Dean countered. "I'll post ads in the usual places, and I guarantee we'll get a solid response. This is L.A., after all, musicians everywhere, and since we're offering pay, not usually the case with original projects, it's more likely we'll have to bar the door."

"Then that's the plan," Gwen agreed. "I'll Venmo over the money—Dean, shoot me your account info when you can—and you two will let me know when you've got the auditions set up. I'll be there with glitter in my hair and Pop Rocks for all. Oh, and no Bart on this chapter, kids; lips zipped. He's never been good at keeping secrets, and this one is too big to burden him with."

As they ended the call, Dean closed his laptop and glanced at Bridget, quietly scrolling through her phone messages with a casualness she clearly didn't feel.

"You okay over there?"

She looked up, smiled brightly, though with a faint edge of panic. "Sure. Just got another text from Ellie Scamehorn wondering if I want to book a spot for the next round of presentations. At this point, I'm not sure when I could possibly commit to having this project done."

"Bridge." He sat down next to her, picked up her hand. "I promise you; this part isn't as out of control as it seems to you right now. I've helped audition players plenty of times before; I know how to do it. And I'll work out the timing with the school— they've always been very amenable to my side gigs. When we've got the players, we book the rehearsals, and when they're ready, we set up a showcase at S.I.R. It's all doable, all pretty simple."

"But you're doing so much; I feel like I'm just sitting around letting you and Gwen run the show, and this is supposed to be *my* project to get *my* ass into the school. It's like my parents are doing my homework."

He leaned back. "Hey, if you feel like I'm steamrolling you, I can—"

"No, no, no, I don't feel like that at all. I think you're being unbelievably generous and helpful; I just feel like a slacker."

"That's crazy. You're working a full-time job *and* doing everything you can on this. It's a lot." He got up and moved toward the kitchen. "I think we need to eat. Wanna order a pizza?"

"Sure." She looked at him, a bit woebegone. "I'm sorry if I'm being an ass. I'm just out of my comfort zone."

"I get it, no apologies necessary. Just focus on what you *are* contributing. It's a lot. You're writing it, you'll photograph the band, you're videotaping everything we do, then you'll edit it together when it's done, the hardest part. That's a shit-ton of work. Me and Gwen are just moving pieces around; you're the one who'll be bringing it to life."

Bridget smiled. That sounded both poetic and accurate. It also succeeded in assuaging her immediate angst. "Okay, Dean Park. Let's make a band."

CHAPTER 34

O nce Dean acquired the school's permission (at a reasona-
ble cost) to not only conduct auditions but hold the two
required rehearsals in his studio space, the big room was set up
with an assembled drum kit, guitar and bass amps, a Roland
keyboard, and mics all around. Each auditionee had been sent
the tracks, "What Can I Do" and "He Used to Know Me," with
instructions to "do your best to capture the sounds and sensibilities on the recordings." This sparked some confusion, requiring
diplomatic explanation.

"You want us to *mimic* exact riffs and stuff?"

"Should I try to get my voice to sound exactly like the singer
on the tracks?"

"Is this some kind of tribute band?"

"I like the tunes, but I don't really want to imitate anybody."

"Is this for a reality show?"

Both Dean and Bridget took calls to explain some version
of the following: "No, you don't have to mimic or imitate anyone, but the label really likes the way the songs sound on the
tracks. They expect to see a band that sounds like the band that
made those recordings, so we want to get as close as possible. If
something good comes out of it, we can get a little more original
later."

Neither of them had any fantasies about pulling this off in
the real world, but even Bridget had to admit there was something subversively entertaining in the effort. Keeping it from
Libby was fairly simple at the moment. She was madly prepping

for her CPA exam, the first round of which was booked for the following weekend, occupied enough to accept without question Bridget's blithe announcement that, 'I'll be working with Dean on the project all weekend, so don't expect to hear from me."

And so they began. As promised, Dean ran the operation like the professional he was, Bridget was pathologically nervous, while Gwen planted on the couch in front of the console, out of standard business wear and into a vintage leather jacket and tight jeans, making notes and getting up from time to time to whisper opinions in Bridget's ear. She'd been introduced as their "executive producer," which seemed about right.

Dean and Bridget had designated themselves as "co-managers." With him running the tech and her behind the camera, they presented as a cohesive, believable team. Hopefully, despite Bridget's raging case of imposter syndrome, it would hold.

The first slate of performers were three different drummers, as Dean scheduled each instrument in its own time block. One and three were good; the second one was phenomenal. All were told they'd hear from them either way.

There were similar scenarios with the guitarists, keyboardists, and bass players, each group featuring at least one, sometimes two, players who stood out. The singer, however, proved a trickier proposition. The first auditionee insisted on singing a Pat Benatar song (acapella), asserting that, "if you want '80s, who better?" The second was weak on vocals, but quite handy with the mic stand; upon her exit, Gwen remarked that pole dancing might be more in her wheelhouse. They had two more coming in, but Bridget got the sense that this part of the assignment would be a bigger challenge than the rest.

Because it was an odd task, frankly. To find a singer with true talent and vocal chops, yet a voice close enough to Libby's to convince an A&R guy that this was, in fact, the band from the recordings. That was the sticky part as far as Bridget was concerned. The pretense of it. It kept popping up as an alarm bell, and in between auditions, she somehow managed to get Dean and Gwen repeatedly debating this aspect of their activities.

"Sweetheart, we aren't duping investors or running a Ponzi scheme," Gwen insisted. "It's just a musical experiment; no malice intended."

"I know, I understand that, but all of these people have asked what the goal is here, and it's hard to explain without sounding like we're attempting to pull off a scam."

"Scam?" Dean's reaction was immediate. "Seriously, Bridget? You really feel that way?"

She hesitated. "Well, kinda. Aren't we? Kinda?"

"No. There's no scam here. We're going to present Aaron with a band. We're not going state, 'this is the band that recorded the songs.' We're just going to put them on a stage, have them play the songs, and see what he thinks. If we hire the right people—and I think we've got some excellent choices with the instrumentalists—they'll be good enough and rehearsed enough to translate the tunes with real conviction. He'll either like them or he won't, but we're not going to waste his time with a crappy band. It'll be a great band; I promise you that. The worst that happens is he walks away and that's that. The players are getting paid, so no harm done to them."

"And Bridgie," Gwen added. "I bet we'll knock the guy's socks off."

Bridget shrugged. "Okay, if you guys are convinced this is morally defensible—"

Gwen grabbed her shoulders and literally shook her. "Stop it. Now you're starting to sound like your dad—what does Dean call him? Eeyore? Come *on*; if nothing else this is fun, the most fun I've had in a long time. Aren't you having fun, sweetheart?"

Finally laughing, Bridget remarked, "A little. I'm having a little fun."

"Good enough." Dean sighed with some relief, looking over his scheduling sheet. "Okay, we gotta get back to it; there's another singer up. She's a friend of mine, so let's see how she does." He opened the studio door and a twenty-something woman with dyed blue hair, head to toe black, and a silver nose ring, stepped in, her body language immediately awkward.

"Hey." She didn't seem thrilled to be there.

"Guys, this is Georgia Prather. Georgia, I'm glad you—"

"Yeah, Dean, listen, I tried to call you earlier, but you didn't pick up, and I guess you didn't check your texts either, so I figured I should at least show up to talk to you."

"Oh, sorry. We've been auditioning all day, so I wasn't paying too much attention to my phone. What's up?"

She glanced at Bridget and Gwen, then pulled Dean closer to the door. They could still hear her. It was all very strange. "We had a gig last night, so I didn't get a chance to listen to the tunes till this morning. And thanks and all for the invitation to audition, but they're just not my thing, you know? A little too light and poppy for my voice, so I'm gonna pass. Sorry." She looked over at the two women peering at her from across the room. "Good luck, though." Back to Dean. "And thanks for those last mixes you did for us. They totally kicked; the guys were knocked out."

"Um, glad you were happy with them." Dean couldn't hide his discomfort.

"Yeah, totally. Okay, later." With a quick turn, she was gone.

"That was weird," he said to Gwen and Bridget, moderately embarrassed.

Bridget was suddenly struck by a thought. "Is that the girl on the tracks you played me way back when, the one whose voice I wasn't wild about?" she asked, frowning.

He actually blushed. "Yeah. But I thought if you could hear her on your mom's tunes, something quite a bit different from what she does with her own band, you might like her. But, whatever. Not the right fit; we move on."

"Nope. Not the right fit at all. But kind of weird, really, that you even invited her, since I already said I didn't like her voice—"

"Then it's good we didn't waste any time with her." Dean, who rarely got testy, got a little testy.

"Guys, guys," Gwen cut in, "it doesn't matter either way. We're open to suggestions, and not all of them are going to pan out, so let's calm down and get on with it."

There was a knock at the studio door, and when Dean opened it, a tall, exceedingly attractive, woman walked in. Smartly attired, lyric sheets in her hand, she smiled wide and looked around the room, breaking the tension of the preceding moment. "Sorry to interrupt. Am I in the right place for the Minor Rebellion auditions?"

"Yes," Dean nodded. "The right place." He checked the time on his phone.

"I know I'm a little early," she remarked. "I just saw the last singer leave, so figured I was up next. If you'd rather I wait outside till my set time, that's fine."

"No, no, your timing's perfect!" Gwen chirped from across the room.

"Oh, good!" She reached out her hand to Bridget, who somewhat stiffly returned the gesture. "I'm Maya Bell."

"Bridget Conlin."

"I really love these songs. Are they yours?"

"Um, no, we just—"

"The band writes together," Dean jumped in. "And thanks. We think they're pretty great too. You ready to give it a try?"

"Absolutely. Let's do it." Maya walked into the performance room like she knew what she was doing. She placed the lyric sheets on the music stand, slipped on headphones, and adjusted the pop filter, exuding "professional" with every move. Then the track started, and she began singing.

Gwen turned to look at Bridget and Dean with wide eyes. "I believe, my budding impresarios, we've got ourselves a band."

CHAPTER 35

After the long ramp-up of classes and studying and cramming and worrying, Libby was on the CPA test roster for the next two Saturdays—two tests a day, eight hours the first day; seven the next—and she was feeling the pressure. She could have stretched the process out over eighteen months (per the CPA Board and Jonah Hill), but she wanted it done. She expected it to be brutal and, consequently, was moderately to majorly anxious about the endeavor.

Because, after the weeks of classes financed by her employers, plus the many additional hours of study and prep outside class, there were no options for her to not do well. She'd researched enough to know that the pass rate on the first try hovered around twenty percent. She didn't like those odds, so she'd put in even more study time than planned, which largely meant keeping Jeff at bay until the task was completed. His response was, "I don't love it, of course, I want to see you, but I totally understand." She hoped he meant it because she felt she had no choice.

Bridget had essentially gone AWOL. Though there were nights here and there when she'd stop by the house for more clothes or to do laundry, most time was spent at Dean's. Which was fine with Libby; actually, preferred at the moment. It left her with fewer distractions and demands to accommodate. There were brief conversations, occasional phone calls and texts, all of which assured Libby her daughter was fine, busy with work

184 | LORRAINE DEVON WILKE

and the mysterious project, and would soon come up for air. It appeared they were both on a mission.

Gwen had been conspicuously quiet for a while, but Libby figured she was finally starting her great American novel or reveling in all things Otto. As it was with Bridget's absence, Libby welcomed the unusual quietude from her usually noisy friend, which allowed her to stay laser focused. Plus, she knew the quiet wouldn't last long and relished the temporary peace.

She'd Facetimed with Robbie, who remained immersed and excited about his job, announcing that he planned to stick with it even when school started ("Just make sure you keep your studies up," she couldn't help but interject.). He confirmed that his tutoring was "endurable," and he'd be retesting for course credit sometime before the next semester began. He showed some interest in her CPA progress, asked about Jeff, said nothing about Dustin, and filled her in on the latest with Bart, who, apparently, had garnered some new clients, courtesy of Dean.

With all essential parties under control for the duration, she settled down to a dinner of yogurt and a stale protein bar, remembering that she wanted to grab her old canvas briefcase from the attic. It was the one she'd used when taking her first QuickBooks course way back when, the one that went with her on all her early on-site client jobs, and she decided it was some kind of good luck charm she ought to have for the upcoming test.

Making her way up to the dingy loft, she couldn't help but notice how scrubby and unappealing the space was these days. She was so rarely up there its aesthetic deterioration (had it ever been aesthetic?) had fully evaded her attention. There'd been a quick thought about trying to do something about it at some point, but it was immediately dismissed. Pushing open the hobbit door to the attic, she pulled the light cord to illuminate the space beyond, a dark, dusty expanse of familial flotsam and jetsam.

"Ugh," captured her immediate reaction. Wandering through the piles of old furniture, remnants of previous eras, detritus inherited from her parents, she coughed as dust skittered and the gloomy light made the place even creepier than it might have been. Digging through a box labeled *old clothes & stuff*, she found the coveted bag. It didn't appear quite as smart as she remembered but figured a good clean-up would return it to its professional status.

She stood and stretched her back. As if drawn to it, she glanced over to the pile of tapes hidden under a faded quilt. With her bag slung over her shoulder, she walked over and peeled off the quilt, gazing down at the evidence of her earlier life. With so many boxes stacked in the pile, she didn't notice that any had been removed. Picking up one of the larger boxes, she opened it to find the track sheet listing all the players, instruments, and their corresponding tracks. She sank down to a ratty stool nearby and let her mind swirl, to that time, to those people; to a moment in her life when she knew who she was, when everything seemed possible, and joy, excitement, and creativity were daily components of her existence. Chris, Gavin, August, and Pat. Nick ... Nick. Their crazy manager, Damon, who once said he "loved her like a daughter," and for a time made her feel like she was a star, and her destiny was assured. It had been unforgettable, that time; it remained unforgettable.

Tears welled as she softly sang one of the songs tracked on the sheet. Her voice was rough and scratchy, the notes went where they shouldn't, but as she sat in this dusty place that held her history, she let the quiet memory of music escape her tightened throat.

CHAPTER 36

Starbucks was crowded, but they'd picked it because it had ample outdoor seating, and was midway between Delgany Records and S.I.R., making it a convenient stop for Aaron Leifer.

Bridget had taken the afternoon off to attend the meeting ("family emergency," which was marginally true), and now sat sipping a latte, decked out in a very *InStyle* outfit and full makeup. Dean sat across from her with his hair slicked back and an uncustomary, but inarguably hip, sport jacket. He caught her grinning at him.

"What?"

"You look cool. Very music manager."

"That was the assignment, wasn't it?"

"It was. Well done."

"And you're looking exceedingly music manager yourself, Miz Conlin."

They laughed, but it was clear both carried some nerves. Her fingers hadn't stopped tapping the table since they sat down.

"You okay?" he asked.

"I might throw up," she confessed. Her face did appear pale.

"Just drink lots of water and keep the focus on the band. That's what they're interested in; not us. I doubt they'll even ask any questions about us."

"Let's hope you're right."

On the table was a folder, some CDs, and a neatly arranged stack of photos. They were prepped. Just as Bridget checked the time on her phone, two thirty-something men with substantial hip quotient walked onto the patio. Dean nodded in their direction, and they headed over. The older of the two reached out for Dean's hand.

"Dean Park?"

Dean rose and grabbed his hand. "Yes, you must be Aaron."

"Nice to meet you."

"This is my partner, Bridget Conlin."

Bridget offered Aaron a firm handshake.

"Good to meet you, Bridget." He turned toward the man standing next to him. "Tyler Williams, from our A&R department."

More hand shaking, then they all sat. Dean slid a cup in front of Aaron. "I went ahead and ordered you a latte. Tyler, anything I can get you?"

"Thanks. I'm set."

As Aaron took a sip of his drink, he noticed the items in the middle of the table. "So what have you got there for us?"

Dean handed the photos to Aaron, who looked through them, passing them on to Tyler.

"Great looking group," Tyler commented.

"I'm curious, Dean." Aaron took the pictures back and flipped through them again. "Why didn't you include these on your social media pages? They've got the look, she's gorgeous; it seems like you'd want to promote that."

Bridget squirmed, grabbed her coffee to cover her ratcheting anxiety.

"Oh, we do, certainly, but we had some personnel changes and couldn't get new pictures till we landed a replacement. They're up there now."

"Oh, yeah? Who left the group?"

Dean took a beat. "The original vocalist."

There was a pause.

"Wow. She was a pretty strong selling point. What happened?"

"Um, just some personal stuff. She was a little vague about it."

Tyler leaned forward with a grin. "Well, if your new girl sings as good as she looks, you should be okay."

Bridget shot him a look; Dean leaned into her.

"*Is* she as good?" Aaron asked the obvious question.

Dean and Bridget answered simultaneously. "She's excellent/ she's very good."

"Great. When do we hear them?"

Dean shuffled to rise. "If you've got time, they're set up at S.I.R. just down the street."

CHAPTER 37

Bridget decided to go ahead and alert the band of Aaron and Tyler's imminent arrival. Mostly she wanted to pull away from the men in hopes of shaking off some of her burgeoning anxiety. She'd said so little during the meeting she was certain she'd come off like an idiot; on the other hand, this all felt so surreal she didn't know what she would have said anyway.

As she opened the door of Stage 3, and before the players saw her, she heard muted conversation; she stopped to listen. With Norm, the studio manager, fiddling with the soundboard at the back of the room, the group of photogenic twenty-some-things—drummer, bass player, two guitarists, keyboards, and Maya—huddled together at the edge of the stage.

"But it *is* weird, isn't it?" the drummer commented. "Dean wants us to act like we've been playing together for a while, and I don't get it."

The guitarist piped up. "It's a bit for some doc, I think, like a reality show. If we get the deal, I guess we come clean then."

"I'm supposed to be new, though," Maya remarked, head tilted as if she, too, was confused.

"Are those two really managers?" the other guitarist asked with raised eyebrows. "I mean, Dean's cool, but Bridget seems a little lost."

Bridget, still tucked behind the door, blushed. But he was right. She was lost.

"I don't know; I just hope the A&R dude doesn't ask too many questions," the keyboardist threw in.

"Seriously? We'll be lucky if he sits through the set!" They all laughed; clearly they'd been down this road before.

Bridget was forced from her hiding place when Dean pushed through the door, Aaron and Tyler steps behind. He looked at Bridget with surprise.

"Are you hiding from the band?" he asked, grinning.

"Pretty much."

He grabbed her arm and as the four of them walked in, the band hopped to their feet.

"Hey, everybody," Dean called out. "This is Aaron Leifer and Tyler Moore from Delgany Records. Gentlemen, this is Minor Rebellion."

Aaron and Tyler waved perfunctorily and sat down. Bridget readied her iPhone to video the proceedings as the band got into place behind their instruments; Maya smiled, ready at the microphone stand.

"Okay, guys, I'd like to hear 'What Can I Do' first, if you don't mind," Aaron said.

Bridget, too nervous to sit at the table, stood next to the soundboard with Norm, happy to capture longer, wider shots. As she found herself holding her breath, the band kicked into the song. They sounded good; Maya, committed and charismatic, carried the tune, but it was a little ragged around the edges. And, she had to admit, didn't sound like the recording.

Aaron leaned into Dean. "They're good, but they're missing that *thing* that grabbed me; the sound, the style. Maybe it's the new singer, I don't know. She's great, but not what my ear was listening for. The recording's got it, but I'm not hearing it here."

Dean's stomach sank.

The band finished, ready to play on, but Aaron and Tyler stood up, making clear the showcase was over. Aaron shook Dean's hand, commenting, "I love the tunes, but the group needs work. Get them closer to their original sound and if it pulls together, give me a call." He turned to the band. "Thanks, guys. Sounds good." With a quick wave, Delgany Records left the building.

The band, shellshocked by the quick exit, began whispering amongst themselves.

Bridget finally joined Dean at the table, whiplashed. "That was brutal."

"No shit."

He turned and called out to the band. "Listen, you guys did a really good job; I'm sorry they didn't hang around for a few more songs. But I want to talk about their response and where we'd like to go from here. Come sit with us when you're done." He then turned to Bridget. "I think it's time to talk to your mom."

CHAPTER 38

Done. Over. Complete. Libby was mentally and physically exhausted, so much so that, instead of spending her first post-exam night with Jeff in the luxury of his luxurious home, she asked him to trek to Hollywood to sleep in her bed. He was very accommodating. It was a lovely, tender night of takeout sushi and "let's get reacquainted" sex, during which she fell asleep before the anticipated conclusion.

In the morning, the first Sunday in many months when she had no studying to do and no errands to run, Jeff got up early to make coffee and cornbread pancakes. An early, and surprising, text from Bridget requested, "some time with you today to discuss a few ideas regarding my admissions project." Despite preferring that any family discussions be put off to another day, she missed her daughter and wondered what ideas regarding the mysterious project could possibly involve her, so a two o'clock gathering at the house was arranged.

When Dean and Bridget arrived, Jeff said his hellos, then headed out. Libby hoped they'd reconvene later to pick up where they left off and said so as she kissed him at the door. He smiled and whispered in her ear, "Just head over when you're done here."

After Libby got situated on the couch, a cup of coffee in her hand and an expectant look on her face, Bridget, iPad set on the coffee table and a frisson of nerves tickling her limbs, began a slightly awkward explanation of the general outlines of the project, which, of course, Libby already knew. This went on for long enough that she finally interrupted.

"Honey, I'm curious, what specific *new* ideas did you want to talk about with me? I'm aware of the foundation of what you're doing—we did our little interview, for whatever that was worth—but I'm not clear on how else I might help."

There was a pause as Dean and Bridget looked at each other.

"What?" Libby asked, surprised by their tension. "Has something happened?"

"Mom ..." Bridget squirmed while pulling up her iPad. "I want you to keep a really open mind about what I'm going to show you."

"What does that mean?" Libby's alarm was immediate.

"No, no, nothing bad, it's just on a topic you're very, well, secretive about. It's about your music."

"Okay, but isn't that why we did the interview, to talk about that era of music? Have you decided to go in a different direction?"

Dean, who'd been quiet in deference to Bridget's introduction, saw Libby's confusion and jumped in.

"In a way. It's important that you know, Mrs. C—uh, Libby—that all this started with my curiosity about your music. After you told us about your band, I was not only impressed, but really wanted to hear your recordings. I don't know if you remember me mentioning that at the time—"

"Yes, Dean, of course I remember." Their meandering ramp-up was starting to make her anxious and slightly annoyed.

"And *I* figured, Mom, since you were pretty dismissive about it at the time, you wouldn't likely be rushing up to the attic to find tapes for Dean to listen to, so when he got the idea that maybe my project could involve drawing parallels between the music scenes of now and then, we wanted to listen. To your songs, to your specific music. So we did. And Mom, we were blown away. Really, truly blown away. You were so amazing, and the songs were—"

"Wait, wait, *wait*." Libby rose from the couch. "You're saying you went up to the attic, ferreted through my private stuff, took some of my tapes, and snuck them out of here so you two could listen to them? Is that what you're saying?" Libby's face had paled.

Bridget was shaken by her tone. "No, I didn't 'ferret' through your stuff, Mom. It's all just sitting there, out in the open under Grandma's quilts gathering dust. They weren't even hard to find."

"And you didn't think you should maybe *ask* me before you absconded with them?" Libby's face had hardened.

"I *did* think about it." Bridget was now fully panicked by the turn this had taken. "But in weighing the pros and cons, it seemed wiser not to stir up another big conversation about it, which I know upsets you, if ultimately, we didn't end up using any of the songs. What made sense was to hear the music first—"

"*Using* the songs? For what?"

There was a pause.

Dean quickly picked up the relay. "I mentioned to Bridget that it would be cool to have some music from the actual era to use as a point of comparison, of reference, so we—"

"Wanted to see if it was good enough, if *I* was good enough, for you to use the songs, yes?"

"Uh, yeah, basically." Bridget replied softly. "But please don't take that as any kind of insult to you or your band. It was only because, to be completely honest, I had no idea if any of it *was* good, if *you* were good, because you hadn't shared it with me, and I had no memory of the music at all. So we wanted to listen first, and if it worked, we figured then we'd ask if we could use it."

"Okay, so that's what this is, this conversation; you asking me? If you can use it? For what, by the way? Use it for what?"

Libby had stopped pacing in front of Bridget, who appeared cowed at this point. Dean jumped in again.

"Libby, I hope you won't get mad at Bridget because it was really me who got this part of it going. But after we listened, we were so completely blown away, like Bridget said, we thought about how to incorporate your songs into the concept we were brainstorming, the 'then and now' thing. That was when we decided to get some background on you and your band—"

"Yes, yes, our little kitchen interview; go on."

Dean, thrown by her tone, continued. "Then Bridget and I talked about putting a couple of your tunes together with a made-up band name and some cool artwork; updating the mixes just a little to present it like a contemporary band, then post everything online to see if it could compete with actual contemporary music out there. Bridget's been video-documenting the steps along the way, which she'll conclude with whatever the experiment ultimately reveals. And that will be her admissions project. Which I think will be a slam-dunk in terms of getting her into SCC."

There was a ponderous pause.

"So, let me understand: you created a package with *my* music, *my* voice, and some fake band name, yeah?"

"Yes." Bridget looked queasy.

"Who did the artwork for you?"

Bridget hesitated. "I did some of it. Dad helped us with that."

"I see. And who covered the expenses? I assume there were expenses?"

Again Bridget looked at Dean, trapped in what was devolving into a conversational ambush.

"Gwen paid for everything," Dean replied.

"Oh, of course she did. And why not? Why wouldn't my entire circle of family and friends collude behind my back to co-opt my work and history for the sake of some fun little school project?"

"No, Mom, it's not like that," Bridget insisted. "We are in awe of your voice. Your songs are incredible, and you really were a star, and even though I have no idea why you didn't make it back in the '80s, right now people are loving your music."

"Is that right? You already know that?"

"Yes."

"You've already posted it online and people are listening to it, downloading it, whatever? Again, *my* music, *my* voice, *my* band? It's all out there, and I didn't even know it had ever left the attic?"

Bridget seemed to have sunk into the upholstery of the couch. "I kept waiting for the next thing to happen to figure out when to bring it to you. I thought it would be better to wait until the whole project was done, and I could present you with the completed documentary showing what an amazing singer you were, how incredible and viable your music was and still is, but then ..." Her voice trailed off.

"Then *what*?" Libby snapped.

"Things took an unexpected turn." Even Dean seemed rattled at this point. "And we knew it was definitely time to talk to you."

Libby dropped into a chair across the room. "What unexpected turn?"

Bridget then explained the situation with Delgany Records and Aaron Leifer; about them putting Minor Rebellion together as an actual band, doing the showcase, and getting the feedback they did. Figuring she had nothing to lose at this point, it was a purging, throw-it-all-out-on-the-table verbal dump. When she got to their last "crazy idea," the lightbulb that came to Dean after the showcase, she deferred to him.

"We feel like we need to play out every possibility, a leave no stone unturned kind of thing, to take advantage of Delgany's interest." Dean was almost breathless at this point. "The new guys aren't fully getting the vibe of the music and we thought it would be really cool to reach out to your original players and, if they were still around and up for it, bring them in to work with the newbies."

"I mean, Mom, think about how incredible it would be if now, all these years later, your music finally breaks out with a record deal or a publishing deal. It was just too amazing a possibility to ignore, and when Gwen said she'd probably be able to track the guys down and—"

Jarringly, without warning, Libby suddenly stood up, slammed her foot hard to the floor and let out a cacophonous, hair-raising scream that had tears literally bursting from her eyes.

The sound stunned Bridget and Dean into immediate silence.

Bridget stood, panicked, and reached out to her mother. "Mom, Mom, I'm so sorry. I honestly didn't think it would make you this upset. I thought you'd love that we loved your music and—"

Libby could barely breathe as she bellowed. "It was *mine*, Bridget, my past to deal with. To forget, to hide, to do with whatever I chose. *Mine.* It wasn't yours to dredge up like some fun little social media experiment, to put out into the world like it had no legacy or story behind it. You have no idea, *no idea*, what happened or why—"

"*Because you won't tell me!*" Bridget finally yelled back. "That's why I have no idea. Tell me. Make me understand. I didn't know how good you were and now that I do it's even more impossible to understand how you walked away from what you loved, what you dreamed about, without a look back."

Now Bridget was crying; Dean sank to the couch, overwhelmed.

"You say it wasn't because of me, but what other reason is there? Why don't you explain it to me, Mother, so I *do* have an idea."

Libby turned to her; her face white. *"Because it's none of your fucking business!"*

With that, the air seemed to be sucked from the room.

Bridget stood shocked and speechless; the two women locked in a standoff. A beat, then she lurched for her iPad and purse and flew out the door. Dean, unclear on the appropriate response simply said, "I'm so sorry," to Libby and followed Bridget out.

When the door closed, and heavy quiet filled every inch of the space, Libby collapsed to the chair, battered by what had now become a full-fledged hurricane.

CHAPTER 39

Gwen stood in Libby's kitchen with a bag of donuts and a face flooded with concern. After receiving a hysterical call from Bridget, and a commensurately worried follow-up from Bart, who'd also received a hysterical call from Bridget, she got in her car and drove from downtown to Beachwood Canyon. She'd let herself in the house with her spare key, and now watched as Libby deconstructed in front of her on the couch, replaying the events of the day with jagged sobs.

When she'd finally depleted herself, Libby looked up at the tense woman standing in front of her with a bag of Yum Yums and the mien of contrition, and hissed, "Do you honestly think donuts will assuage me in this hideous fucking moment?"

"It crossed my mind. I've never seen you unhappy with a fritter in your hand."

"*Stop.* Just stop, will you? I'm not feeling quippy in the least."

"Yeah." Gwen set the bag on the dining room table, then settled in a chair across from Libby. "Do you want me to try to explain things, do you want to continue screaming, or do you want me to get up and leave?"

"All the above."

Gwen stood. "Okay, then. I'll just—"

"*Sit down*, for fuck's sake." Libby barked. "I don't want you to leave. I don't ... I don't know what I want."

Gwen sat back down. Deciding silence might create a sound vacuum that Libby would be compelled to fill, she said nothing. It worked.

"I think I need mental help." Libby's voice was strained and exhausted. "Honestly. I cannot believe I just treated my daughter like she slit my guts open and threw them on the internet for all the world to see—though that's exactly what it feels like, even if she doesn't know it. Even if she didn't mean to. And now that I've behaved like a complete fucking madwoman asshole, I don't know how to fix things."

"The situation with her, or the situation more historically?"

Libby finally looked up at Gwen, who kindly offered no reaction to the red, bloated condition of her face. "What does that mean, more historically?"

"Seriously?"

"You mean tell her what happened?"

"Of course I mean 'tell her what happened.'" Gwen snapped. "It's time. It's past time."

Libby curled deeper into the couch with a moan. "I can't. I don't want to."

"Yet somehow you must. Especially now. You cannot allow your daughter to think you're either crazy, or a dilettante, which she suspects, or, more horribly, and what she truly fears, that she really *is* the reason you walked away from your grand life dreams."

Libby slowly pulled herself up, looking as bedraggled as a person could. "I honestly don't know if I can. I mean that. I haven't talked about what happened with anyone but you and Bart. Well, there was Damon, but we both know what a clusterfuck that was."

"Your ex-manager was an unmitigated asshole of epic proportions. But you know who else you *should* have talked to? A fucking therapist, who might have been able to save you from yourself."

"You've said that before. Many times. But I couldn't. I still don't want to talk about it ever again, with anyone. I cannot dredge it all up."

"Then please tell me—how do you plan to fix this colossal fuck-up with Bridget?"

Libby's eyes flashed. "There would be no colossal fuck-up if she'd stayed out of my business and wasn't supported in her subterfuge by the willing collusion of you and Bart. You are both as responsible for this mess as she is!"

Gwen went to the bag of donuts on the table, proceeded to pull one out and take a big bite. "Yum. *So* good." Her tone was intentionally goofy. "I can see why they call the place Yum Yums. Want one, Lib? They're yummy."

Libby couldn't help but smile. "Sit down, asshole, and admit to your evil acts."

Gwen sighed, put her donut down, and walked back to the chair. "I have a slightly different perspective on it all."

"I expect no sensitivity when it comes to Bart, but when I heard you were secretly involved, it fucking hurt me, Gwen. *Do you get that?* It felt so sneaky and awful."

"Lib." Gwen sighed, marginally chastised. "I'm sorry you're hurt. I'm sorry it was secretive. But it wasn't sneaky in a creepy way, and it definitely wasn't awful. I thought they had a really clever, wonderful idea, one that *honored* you and your music, your talent, and I thought there would be a way to peacefully present it to you when it was done, a way that would make you *feel* honored. So, yes, I took a chance."

"Uh huh. And while you were all so busy *honoring* me, you ignored what I really needed and wanted. Which was to leave it the fuck alone."

"Yet, I'll counter that this thing has come to a head for a very essential reason." Gwen's expression was fierce.

"What's that?"

"You need to stop pretending."

"How am I pretending?" Libby's eyes flared.

"You're pretending that if you never talk about what happened it won't have actually happened. That it didn't smash your life to bits. That it didn't destroy you for a time. But it *did* happen, and it's had a profound effect on your life, your *whole* life."

With that, Libby visibly deflated, leaning back on the couch.

Gwen continued. "I've known you since we were fourteen years old, and no one knows better than me who you are and what matters to you, what *mattered* to you. I stopped agreeing a long time ago that burying your past was an acceptable measure, but you were immovable, even to your own mental and emotional detriment. So when Bridget and Dean presented me with their idea, I got excited thinking about your music, about breathing life into it again, into you as a singer, something I was in awe of back then and remain so now. I got serious goosebumps listening to those songs again, Libby, and Bridget was beyond words. Slayed, literally. Really get that in your head: *your daughter was brought to tears listening to you sing.*"

Libby looked at her, a smile flitting.

"So, yeah, I honestly thought, given what they proposed and their individual talents, that you'd ultimately be moved and delighted by it too. Even if you still wanted to keep the reasons for band's demise private, you could've enjoyed their mini resurgence of your art, created solely for the sake of your daughter's scholarly evolution and advancement. But instead you decided to cut her head off."

"That's a bit much." Libby huffed. She got up and wandered over to the table, pulled an apple fritter out of the bag. "You make me sound like an ogre." She took a bite. "Damn, these *are* good."

"Not an ogre, Lib, but perhaps you experienced some over-reaction. Their intentions were true and loving, I promise you."

Libby put the fritter back in the bag and sank to a dining room chair. "I can't believe how angry I got. It was like I was out of my body. I wanted to hit her. I honestly felt like I could've killed her. I mean, not really, but *you know?*"

"And she got that. You can be one terrifying bitch."

"Apparently."

Gwen leaned forward, arms resting on her knees, hands clasped, face serious. "Libby, my friend, my dearest, darling bestie; you've been holding this tight to yourself since you were nineteen years old, and it's time for an unburdening. I was there. I am here. I have been a witness to your life. And I have watched this hidden, dreaded event metastasize to levels that have nega-tively affected too much of who you are, how you traverse your life, and how you relate to the people in it, including and espe-cially your daughter—"

"I've never held any of it against Bridget."

"Not intentionally, no. But it would've been impossible for anyone to experience what you did and *not* feel conflicting emo-tions, *not* see some representation of what hurt you in her very existence."

"So you *do* think I did that." Libby stared hard at Gwen, then crumbled. "Did I? *Did* I?" she wailed.

"Libby, I think it's—"

"I've thought about that possibility so many times. We even talked about it recently—"

"We did."

"I've been cyclically terrified that I might have ruined her, hurt her with my own emotional chaos. *Did* I see her as a reminder of what happened, even just a little bit? *Have* I? I love her beyond words, have always loved her beyond words, but did my mess eke out and taint her little developing psyche enough to poison our relationship?"

"Listen to me right now." Gwen got down on her knees in front of Libby's chair, forcing her beleaguered friend to look at her. "You showered that child with nothing but love and devotion, and *still* she's always been a feisty thing, all on her own. We did already talk about this but if you're still beating yourself up about the impact of your childhood angst, let me reiterate my deep and profound thoughts once again. I think we each come into this world who and what we are, and regardless of what may or may not have 'eked' out of your subconscious, you do not get to blame yourself for Bridget's personality. I've seen her go off on her brother, her father, me, an Uber driver, that snotty barista at the corner Starbucks, and none of us were doing any eking around her, I promise."

Libby had to smile. "Maybe," she replied weakly.

"Not maybe. *Yes*. But ... *but* ... I remain convinced, especially after what's happened today, that it is time. If you talk about it with no one else in this lifetime, you must talk about it with Bridget. Sooner as opposed to later. Because, regardless of what did or didn't happen between you two in the past, you *will* break the relationship now if, in this moment, you don't unpack that box with her."

Libby said nothing.

Gwen stood up and went to the door. "Okay, I'm done. I've expended my wisdom, though I am leaving the donuts for you. There's an extra apple fritter in there. I know my girl." She opened the door. "You think about things. If you want to talk more, call. If you want me to come back, I'm here in a nanosecond. Just know I love you as much as my own skin. So does Bridget. Let's fix this." And she was out the door.

CHAPTER 40

Los Angeles, 1989

At some point during the time Eric Burrows and his team at Mount Cloud Records had taken to put the pieces of the Liberty deal together, he'd requested to meet with each band member privately to get a sense of their individual goals, their musical vision; what they wanted from the deal they were about to sign, and what they were prepared to dedicate to their eventual success. It was determined he'd meet with Libby first—"You are, after all, the voice and face of this band"—and after delivering that news at a rehearsal, Damon offered to drive her to the meeting.

"I can drive myself, Damon," she insisted.

"And it's no problem for me to get her there," Bart spoke up. He was never fond of the position-jockeying that seemed to happen with their oft-times too-controlling manager.

"I have no doubt either of you can drive a damn car, but I want to be there for this meeting, to make sure things go smoothly—also to be available for any legal or logistical questions that might come up."

A look was exchanged between Bart and Libby. Some tension was conveyed, subtle enough, however, that the others didn't notice.

Two days later, Libby, dressed in her finest "rock chick" outfit, hair teased high and make-up dark and dramatic, sat in the passenger seat of Damon's canary yellow Porsche 911 Carrera as he flew west on Sunset Boulevard toward the Mount Cloud offices. He was making mindless conversation, likely an attempt to quell her obvious nerves, but she was distracted enough that he finally noticed.

"What's up with you, sweetheart? Are you nervous about this meeting?"

She kept her gaze out the passenger window. "A little. He's kind of a strange guy."

Damon shot her a startled look. "Is he? I've never noticed anything strange about him, and believe me, when it comes to protecting my artists, I look for that kind of stuff. What's so strange about him?"

She shrugged. "I don't know. Maybe I'm being oversensitive. But he gets dismissive with me sometimes, acts like he doesn't take me as seriously as the guys. I keep thinking he's going to pat my head or call me a little girl."

"Oh, come on, Libby; he thinks you're the bee's knees. I've heard him say plenty of times that without you they'd just be another band. He's wild about you."

"That's good to know. But, wow, 'bee's knees'?" She grinned. "You sound like my grandmother."

"Hey, I'm old." He shot her a wink. "Is that it? Everything else okay? You ready for this meeting?"

She looked away again.

"What?"

"Damon, um, I do need to—"

Suddenly he was at the parking kiosk at Mount Cloud, names being given, passes delivered, and the moment for further conversation passed. Libby took a deep breath and stared out the window.

★ ★ ★

Damon told her he'd be down in the cafeteria, confirming that he'd left instructions with Eric's assistant to alert him when the meeting was over, or if he was needed inside. "Sparkle, Liberty, this is your moment," he trilled as he gave her a quick hug.

Inside the legendary suite, Eric sat perched at the edge of his desk, surrounded by walls papered with framed gold and platinum records, shiny band posters, and photographs of him cozying up to a remarkable roster of big-name stars. Hair gelled to perfection, jacket sleeves jammed up to his elbows, he presented as confident and cocky in a way that likely served him well in the job; to Libby he just exuded arrogance. Something about him was smarmy and off-putting, and she was convinced he either saw her as stupid or a potential piece of ass.

He rattled down a list of "all the exciting things we've got planned for you," and at about fifteen minutes in, when she could no longer listen without interruption, Libby cleared her throat, sat up straight, and reluctantly revealed to Eric Burrows that she was unexpectedly and inconveniently pregnant. It was as hard a confession as any she'd ever made, and his immediate stone-cold reaction was exactly what she'd feared.

With a quick catch of his breath, he readjusted his face. "Okay. That's a shocker I didn't see coming, but it's not the end of the world. Thank you for telling me. I assume you'll take care of business ASAP, give yourself a few days to get back on track, then we'll move forward, yes?" His smile was forced.

As she listened to his words and noted his cavalier dismissal of the situation's gravity, at least to her, she realized she hadn't given enough thought to how, exactly, she saw all this

212 I LORRAINE DEVON WILKE

playing out, what she saw herself saying to him, what she saw herself doing. She'd read enough articles about female singers with kids making it work on the road to assume it would be a viable option for her too. When she'd broken the news to Bart days earlier, and once past his initial shock, he agreed there was no reason the band couldn't work around it, the two of them couldn't work around it.

They also discussed the other obvious option. Clearly this wasn't the optimal time to have a baby. Beyond the dangling carrot of the record deal, they weren't married, had never even discussed getting married, were making little money between them, and, most obviously, she was a teenager far from ready to raise a child. That second option presented as the clear and most logical choice.

Yet in this moment, as Eric presumed in his facile, condescending manner that an abortion was a foregone conclusion, something in her rebelled.

"I haven't decided what I'm doing yet," she quietly asserted.

His eyes got hard. "Is that right?" He stood and walked to the window, staring out. "Well, I can't say I picked up on this until now, but maybe you're one of those pathological chicks who doesn't really want success. You talk about it, you say you dream about it, but when you get right up to it, it's smack dab in your face, you find a way to sabotage yourself. I think that might be you."

"That's not even close to me." she snapped.

"No? Then tell me, Liberty Conlin, girl the damn band is named after, why does a nineteen-year-old singer on the brink of stardom get herself knocked-up, then think for even one fucking moment about keeping it and throwing away everything she's ever worked for?"

"First of all, I didn't plan this. It wouldn't have been my choice. I thought we were being careful. But it happened and now, well, I'm prepared to work around it. I'm certainly not the first singer in musical history to have a baby; lots of famous women have managed to make it work, and I—"

His laugh was caustic. "One problem, honey—you ain't famous. In fact, as far as this business is concerned, you don't even exist. You're not an established act, not a star, and at this rate, you never will be."

Tears crept to her eyes, but she was determined to keep them from tumbling. "Look, Eric, I know I've surprised you with this and for that I'm sorry. But all the amazing things about this band, the things you said you love and are so excited about, are still there. I'm still here and I honestly believe we can make it work. We already have our basic tracks done; I won't be showing for a while, so there's plenty of time for a short tour after the record comes out and—"

"What about after the record breaks? How does a new band on a tight budget support an album on the road when their teenage singer has a screaming rugrat, a shitload of mommy paraphernalia, and fifty pounds of fucking baby fat to lose?"

Libby was stunned. Whatever else she felt or thought about Eric, she did not expect his crassness. She got up and moved toward the door.

"Yeah, there you go. Just walk out and throw this deal away; fuck the rest of your bandmates, atta girl." His sneer cut like a knife.

She turned in a fury. "I am *not* doing that; I would never do that. I'm the one trying to make this work; you're the one making it a problem."

"Oh, it *is* a problem, and if you're too caught up in fairyland to figure that out, you don't deserve this damn deal."

At that point she couldn't hold back the tears. Standing at the door she sobbed, "I don't understand why you're being such a—"

"What? Asshole? Prick? Bully? No, sweetheart, just a businessman, a pragmatic and very successful businessman." Jaw clenched, he came across the room and loomed within inches of her. "Here are the facts: There is a deal on the table, but let me be very, very clear. As good as you are, trust me, you are not important enough, and this deal is not big enough, to weigh it down with a bunch of ancillary bullshit that has nothing to do with music and success. It's lean, mean, and streamlined. You told me you wanted this more than anything in the world, so I'm simply calling you on that. Your move, little girl."

He was so close Libby could feel his breath on her forehead and her entire body stiffened. "What does that mean?"

"You can't be that fucking naïve." Then, in a stunning move, he pushed his body hard against hers, shoved his hand down the front of her skirt and under her panties, and grabbed her crotch, tightly, painfully. Before she could move, react; scream, he leaned into her ear. "It means we're ready to sign a band of six young rock and roll maniacs who come to the table with no baggage, no bullshit, nothing to slow the train down. Your rosy little family life is not in the plan, not in the budget. You want the deal?" He pulled his hand up and squeezed her belly so hard she whimpered. "Fix this problem. You don't? We're done. Your band is done. You're done. I will see to that, little girl."

He yanked his hand from her clothes, walked to his desk, and wiped his fingers with a Kleenex. Tears streaked down Libby's face as she fumbled with the doorknob and flung herself out of the room.

★ ★ ★

Damon, speeding down Sunset, now in the opposite direction, focused fiercely on the road ahead, shellshocked by her report, which was relayed with frantic, wrenching sobs.

In the dimming light of dusk, he attempted assuagement with useless platitudes but only succeeded in exacerbating the situation.

"You're not listening to me, Damon!"

"I am, sweetheart, I am. I guess Eric *can* be a real dick, I get that now. I have heard other people mention that. But honey, I have never heard of him doing anything like that, ever, and if it happened, it—"

"*If* it happened? It happened, Damon!"

"Okay, okay, I'm sorry. If you say it happened, something must have happened, which is obviously uncool. Very uncool. But you also gotta look at it from his point of view. After the long set-up we've had with meetings and lawyers and all the steps we've taken to get this deal worked out, you basically ambushed him with this baby thing. I mean, I'm shocked as hell about it myself, to be honest. Really, really bad timing. I mean, Jesus fucking Christ, Libby, we're about to sign a deal with this guy, top brass at one of the best labels in the industry, and you pull this shit? It's a lot, let me tell you, so maybe give him some leeway, whatever happened. After a few days he'll calm down, you'll calm down; you and Bart will take care of things, and when you're back on your feet, I'll go in with you, and we'll sit down and talk it out with him, clear everything up, get an apology from the asshole, and get the deal signed."

He couldn't look at her after that. Sucker punched, she had nothing left to say.

CHAPTER 41

They were in Bronson Canyon, in the tiny park tucked into the foot of the Hollywood Hills where Libby used to bring Bridget and Robbie to ride bikes and hide Matchbox cars in the sandbox. It was a nostalgic place of warm memories and sweet moments and, therefore, a perfect location for the unburdening of her long held and agonizing story.

Libby was stretched out on the blanket Gwen had thrown down on the grass, eyes red-rimmed and staring up at the sky, her body tensed as if replaying the memory had physically knotted her. Gwen sat cross-legged on the other end of the blanket, arm around her teary-eyed goddaughter, who appeared devastated by her mother's story.

"I had a hand-mark bruise on my stomach for over a week, which I hid from your dad for obvious reasons. He would've gone ballistic, and I was too overwhelmed to deal with that on top of everything else. Damon did go in and talk to Eric, who told him nothing had happened, that I'd completely made it up; that I was 'mentally unhinged,' and he was 'outraged by my false accusation,' even threatening to take legal action against me. Can you imagine how terrifying that was?"

"No. Yes. It's horrible," Bridget softly responded, her head shaking.

"Damon believed Eric's bullshit. Or at least pretended to. Of course he was always angling to save his own ass businesswise, quite comfortable throwing me under the bus if that's what it took. But in a feat of patriarchal condescension, he assured me that he and Eric had 'figured out' how they could work around my emotional instability and personality flaws, which entailed all sorts of weird restrictions on me, and, of course, the non-negotiable demand that I get an abortion." She sat up, as if stronger posture was needed at this point of the story. "But there was a problem with all that. *I wanted you.*" She looked at Bridget to emphasize the point. "*We* wanted you, Dad and me. And secondly, I knew I couldn't, I *wouldn't*, work with that predatory asshole under any circumstances. I kept hoping they would assign us a different point person at the label, a sane one who *wouldn't* make demands on my personal decisions, who *would* know how to work around my pregnancy. That seemed doable to me, considering how excited they'd been to sign us. But when I conveyed that to Damon, his response was that I was immature, unbalanced, and self-sabotaging; no one at the label would work with me under those circumstances, he said. He then dumped me as a client, and, of course, the deal imploded."

"Unreal." Bridget's voice was barely audible. "And I swear I'm not trying to make this all about me, but wow. My simple existence was all caught up in the middle of that mess, and I can't help but feel a little terrible about that."

Gwen gave her a shake. "Bridgie, stop it!"

"How can I not feel that?" she insisted.

Libby leaned forward. "Listen to me, Bridget, and really look at all the moving parts here, not just that one. Your simple existence, as you put it, had us over the moon, we were already so in love with you. And now really get this point too: there was no reason, *zero reason*, the label couldn't have worked it out with me if it hadn't been run by a sociopath. This was not an unheard-of situation, and other labels did figure it out. Just not *this* one."

"That's true, Bridge." Gwen interjected. "The late, great Sinead O'Connor wrote about something similar happening to her. Her label tried to force her to have an abortion when she was recording her first album, but she refused. Lucky for her—unlike in your mom's case—they were already too invested to cut her loose. Which gave her leverage. Women with leverage had more options."

"And that was an incredible album," Libby added wistfully.

"As yours would have been," Gwen rejoined.

Bridget leaned into Gwen's shoulder. "When I think about how huge and impactful everything was for me at nineteen—and that was just stupid stuff like bad dates or horrible haircuts—it's easy to understand how something *this* monumental would have wrecked you."

"It did." Libby reached out her hand; Bridget took it. "It was the worst experience I'd ever had, so I locked it up in a box just to get through the day, get through my life, and, over time, that box stayed locked. Which is how we ended up here."

"I get it now, I really do." Bridget assured her. "I don't think anyone would want to talk about something like that. How did the band deal with it?"

"That was the hard part. Probably the wrong part. I don't know. I didn't tell them."

Bridget was stunned. "How could you not tell them? What did they think happened to the deal?"

"After Eric's lies and Damon's reaction, I was terrified they wouldn't believe me either. So much so that I completely shut down. Then Eric got to Nicky, which I found out later from Gwen." She looked over at her best friend, who picked up the thread.

"I didn't know what had happened at that point; your mom and I hadn't talked yet. So when Nick called, trying to get to her through me—" She looked at Libby. "Because apparently you weren't answering your calls."

"I ... couldn't."

"I understand. But he was out of his mind because Damon had left him a message saying, 'Libby blew up the deal.' Since he couldn't get to your mom, and I didn't know anything, he made the hideous mistake of going to see that sleazy prick Eric, who proceeded to tell him that 'Libby decided on a whim to walk away from the music business to play house with Bart and purposely blew off the deal.' For some stupid reason I cannot fathom to this day—because he should have known her damn well enough to know that could never be true—Nick believed that motherfucker and went insane. I mean, truly insane. He then, of course, passed on all the lies and bullshit to the rest of the guys. Who also, understandably, completely flipped out."

"Each of them tried to call me at different times," Libby continued the story, "screaming into the phone machine, demanding that I give them answers, but I was so traumatized, so gutted, I couldn't speak. Every message shut me down further. It was like I was literally frozen. I kept running pictures through my head of his hand shoved down my crotch, him touching me with his fingers, hurting me, threatening me, and I couldn't find a way to talk about it with the guys; it all felt so shameful to me."

"Oh, Mom, how sad that *you* felt shameful; you were the one who was assaulted."

"Yes, perverse from where I sit now. But back then I was a traumatized teenager with no tools to deal with it. Thought about talking to my parents, but they couldn't have handled it. I even made Dad promise to keep it to himself; told him it was my story to tell, not his."

"Did he? Keep it to himself?" Bridget asked.

"He did. Which shattered his relationship with the guys, especially Nick. Of course, Dad was furious at him for not seeing through the bullshit and taking my side even without knowing all the details."

Bridget kept shaking her head. "It's just so really, really awful, Mom."

"I wish I'd been stronger back then, more assertive." Libby lay back on the blanket, exhausted. "Not only did I lose my dream, but I lost my guys, my friends. I lost Nicky. He'd taken me under his wing when I was just sixteen, mentored me with so much care and respect. I can honestly see how he felt betrayed by me."

"Yeah, but I'm with Bart on that one," Gwen almost growled. "Even if you didn't pick up the damn phone for the next twenty years, he should've known you well enough to know those lies could never be true."

"Probably." Libby nodded weakly. "We were all young and stupid, I think."

"What that guy did to you was criminal," Bridget seethed. "You should have reported him."

"I should have. But you need to understand, honey. This was a very different time, long before 'Me Too' and 'Time's Up.' Back then people either didn't believe women, or, if they did, they just brushed stuff like that under the rug. It was a 'cost of doing business,' as Damon put it. Especially if reporting it would cause a ruckus with powerful people or fuck up the commerce of a situation. Eric was a big name in the industry. Mount Cloud was a cover story on *Rolling Stone* right before this happened. No one would've messed with that. And no one would've likely believed me anyway. Look how hard it was to take down Harvey Weinstein or Bill Cosby. It's *still* hard to get guys like that; back then it wouldn't have even been considered."

Bridget remained churned. "But wouldn't the band have fought for you if they knew?"

Libby sat up and slid next to Bridget; put her arms around her. "Bridge, you know me now, a middle-aged loudmouth who wouldn't let assholes like Damon and Eric manhandle me in a million years. And you're right; I *should* have made a fuss. I *should* have told the band. I *should* have reported it. But the most salient, driving reason I didn't was because I didn't think anyone would believe me, not even the band."

Bridget leaned her head on her mother's shoulder. "Mama ..." she said softly.

"And not to get all hateful and schadenfreudey," Gwen smirked, "but Eric did finally get nailed for sexual harassment about fifteen years ago, five different female execs took him on. He was ousted from the label, which ended up going under after all the bad publicity, and just a few years ago that motherfucker died of prostate cancer. As for Damon, that mewling toad did time for dealing coke; was actually set up in an FBI sting and went to federal prison for three years. Killed his marriage and his career. I hear he's now a pit boss at one of the dumpier casinos in downtown Vegas, fat, bald, with a ketamine habit. So I guess karma did get a little busy on your behalf, Lib."

"Wow." Libby looked stunned. "I can't believe you never told me any of that."

"I have tried to avoid, over all these many years, ever mentioning anything to do with either of those two cretins for your mental health and mine."

"Good bestie." Libby had to smile. "Although I'd never want to celebrate anyone's death or detainment, I must admit to feeling some evil satisfaction with that news."

"Yep." Gwen stood up. "Now, I hate to break up this cozy little klatch, but I've got a dinner to get to, and I believe we've covered it." She looked pointedly at Libby. "And just so you know, my dear friend, when all is said and done, I think you *were* pretty brave, even being that anxious, naïve young girl. As we have learned in our long, wizened lives since, it takes great courage to remove yourself from toxic situations, especially when it means losing something as precious as your dreams. I've got nothing but admiration."

Bridget looked at her mother, eyes shining. "Me, too. I also think Dean and I will just let this project go and brainstorm some other ideas. I can't imagine putting you through anything more on this one."

Libby stood, pulled the blanket up and began folding it. "No, I don't think so. It's a great idea, you've already put so much work into it, and ... I'm okay. I really am. Now that we've talked it out, I'm better. I can deal with it."

"Are you sure?" Bridget was understandably wary.

"No. But yes. Yes, I'm sure." She smiled at her daughter. "Besides, I don't want to hold up your next chapter any more than I already have."

"Mom, that's not—"

"I'm kidding, I'm kidding. Sort of."

"Okay. But how much should I tell Dean about all this? He obviously knows something happened that we needed to talk out, but I don't want to share any more than you'd want me to."

"I appreciate you asking." Libby pondered the question. "I'll leave it up to you. You know him, you trust him, and I trust you. He was there for my meltdown, so I guess he deserves to understand the context behind it. Trust your judgment; that's all I ask."

"Okay. I do want him to understand. Are you going to tell Jeff? Or have you already?"

Libby paused. "No, I haven't. At this point, I don't think so. I'm not ready to let him that far into my life yet. It's too new, and I need to see where it's going before I burden him with my deep, dark past."

"Mom."

"I'm mostly kidding. I'm just not ready to share it with him yet. Maybe later."

"Okay, I trust you too." She smiled.

"By the way, how do you two plan to facilitate this unimaginable gathering of the old band?"

Bridget looked at Gwen, who deferred. "Go ahead, sweetheart; lay it out for your mama."

"Okay, well, our plan was to get everybody together for a party, create a reunion vibe sort of thing, and when they're all there Dean and I will ask them about working with the new guys a time or two. Do you think they'd be up for that?"

"I have no idea. How could I? And how do you plan to find these guys? I haven't spoken to any of them in decades. I saw Nick once after you were born, Bridget, but not since, and it was a very awkward experience at the time."

"Well, there is this little thing called social media, or that even bigger thing called Google," Gwen said. "These guys haven't exactly gone underground."

"They're all on social media?" Libby looked as though the thought had never occurred to her.

Gwen cocked her head disbelievingly. "Are you seriously telling me you have never Googled them or tried to track them down on social media?"

Libby wasn't a Luddite, but neither was she a fan, or even an active user, of pertinent social media. She did what was needed for her job with Chloe but remained unwilling to do more than occasionally lurk around the platforms from time to time. Though she had been tempted to Google each of the guys over the years, she'd made a pact with herself not to, for reasons of her own sanity.

Gwen continued to look skeptical as she explained all this. "Wow. When I said you were detached from the world, I had no idea it was as literal as this. I mean, even my mother has a Facebook page. Even *your* mother does; we're actually friends!"

Libby blushed, aware that her attitude was an anomaly. "I'm sorry you find my desire for privacy a strange thing."

"Not so much strange, babe, just a little lonely."

"Once again, trust me when I tell you I'm not lonely and, frankly, I'm quite happy to not have any obligation to share life updates with gaggles of selfie-sated strangers."

Bridget laughed out loud. "Now, there's some poetry!"

Libby had to smile. "It's the old songwriter in me. But listen, if social media and Google help you find these long-lost fellows, go for it. Though I doubt they'll want anything to do with anything that involves me. They still have no reason to believe I *didn't* fuck them over."

"Well, maybe not so much these days." Gwen cleared her throat.

"What does that mean?"

"See, while *you* may not have talked to them in a long time, I have stayed in touch over these many years—and not just online. Didn't I ever mention that?" She attempted innocence. It failed.

"Nope. How in touch?" Libby asked.

"Occasional bump-ins at events, texts or calls now and again. There might have been drinks or dinners, briefly, from time to time."

"I see. Very surprised to hear this. Feels like another example of subterfuge, but then again, I'm not sure. Depends on what you mean by 'not so much these days' in regard to their historical perspective on past events."

The three women were now standing in a huddle: Bridget fascinated to see where this was going; Libby, eyes curious, expression tense, while Gwen stood with her arms crossed, slightly defensive, as she continued.

"Now, I promised you way back when that I would never tell your story to anyone, and I haven't. *But,* over the years, when

I've had occasion to get into conversations with any of the guys and the subject came up, as it obviously would since we were all swirling in the orbit of what happened back then, I made sure to indicate, quite strongly and with clear intent, that there was *lots* more to the story than they were told, but if they wanted to know the details, they'd have to get in touch with you. But I made sure they knew and understood that you'd been very badly treated by Mr. Eric Burrows, enough that things fell apart."

Libby's expression was inscrutable. "Interesting, then, that none of them ever reached out to me for those details."

"Each of them, at one time or another, said they were going to, they wanted to, but, Lib, you know how life is; you know how men are. Awkward conversations after years of *no* conversations are like eating glass for basic guys who lack higher consciousness tendencies."

"Not even Nicky?"

"Oh, I never talked to Nicky. Never ran into him, he never called; I never called him. He's the only one. He's not much for social media either, so that man sort of disappeared into the ethers. I know some of the guys are in touch with him, though, so who knows what they might have passed on. But I haven't seen that little rock god since we were children." She gave Libby a sly look. "But I can get in touch with him now. You really okay with that? Okay with me dragging the Neanderthals back into the light to help these poor desperate youngsters with their clever and very imaginative project?"

All eyes went to Libby.

It was a big ask, an epic plate-shift given the history she'd been carrying around most of her life. She looked at Bridget's anticipatory face, one that had snarled and snapped at her over the many months she'd been in Los Angeles and now bore a tenderness that had never been part of their mother/daughter lexicon. That was worth the discomfort.

"Fine. Do what you do, Gwennie. You're the exec producer of this madness. Just let me know the results in enough time to mentally prepare myself. 'Cause it's gonna take some damn mental preparation."

She meant that. But there was also a bump of anticipation. It was the first time she'd felt anything but anger, hurt, shame, and regret on the topic. Anticipation was refreshing.

CHAPTER 42

Dean had given Bridget the key to his apartment. It was a pivotal development in their relationship, and something that left her feeling warm and attached. Today, she was using it for the first time despite knowing his schedule wouldn't get him home for at least another hour. She needed time to herself after the afternoon in the park; time to process what she had learned and how it made her feel.

It made her feel like an asshole, a petty, judgmental, entitled brat who had treated her mother like crap for most of her life without a scintilla of interest, awareness, or empathy. She'd seen her as simply the fulfillment of a role—*mother*—without considering she was also a human, a woman; an artist, one who'd lived a life, been hurt and abandoned, who struggled with anxieties and confusions, and in the midst of it all had raised two children, cobbled together a career, and wrangled a difficult marriage.

Bridget threw herself on the bed and, unable to hold back, wept, loudly and without restraint. The knot in her stomach was so big, so heavy and pressuring, it seemed certain that only ferocity and volume could dispel it. She curled in a ball, shoved her face in a pillow, and wailed.

When Dean arrived home an hour later, he found her sitting on the couch, her face a swollen mess of red and mascara. Because he was aware she'd met with her mother to discuss the prevailing situation, he'd had some anticipation of turmoil. What he didn't realize as he caressed her face and brought her cool cloths and a bottle of ginger ale, was that though she was drained and depleted, she'd had a breakthrough, an emotional transformation that left her suffused with love and compassion. For her mother.

And because she trusted him and knew it would only expand his level of understanding, she transmitted every detail to him, every one—from the crass, violent assault of a predatory man, and the betrayal of a manager, to the obliteration of a dream, the abandonment of her creative collaborators, and the inevitable shattering of a young girl's spirit.

"When we listened to her voice for the first time, I felt like I was suddenly being asked to embrace this wildly talented singer as my mother, after a lifetime of never knowing that person. But after today, after hearing her story, the *why* behind it all, I could just weep forever." And she did, indeed, start crying again. "I've been so hard on her, so dismissive and denigrating, never once considering *her* origin story, her pain and hurt, always so focused on my own stuff, my own frustrations and needs and wants. I've not only been a horrible roommate; I've been a horrible daughter." What that, she was wailing.

Dean held her until she'd exhausted her latest round. When she sat back up and took a sip of ginger ale, he finally stepped into the fray.

"Bridget, you haven't been a horrible daughter; you've been a daughter who had some stuff to learn. If you think about it, this whole thing we started is pretty fucking amazing, like some kind of karmic trigger. For the first time in your life, in her life, the two of you have gotten past all your bullshit and bad habits, and talked about her deepest, darkest, most painful secret. The one that blew her life apart. And she shared it with you, even though it was really hard for her to do, because it was that important to her that you really understood what happened, and that you knew it *wasn't you* who blew up those dreams. I know you think I'm an optimism junky, and I might be, but I think this might be the most healing, life-changing thing that could've happened for either of you. *And* we get to move ahead with the project. How cool is all that?"

His face was so lit up, so flushed with love and excitement, Bridget could do nothing but pull him close and hold him as tightly as her arms would allow.

CHAPTER 43

On a bright sunny morning with nary a cloud in the sky, a perfect tribute to the news of the day, Libby learned she passed the CPA certification exam.

"And on the first try!" Chloe gleefully exclaimed. This sent her tittering to the phone to inform her husband, Martin, that they'd be hosting dinner at The Capital Grille, their favorite restaurant in downtown Los Angeles, one so expensive that Libby had not only never been there but had never even heard of it.

"You are available tonight, yes?" she asked Libby, still on the phone with Martin. "And you must bring your new boyfriend; it's time we meet him!"

Libby nodded to both requests, unclear if Jeff was free or would want to join them, but while Chloe was on the phone with the restaurant, her quick text to him elicited an enthusiastic thumbs-up. It seemed his status would now move into a more official territory.

★ ★ ★

Jeff was, of course, well-versed in the appeal of the restaurant ("it's a favorite of some of my dental colleagues") and was charmed by Libby's employers. The food and drink were exceptional, the conversation sparkling; the celebratory theme well acknowledged. At one point, Chloe slipped Libby an ornate envelope, patting her hand with a warm smile and whispered instructions to "open it later." Too curious/anxious to wait till then, she slipped into the ladies' room and was stunned to see, inscribed on a beautiful ivory card, the unexpected figure that defined her new salary.

When she returned to the table with tears in her eyes and an expression of sincere gratitude, Chloe simply replied, "It's well deserved, my dear."

"We are so impressed with your dedication and hard work, Libby." Martin, a tall, nattily dressed Englishman who typically countered Chloe's natural ebullience with an almost stern countenance, reached across the table and took her hand. "I've had friends who could not accomplish what you did in the time frame you managed, all while continuing to be exemplary at the store. We want you part of our business for a long time to come."

Clearly being a CPA had its perks.

Glowing from the accolades, the celebration; the salary bump, and Jeff's hand on her knee under the table, Libby didn't even flinch when he unexpectedly brought up the topic of "Libby's band." She had explained the outline of the story to him the previous night (with no mention of its darker chapters), and he got very excited about the prospect of potentially meeting her old bandmates.

"I've even offered my place for this grand reunion." Which he had. Which she'd accepted with the caveat that it might not come to fruition. "Should be quite a shindig if it does!"

"My best friend, Gwen, is the pseudo exec-producer of this crazy venture," Libby explained to Chloe and Martin. "She's trying to track them all down, but it's been a very long time, and I have no idea how successful she'll be."

"Well, my goodness, Libby, I'm just gobsmacked that you have this hidden, secret history!" Chloe chortled. "With your great visual eye, I had no doubt of your creative aptitudes, but this is just extraordinary."

They—she and Martin—then went on to inquire about the details, from the clothes she wore to the kinds of songs she sang, even the personalities of the "boys in the band." Libby couldn't help but feel giddy at the attention but given the dearth of conversation on this topic over the last thirty-some years, it was also a bit exhausting. By the time she and Jeff were headed back to the Hollywood Hills she could barely keep her eyes open. Then she couldn't.

When he pulled into the cul de sac and stopped the car, she jolted awake, looked at him with chagrin. "Was I snoring?"

He laughed. "Just the gentle girly kind."

"Sorry. Guess I'm more tired than I thought."

"No apologies necessary. It was a big night after a demanding few months; I'm impressed you're still standing. Or sitting, as it were. But, given the look on your face, my guess is you'd prefer to be alone tonight. Am I right?"

"What gave it away? The eyes that won't stay open?" She liked that he noticed and responded accordingly. She also liked that he enjoyed meeting her bosses and engaged with interest, stepping into his now proclaimed role of "Libby's boyfriend," as Chloe had introduced him to Martin, with ease and clear approval.

"I know your tells, lady." He grinned back.

"I *am* wiped out. I hope you understand. I need to start catching up on my sleep, and you are not at all helpful in that regard," she offered with a sly smile.

He leaned in and pulled her close. "I could always restrain myself and just sleep. I'm a very disciplined fellow."

Her response was a deep, unrestrained kiss. "I wouldn't want you disciplined." She unbuckled her seatbelt and opened the car door. "I like your wild side too much. Now go home."

★ ★ ★

But sleep evaded. Laying wide awake for what had now been several hours, Libby raced through the litany of thoughts and emotions that rolled around on repeat. She'd arrived home to a long voicemail from Gwen, breathless to report that she'd talked to *"every one of the guys, even Nicky,"* and without hesitation, she insisted, they were up for the soiree:

"They did talk a bit about what happened, each of them, and I again gave as much context as you'd allow. But there were mostly just lots of 'it's all in the past' and 'I've moved on, would love to see the Libster' kind of stuff, which I thought you'd appreciate. I threw out the dates Jeff gave you, and it looks like that second Saturday will work, okay? Wow. Amazing, huh?"

It was. It was also horrifying. She was just getting her life in order—a solid relationship, a major raise, her son was flourishing in a new semester, her daughter evolving—so the specter of scraping the scab, potentially setting off fireworks about things she couldn't change even if she wanted to, was daunting.

In this fraught moment in the middle of the night, with her heart beating too fast and her head swimming with anxiety, she wished she'd never agreed to it; hadn't felt so acquiescent to the nascent goodwill budding between her and Bridget, and had just said *no*. It was too late now. Blowing it all up at this point would shatter whatever fragile peace they'd brokered, and that was untenable. Once again, she'd buck up and get through whatever was required of her.

Dammit.

CHAPTER 44

It was party day.

When she pulled up to Jeff's house two hours before the event's start time, Libby struggled to find parking amidst the various trucks—caterers, bouncy house, liquor supply store— and Gwen's and Bridget's cars. Despite her admonition to Jeff that, "We don't need a big hoopla. Gwen's covering the liquor, and I'll just get stuff to barbecue, salads and chips from the deli," he'd adamantly rejected the plan.

"It's the first party I've thrown since my divorce, and it's a big deal, you getting together with these guys, Bridget and Dean's project, the whole thing. I want to do it up right and you can't stop me."

So she'd accepted with gratitude, and the result was this wild congregation of party preppers. Decorative lights were being strung around the patio and yard; tables were set in strategic spots; a bar was being assembled. Everything sparkled and shined, the overall effect took what was already a startlingly gorgeous house and surrounds into the stratosphere of spectacular.

With her outfit thrown over her arm, Libby made her way inside to find Jeff in a natty ensemble of beige linen slacks and a Tommy Bahama shirt. His wet hair (clearly just out of the shower) was plastered to his head, so much so that Libby was compelled to grab him in a hug and simultaneously muss it into more fashionable disarray. He let her, but not without comment.

"Too buttoned up for the rock and roll crowd?"

She had to smile because it sort of was. "No, you just look better when I've run my hands through it."

He pulled her closer. "I like the sound of that."

She laughed and pushed him away. "Stop, you'll wrinkle my outfit!"

"What have you got there? Show me."

"Nope. You'll have to wait until I make my very dramatic entrance once everyone's here."

"Okay. Nothing wrong with a little drama. I just hope you aren't disappointed if the crowd that shows up is a little more Spinal Tap than Rolling Stones."

She thought she detected a hint of snark, which wasn't like him. "I won't be because, frankly, I have no expectations either way. But now I'm going to join Bridget and Gwen, who've texted me from the suite upstairs which you graciously designated as our girl-space, and I'll see you back down here later." She leaned in and gave him a kiss. "And thank you again for doing this, for my kid, for me; I don't know, for all of it. Even allowing my ex to partake. It means a lot."

"I'm happy to do it, Libby. And I'm having fun, I promise. I'm fascinated to meet all these various men from your past. Now go get dressed; I want you to dazzle those old farts." He gently swatted her butt, then headed out to the patio. She took a moment of pause, considering whether the smack was sweet and allowable. Or neither.

I'm being ridiculous now, she snapped to herself and headed upstairs.

★ ★ ★

Bridget, recycling her outfit from the first Aaron meeting, looking smart and stylish, sat on the bed of a very large and beautifully decorated guest suite watching as Gwen primped over an anxious Libby's hair. Gorgeous in her stunning but carefully casual outfit of vintage flared jeans, chunky leather belt, and white poet's shirt, Libby was a long way from the housewife of old.

"You look incredible, Mom."

"Thank you, sweetheart. Gwen took me shopping, and she's always had impeccable taste."

"Yeah, I've got an eye for what looks good on aging bodies. I think I did well." Gwen looked her over with a nod.

Libby shoved her good-naturedly.

"But not just the clothes, Mom; *you* look fantastic."

A warm smile passed between them. "You're not so bad yourself, kiddo."

Bridget had recovered from those early months of mourning and depression to blossom into the fit, well dressed, exceedingly gorgeous young woman who was now standing in this room ready to take on the unknown. "I felt obligated to be an impressive as I could get, given what we'll be asking of them, so thank you. How do you honestly think they'll respond?"

"I have no idea, Bridge. I had no idea they'd even show up, so it's all a mystery to me." She shook her hands out if tossing off nerves. "And why am I so damn twitchy?

"Seriously?" Gwen snorted. "New guy, old guy, a bunch of old guys, and wish-he-coulda-been-my-guy. Do the math."

"What are the odds of Nick even showing up?" Libby asked her.

"He said he would, but who knows? If he does, he'll be late. Count on that. No one likes an entrance better than Nicky."

"But you talked to him? Personally?"

"I did."

"Are you going to tell me about the conversation?"

"Maybe later. Right now I want you to go into this with a clear head, a clean slate, no preconceived ideas, no percolating anxieties. I can report that he said he was looking forward to seeing you which I have no doubt he meant."

Libby's face flushed.

Bridget broke in. "I am now at peak level curiosity. I've heard so much about this guy I feel like I might need a trigger warning. Will I want to punch him or ask for his autograph?"

Playfully ignoring her, Libby walked to the mirror. Examining her face, even she was impressed at how fabulous she looked. "Excellent job on the makeup, Gwen. I almost look like a woman in her mid-fifties."

Gwen bowed, fluffing her own hair. "Thank you, ma'am. Your face was unusually cooperative today. I wonder why?"

Bridget shook her head, laughing. "Oh, so no one's going to respond to my question? No one's going to explain Nick to me?"

Libby motioned to Gwen. "I think you should take this."

"Okay." Gwen zoned in on Bridget with gleaming eyes. "You've heard the dark side of this tawdry tale, its horrible creatures and ugly denouement, but what we haven't told you is all the sweet, happy days that preceded that ending. Nick is—how shall I put it? Well, actually, let me put it in past tense because I have no idea what Nick is now. Back then, Nick was that guy you couldn't help but fall in love with, at least a little bit. Every woman I knew who knew him *did*, some more than just a little. He had charisma by the boatload, was an incredible musician, a sweet man with a gorgeous face and a good heart. *And* I've wanted to punch that face many times over the last thirty-some years, so your guess is as good as mine as to what your own impression will be, Bridgie."

"But he was a solid person, you know, a stand-up guy." Libby added wistfully. "Maybe more mature than most guys his age. He always had a girlfriend, never got into the whole groupie thing like the rest of them, which I saw as very admirable at the time. Remember Mercy Harlan, Gwen?"

"Scottish punk queen. Loved her."

"I did too. But as I mentioned, dear daughter, I did have a little teenage crush, despite Miss Mercy's presence."

"Little?" Gwen bleated with one of her signature guffaws.

Libby flopped on the bed and got all starry-eyed. "He was a guitar wizard and when he'd play his wild solos, he'd look at me with those dreamy blue eyes, and I'd melt every time, just besotted. There was even a kiss once—just once and it didn't go anywhere; Mercy was still around. I don't know what might have happened if she wasn't, and we never talked about it, so I never knew how mutual it was—"

"Oh, it was mutual," Gwen responded. "But our Nick was a man of honor with his Mercy, so he and your mama just made those googly eyes at each other every now and again. And by the time he and Mercy broke up, your mom was dating your dad."

Bridget dropped to the bed next to Libby. "Wow. I could've never existed."

Libby grabbed her in a hug. "Which is why everything happens in its divine right order."

The noise from the patio had grown exponentially louder as the women chatted, and when a burst of greetings and laughter erupted from below, Gwen rushed to the wide bedroom window to take in the scene. "Oh, would you look at that, Gavin's a little butterball!"

Libby and Bridget joined her at the window, peeking surreptitiously from behind the curtain. Libby felt an immediate flush of heat. Looking down at these men who'd been so absent from her life after having once been so essential, was surreal. She joined the banter.

"He is! He was such a great bassist. I wonder if he still plays."

"He does, I guess. Works all the time, he says; where, I don't know."

"And there's Chris. He was the keyboardist, Bridge. Oh, Gwennie, look at Chris's hair. He will not give up the Simon le Bon. Come into the twenty-first century, Chrissie, you'll love it here!"

"At least he's still got hair. Now, August ..." Gwen pointed. "Over by the bar. Dear lord, he's fat *and* bald. Never thought that man would get fat and bald." She turned to Bridget. "He was the rhythm guitarist. Very funny guy. Sexy, a little wild, all the girls loved him. Now he's fat, bald, and divorced."

"But, oh, still so cute, our little Auggie." Libby laughed. "And remember those amazing stews he used to make? Such a good cook."

"Probably why he's now fat. The hair, no excuse." She was grinning from ear to ear. "And, Brandon, of course, still the little stud-muffin."

"Which one is he?" Bridget leaned as close to the window as she could without outing their viewing station.

"Standing there next to that terrifyingly gorgeous model person," Gwen responded. "What is it with these rock guys? Is there just some imprint from birth about being with models?"

Bridget giggled. "If I've kept up with the list, he must be the drummer, right?"

"Yep." Libby answered. "An amazing drummer. Also an asshole. He once said his best advice to me as a young singer was to not gain weight. Let me see, how did he put it? 'Most chick singers end up getting fat. Don't get fat, Libby.' I hated him for that, but I do tend to think of him whenever I jump a jeans size. Of course, I've excused myself as not being a chick singer anymore, so fuck him!"

They collapsed into laughter. Standing next to each other, all spiffed and giddy, they made a hilarious Greek chorus.

"And why are there so many youngsters out there? Aren't they all too old to have that many kids running around or are those actual grandbabies?" Gwen pointed out the window. "There, there, over there. Tons o' youngsters."

"As you've noted, old friend, aging rock stars are not only imprinted about models, they're imprinted about *young*. Just look at all the stunning women in that group. If there's one over forty, I'd be surprised."

"You are correct. And now that I think about it, I do believe there are scads of older progeny from various first and forgotten marriages, the cads." Gwen looked to other side of the large deck with a big grin. "And then there's the three amigos."

Jeff, Bart, and Otto stood huddled around the bar. All three were perusing the growing crowd, leaning into each other with occasional commentary, clearly a breed apart.

"Look at them. They're as bad as we are. Three old hens taking pot shots at the cool guys!" Gwen hooted.

"While Dean walks around being a host." Bridget smiled, pleased.

"Well, Dean's a rockstar in his own right," Gwen asserted. "But, honestly, I think the whole gang out there looks pretty great." She straightened her clothes and checked her makeup in the mirror. "Since we ladies are now appropriately stunning, let's go hit the mosh pit."

CHAPTER 45

Various kids of various ages, hyper from too many sodas and the excitement of having new pals to play with, tore around the deck jumping in and out of the pool, and slamming around the bouncy house Jeff had provided for the day. The mood was rowdy, the volume fever pitched, and watching from the sidelines, drinks in hand, smiles on faces, were the veterans of a band called Liberty.

Chris, the keyboardist with the Simon Le Bon do, was stretched out on a patio chaise with a three-year-old straddling his hips; his postpartum wife, Kiyomi, was nearby nursing their newborn. He looked comfortable and happy to be there, taking in the surrounds with obvious pleasure.

The bassist, Gavin, stood with his wife, Lorna, a beautiful woman of about forty, both occupied trying to keep their two kids from breaking limbs and bashing heads. Lots of hollered admonitions to, "watch out, Miles!" or "don't push anyone, Alex," with Gavin occasionally yelping, "Don't jump so close to the door, buddy!" Joyful chaos.

Seated at one of the cocktail tables was August, the rhythm guitarist. Smiling and sweating in a leather jacket, Fedora atop his shiny pate, he nursed a beer with a heaping plate of hors d'oeuvres, his grin wide as he chatted with myriad guys and gals huddled around him. Three of the kids running around were his, all of whom, ages eleven through fourteen, were either splashing in the pool or flopping around the bouncy house.

The drummer, Brandon, tall and handsome, kept an arm around Giselle, his twenty-something wife who, as it turned out, was "the new face" of some iconic fragrance by a top fashion designer. They made a stunning couple.

As the catering staff whirled around with hors d'oeuvres trays, Jeff, Bart, and Otto held down the bar station, while Dean moved amongst the various clusters taking photographs. Music played loudly and wafts of a well-stoked barbeque filled the air.

Into this convivial scene, in a moment of perfect choreography, Bridget, Gwen and Libby made their entrance like the queens they were. All attention shifted to them. Libby paused nervously at the patio door, then, in what felt like a timed explosion, the boys in the band swarmed, lifting her up with whoops and hollers. Her laughter was part joy, part relief.

They ceremoniously marched her around the deck; kids cheered wildly as the ladies smiled. Bridget captured the scene on video; Dean snapped photos, Bart grabbed another beer, and Jeff simply watched, fascinated.

When they set her down, all manner of good-natured ribbing launched.

"Damn, Conlin, you weigh a ton!" Brandon winked.

"Shut up, you skinny shit," Libby punched him with a grin.

"Ignore him; I think you look fabulous, Lib," August countered with a hug.

"Thank you, sweet Auggie. Keep that cretin away from me, I'll hurt him."

Brandon grabbed her in a bear hug. "Truly, Libby, you look wonderful. For an old broad."

As she playfully shoved him, Gavin approached. "Hey, Brandon, still taking her abuse, I see."

"Gav, my man, what can I say; the woman holds sway over my heart. Always has."

"Liar," Libby retorted. "Come here, Gavin, give me a hug."

As he followed orders, Chris walked up with his newborn.

"Libby, meet my newest offspring. Caleb, this is the finest singer this side of heaven."

Libby glanced at him, touched by the compliment, then took the baby from his arms. "Imagine, little Chris a daddy, you poor, darling baby." She leaned in and kissed his cheek. Looking up with a smile, she said, "Chrissie, he's beautiful. And you haven't changed a bit."

"Hah. How nice of you to try. Come over and meet Kiyomi; see if you can convince her of the same!"

Just then Libby glanced over at Jeff, who was still hovering near the bar looking mildly displaced.

"I'd love to meet Kiyomi but give me a sec." As Gwen swooped in to continue the conversation with the boys, Libby handed her the baby and made her way to the bar.

Jeff looked up. "You look utterly amazing."

She smiled coyly. "Thank you, that was the plan. How are you doing?"

"Fine. Great bunch."

"Yeah? This is all still okay?"

He put down his drink. "Libby, you asked me that when you got here, you texted me that while you were getting ready; you can stop taking my pulse. Believe me, I'm having fun. Though I do wonder what I should know about this Nick fellow before he arrives."

Libby felt a shot of annoyance. "Ah, Bart's been in gossip mode, has he?"

"He's got an interesting take on your old bandmate. I'm doing all right with the ex-husband; I'd just like to know if there's an ex-boyfriend I'll need to deal with too."

"Don't you think I would have told you if that were the case?" Libby's voice had an edge to it. "No, no ex-boyfriends, just old friends. Okay?"

"Then why does Bart have such a beef with him? That clearly seems to be the case."

Libby had no intention of getting into any of it, so she went with: "They worked together for years, and I think they just got on each other's nerves. Doubt there's much else to it."

"Okay, got it." Jeff put his arm around her, his tone conciliatory. "Be patient with me, Libby. I'm a conservative old dentist who's not used to all this rock and roll stuff. I'm doing my best to keep up."

Libby couldn't help but smile, hugging him back. "You're doing just fine. You can keep up with any of them. Now, let's get dinner going. I think the little ones need to eat something besides sugar."

CHAPTER 46

As dinner wound down, kids and adults occupying every available space around the deck and good spirits abounding, Libby felt warmed and grateful for the day. There'd been occasion for each of the guys to find a private moment with her to comment on how sorry they were to have fallen out of contact, how they were aware something untoward had happened; they regretted abandoning her and would "like to get together and talk it out when you have time." She wasn't sure any of them would, wasn't even sure it was necessary at this point, but none of it felt obligatory, all of it felt sincere, and she was deeply touched. She found herself glancing at Gwen from time to time, silently conveying her gratitude for her friend's obvious and meaningful interventions.

But clearly there was attention on Nick's continuing absence. At some point during dinner, Bridget asked Libby, who then checked with Gwen to see if he'd texted or called but there'd been no contact. She tried not to let it impact her enjoyment of the evening but couldn't help but wonder if it was a rebuff of some kind, which would be particularly painful in contrast to the warm entreaties from the rest of the crowd.

An announcement was made that dessert was about to be served, eliciting squeals of delight from the kids and even a few adults—a sundae bar was involved. In the transition, Dean and Bridget grabbed Libby to ask how they should approach the rest of the band with Nick still unaccounted for. She had no idea and was trying to formulate an answer when, as if timed for maximum impact, the patio doors slid open and the notorious Nick Jackson stepped onto the deck, making his predictable, maddening, and very late entrance. At fifty-eight, still striking; very much the aging rocker but with enough contemporary flair to be cool, his face broke into a wide grin as he took in the scene.

"Beasts! Which one of you owes me money?"

A roar followed as the guys leapt up to greet their old cohort. Punched and pummeled in the onslaught, his shouts of laughter seemed to amuse the drop-dead thirty-something woman who'd arrived with him and smiled patiently while observing the commotion.

Libby got up from the table and walked slowly into the circle of testosterone. "Back off, heathens. Let a woman give the prodigal a proper hello." She once again playfully shoved Brandon aside, and she and Nick just looked at each other. A beat, then he grabbed her in a bone-crushing hug.

"Lord, Liberty, you look good enough for VH1."

"What, no MTV?" she quipped.

"Too old for 'em. Hell, you're too old for VH1." All in good fun.

He reached over and pulled his girlfriend into the huddle. "Hey everybody, this is Kyla. Kyla, these are the relics of my past."

Bart, who'd been quiet throughout the day, wandering around for brief conversations while largely uninvolved with the frivolity (though very attached to the beer cooler), suddenly hollered, "Even she can't make a relic like you look any younger, Nick."

Libby's eyes rolled, Bridget squirmed, and Jeff watched without reaction.

Nick, however, didn't flinch. "Have another beer, Barty, and I promise we'll all look good."

Gwen pushed past the awkwardness. "Nicky, go grab Kyla some dinner before the caterer packs it all up. Even August says it's good enough to eat!" And with that, the festivities picked right back up.

★ ★ ★

As the band's music blasted from outdoor speakers delighting everyone in attendance, and kids tore around the backyard with sparklers and bubbles, Libby and Nick moved off to the quieter side of the pool for some private time. The tension between them was palpable, if muted.

"You really do look great, Liberty; held up well." He grinned.

"As did you. I guess time ain't got us yet."

"Nah, we won't let it. So. Life is good?"

"Life is good. Gwen tells me you have a studio that's doing well. Seems you're the only one of us who didn't totally give up the muse."

"Yeah, in some ways I got lucky. In others, there just wasn't anything else for me to do. But, hey, look at you. I hear your son's doing great in school, and Bridget—she's really something. Then there's a new boyfriend, a great job, a sloppy, loud-mouthed ex-husband."

"Ah yes, Bart's got some issues. Maybe someday we'll talk about them. Or the two of you will talk about them, I don't know. But Kyla seems nice."

"She is. She's a producer's rep, very involved in helping build the studio, which was much needed and very appreciated. Nice to have someone that beautiful bring whip-smart business acumen to the picture."

"Ah, still so shamelessly sexist. Here I thought you only went for the brainless beauties." She teased with a grin.

Nick grabbed his chest. "Ouch. You got me there. I just mean she's got it all going on. A great lady. So what about your scene? Bart? Jeff? Torn between two lovers?"

"That's horrifying to consider. No, nothing that dramatic. Bart's a benign pain in the ass and Jeff's my new experiment."

"Sounds romantic."

"Kind of."

"Then ... good?"

"Yeah, good."

"Well, he's gotta be to let this motley crew take over his house. Which is quite the place."

"It is. I guess he'd heard enough about all of you that he was interested to see for himself."

"Hope we didn't disappoint."

"He's an easy guy."

They both smiled. Awkward silence descended as they officially ran out of banal chatter. Libby finally took a deep breath.

"So. We haven't talked in a while. Decades. I wondered if you'd come today. Then I wondered how it would be if you *did* come."

"Of course I was going to come. Gwen wouldn't leave me alone!" He attempted a laugh. When she didn't respond in kind, he got serious. "Look, Liberty, a lot of life's passed since then; it's water under the bridge."

"Is it? Because it was pretty catastrophic, and we never talked about it. That was all on me; I know. I just couldn't for a whole lot of reasons but figured at some point I would. At some point we'd need to. Or you'd want to. I guess I kept waiting for that time to happen."

"Did you?" He shifted in his chair to look at her. "That surprises me because I kept thinking your silence meant the opposite—that you had no intention of talking about things. I practically kicked down your door, and you never once cracked it open."

"I know, but, trust me, it wasn't that I didn't *want* to talk to you. It's that I honestly couldn't. There was so much going on that you didn't know and I—"

"Hey, everybody," Bridget suddenly hollered from the deck. "Could we meet in the living room for a little bit? There's something Dean and I would like to talk about with all of you."

As people started moving toward the patio doors, Nick looked at Libby with a somber expression. "That was interesting timing. Listen, Liberty, I don't know what we should or shouldn't have talked about. Or done. Or not done. It was a long damn time ago. Maybe we weren't meant to hash it all out. Maybe we *can't* hash it all out. Maybe now we're just meant to let it be the past, let it go. What do you think?"

She felt a growing knot in her stomach. He was probably right, but somehow she had hoped he'd want clarity, want to fix what had broken between them. She wasn't sure they could be honest friends in this new moment of time if they just pushed past the old one without discussion or injection of any truth. That seemed to be what he was asking her to do.

"I'm not sure what I think at the moment, but we can give that a go for now, I guess."

He stood up and reached for her hand, pulling her out of the chair. "Okay then. Let's go see what your clever young daughter has in mind for us." He put his arm around her as they walked up to the house, clearly unbothered by the trajectory of their conversation.

She was less unbothered.

CHAPTER 47

The sweeping living room with its vaulted ceilings and dramatic lighting was packed with the adults, while the kids continued their revelry outside.

Bridget and Dean held centerstage. They started at the beginning, explaining the project, why they were all here and what, exactly, was wanted from them. Having reached their conclusion, which clearly stunned all in attendance, each one of the band members displayed some harmonic of curiosity and confusion. Brandon was the first on the floor.

"So, you want us to help these kids sound like us? Am I getting that right?"

"Us from thirty-five years ago." August added. "Wow. That's an interesting ask. When was the last time you hit the skins, Bran?"

"A long time ago. My right knee is shot."

Gavin chimed in. "I play in church every weekend, but that's acoustic guitar. I've had some bass gigs over the years, but those have been few and far between."

Bridget shot Dean a look, and he jumped back in. "I know it sounds a little crazy, but this opportunity came up unexpectedly, and we thought it was worth taking every chance possible to get the label interested in your tunes. They already are, but if that could develop into an actual deal of some kind, the publishing royalties for all of you would be a significant thing, right? And don't get us wrong, these guys are all good players; they just don't have the sound the label heard on the recordings, which is what they want to hear. We figured you could sort of mentor them a little, show them the effects you used, the keyboard settings, stuff like that."

Chris laughed out loud. "Who knew we were so worth imitating? We were just making noise back in the day." They all chortled in unison. "Hey, Dean, while it's flattering that you two are interested in our musical input, I'm not sure what I could contribute or when I would even be available. I've got two babies and a full-time gig, so time is tight in my world. When were you thinking of doing this?"

"We'd totally work around your schedules," Bridget chimed in. "We don't think we'd need more than one rehearsal with them; they already know the tunes. But whatever time you'd all need to work the songs up again for yourselves, we've got it in the budget to pay you each a consulting fee—"

"Aw, sweetheart, we don't need your money," August said. "I just don't know what I could show anyone at this point of my life. Especially young musicians who know what's going on out there, cuz I sure don't."

"And let's face it; it's been a really long time since we played those tunes," Brandon added, echoing the general sentiment. "We *would* have to relearn them all, and that could take more time than any of us have got."

Libby watched Bridget and Dean squirm. She looked over at Gwen, who shrugged helplessly. Jeff wandered around the room quietly refilling wine glasses.

Dean sat down. "Totally understand, you guys. It was a longshot idea and we—"

"I'm in."

Everyone turned to Nick. He looked around, his face serious. "You guys are four of the best players I ever worked with. Seriously. And I don't know about schedules and timing, but I damn well know we could kick some twenty-something butt with our hands tied and knees in a sling. Come on, beasts, it'd be fun!"

They all looked at each other.

Kiyomi peered up from the baby. "I think it sounds like fun too," she said quietly. She leaned over and whispered in Chris's ear. He smiled. "Okay, the boss says if it's nights or weekends, we can work it out."

There was a pause.

"Well, hell, if Nick and Chris are in, I gotta be too. I must have some kick left, for fuck's sake!" Brandon nodded.

Gavin looked at Lorna. "Is my bass still out in the garage?"

"I think so."

"Shit," August barked. "If you losers are on board you know you're gonna need me!"

The tenor of the room completely shifted at this point. As everyone gathered around Bridget and Dean to work out the details, Gwen winked at Libby. When Libby looked over at Nick, their eyes met in a private smile.

* * *

As Jeff and Libby finished last-minute clean-up, the house empty, the chaos settled back to silence, the mood between them was easy but, at least on Libby's part, curious. Jeff caught her gazing his way.

"What?"

"Thank you for doing this. It was a big deal, and your generosity meant a lot to me. I hope it was okay."

"You're welcome and it was, and this should be the last time you thank me, okay? You've thanked me enough." He smiled and pulled her into his arms. "We're in this together at this point, don't you think? I'm here for it all, whatever that ends up being. Were you happy with the way it turned out?"

"Yes, of course. Bridge and Dean got what they came for. Now it'll be incredibly interesting to see how it all works out."

"How did it work out for you, seeing these guys from so far in your distant past?"

Funny, how he put it. Though an apt description, seeing them all today made time almost disappear, as if that "distant past" had no bearing on the "now" they were in. It would be interesting to see how "after" might evolve.

"It was wonderful," was all she could say. It was. Mostly.

CHAPTER 48

The first rehearsal was booked: the upcoming Saturday at Nick's studio. Bridget decided to spend Friday night at the house, wanting private time to put together what she'd be documenting at the next day's gathering.

She and Libby had a quiet, easy dinner together. Since the metamorphic day at the park, the energy, the air, between them had shifted, reconfiguring into something completely altered from what existed before. Both were aware of the change, but it felt fragile enough that any attempt to analyze it seemed foolhardy. *Just be in it,* Libby told herself. Bridget appeared to feel the same.

So they chatted comfortably about work, about how Robbie was doing at school; the men in their respective lives. Bridget told Libby about getting the key to Dean's apartment, "which seems to be a real statement, don't you think?" Libby did, and since she really liked Dean, was happy for her daughter, hopeful that the evolution of their relationship would stay positive.

"What about you and Jeff?"

Libby noted that the question was asked with authentic interest.

"He introduced me as his girlfriend when I stopped by his dental practice the other day. Everyone there seems in awe of him, so that's a good sign."

"So you're still in the assessing his character phase?" Bridget teased.

"I guess. It's been so long since I've been in a real relationship, I'm not sure when I should stop doing that. The pulse-checking. The temperature-taking."

"Well, he's clearly made a decision about you." Bridget grinned. "I don't think he took his eyes off you the whole night of the party."

"Yeah, he's been pretty expressive about his feelings, which, I have to admit, feels a little fast for me. But he's easy to be with, so he makes my time with him easy too. We'll just go with that for now."

Bridget's phone vibrated with a text. "Okay, Mom, Nick says the guys will be at his studio tomorrow at one. Dean and I will get there early to help set up, and you should be there by three, give the guys time to warm up."

Libby smiled at her daughter's efficiency. "Got it, Boss-Lady." A beat. "So you and Nick text each other?"

Bridget looked up with a sly smile. "Yes. Why? Are you jealous?"

"Stop. It's just funny to think about."

Bridget's phone vibrated again. "Oh, he also said to remind you to do your vocal warm-ups. He told me last week to look for an old paisley bag you used to keep your tapes in and, unbelievably, I found it up there in hoarder's paradise. I had Dean digitize them; I'll text you the files so you can just pop them into your phone."

"Damn, you are terrifyingly adept at all this. And I cannot believe he remembered that random detail, my paisley bag. Though he did give it to me." She suddenly had a thought. "But wait, why do I need to vocalize? I thought this was just for the guys to work out the kinks before they meet with your band."

"Mom, they still need a vocalist to follow. That's you, remember?"

"But I wasn't planning on singing." There was real panic in her voice. "I would need weeks, months, who knows how long, to get back into any kind of vocal shape. I don't even sing in my car or the shower. I'm going to sound like—"

Another text came in. "Wow, it's like he actually reads your mind. He said he's planning to drop the keys down at least a half-step—okay, I'm reading this now—'*or maybe a full step, whatever she needs. It'll be easier for her to find her way back to the tunes if she's not pushing the range. Ask her how far we should drop them.*'" Bridget looked at Libby. "Whatever all that means."

Libby shook her head, pondering how Nick was always one step ahead of her when it came to the music. "Tell him a whole step. If I get warmed up enough to raise them later, we can readjust then."

"Okay." She tapped out the message. "The warm-up files have just been sent to you. I'll be in my room working on stuff. Stop whining and start warbling. From what I hear, you haven't sung in a while." Bridget's grin was sardonic; she leaned in, kissed her mother's cheek and was off.

Libby felt slightly ambushed. If she'd given ample thought to unfolding events, of course she'd have realized the guys needed her vocals to work the songs. Somebody's vocals, at least. And who else was there but her?

She went up to the hallway mirror, ruffled her hair, pulled back the skin on her face, smiled like a beauty queen, then let it sink back down to fifty-four. "Nope. No hope there," she mumbled to herself.

She pulled out her phone, tapped the screen to find the mp3s Bridget had just sent. When she hit play, the sound of eighteen-year-old Libby's voice "me-me-me'ing" came through loud and clear. It was as if time, and her daughter, were pulling her back into this incarnation of herself whether she was emotionally—or vocally—equipped to exist there or not.

With a deep sigh, she looked again in the mirror and started singing along with her young, hopeful, breathlessly optimistic self.

CHAPTER 49

Nick's studio was tucked between a block-long army surplus store and a weary stack of office buildings in Burbank. Once inside, however, the smart, contemporary interior (courtesy of the gorgeous Kyla) and top-notch gear made it one of the most coveted recording venues in the city. He was as busy as he wanted to be, he said, and today he was happy to turn the place over to the sweaty pack of men with whom he'd spent his early musical years.

The guys were about two hours into rehearsal, and given the detritus strewn about—coffee cups, beer bottles, equipment, etc., it was clear work was being done here. Bridget had her iPhone set on a tripod and was chronicling the day, which, currently, had gotten a bit testy.

"Correct me if I'm wrong, but we always used a wah-wah here." August looked beleaguered.

"Nope," Nick said. "Never used a wah-wah on this song."

Brandon barked from the drum set. "Fuck the pedal; let's just play, for fuck's sake!"

"Isn't the whole point of this to get it right so we can pass that instrumental wisdom on to the young folk?" August somewhat righteously queried. "Frankly, I'd like to get it right either way."

Bridget shot Dean an anxious look, but he just smiled, leaning in to whisper, "It's okay; this is how it tends to go." She rolled her eyes.

Gavin, who'd been plunking on his bass strings waiting for the question to be settled, finally jumped in. "Aug, buddy, I'm not trying to piss you off, but Nick's right."

"Yup," Chris echoed.

August looked at each of them, then grinned and said, "Fuck it, okay. Let's go."

As relief swept the room, Brandon gave the count and the band kicked into another of their old songs. It was shaky start, but ever so slowly the guys got into sync and rhythm. A smile slowly spread over Brandon's face as he threw his head back with a whoop of joy. The others joined in as the song finally locked and they once more sounded like a band. Bridget found herself welling up; it was like watching something be reborn.

At that precise moment, Libby and Gwen came through the doors. Standing off to the side, taking it all in, they looked at each other in amazement. Time-warp. Libby took off her jacket and popped onto a stool, nervous, but surprisingly instinctive in the space. Nick caught her eye with a wink as the song wrapped up.

"You guys sound awesome," Dean beamed.

"Thanks, buddy," Nick clapped him on the shoulder. "It's like riding a bike. Or a horse. Or one of those cliches." He grinned.

Bridget just glowed; it was all so overwhelmingly cool.

"And Bran-man," Nick continued, "if them's bad knees, I'll take 'em any day. You still got it, my friend."

"Thanks, man." Brandon gave Nick a fist bump.

"The rest of you motherfuckers kicked it too. Dammit, we rock, beasts!" Nick yelped and again hoots went up. The room felt electric.

As the guys went over the rest of the set list, Nick approached Libby.

"So what do you think, Liberty?"

She shook her head softly. "I'm transported. It's like no time has passed, much less three decades."

"Yep. You either got it or you don't. And these boys got it, no matter how old they get."

Gwen heard that. "Hey, loser, you got old too. And you sound like shit."

"Shut up, dragon lady." Grinning, he shoved her. Of course, she shoved back.

"So, Liberty," he said, back to business. "We've been through the set once. It's time to get up and run it with us."

A look of panic flittered across her face as she got off the stool. "Just remember, I haven't sung this century. One or two hours of warm-ups ain't gonna do a whole lot about that, so keep your expectations in check."

"Just take it easy and give us what you got. It was always better than most. The lowered keys should help. Might even sound better in this new incarnation of things."

"We'll see." A mic had been set up for Libby in the center of the circle of instruments. She stood behind it, adjusted her headphones, and cleared her throat, grinning at Bridget with mock terror. Bridget, battling her own nerves, hoped her mother wouldn't choke, wouldn't get self-conscious; hoped she'd be at least a little bit as good as the tapes. She gave her a thumbs up.

"Lib, you ready?" Brandon asked.

"No," Libby replied with a nervous laugh.

"Yes, you are. Okay, boys, 'He Used to Know Me.'"

Brandon counted them in; Libby approached the mic and opened her mouth. Nothing. The mic wasn't on. The band stopped.

"Jesus Christ!" Nick barked. He went to the control room window and banged on it. Behind the glass was Paul, the studio tech working the mixing board.

Nick yelled, "Paul!" He banged again. "Hey, Paul!"

Paul finally looked up. He leaned into the talkback mic. "Not hearing you. Can you speak into the mic." He pointed to the one in front of Libby.

"It's not on, for fuck's sake!" Nick bellowed to the glass. "Can you get her mic on out here, please?"

Paul, finally sussing the issue, nodded. He adjusted some buttons. "Should be on. Sorry about that."

Nick turned to Libby. "Check the mic."

"Check, one, two, one, two. Yep, coming through my headphones."

"Okay, and here we go again," Brandon called out, "One, two, three, four."

The song kicked in. The band was locked. The intro was done. Libby stepped up to the mic. Took a breath and started singing. Her voice was there, if a little tentative. Lots of encouraging nods came her way from all around. She continued, gaining confidence, bar after bar.

At some point, she closed her eyes, forgetting everything, just feeling the music. Gripping her headphones as if they might fly off her head, she belted out the last two choruses with all she had. And it was magic.

When the song ended, there was a deafening silence. Libby stood there, startled. She looked around the room.

Bridget had her hand over her mouth, eyes glistening. She had never seen her mother sing. It was one thing to listen to old tapes, another to watch in real life. It was a revelation; once again, like meeting a new person. Unsettling. Amazing. Electric.

Gwen beamed like a proud mother, and the guys, all smiles, finally chimed in:

"Damn, woman!" August yelped. "You still got it going on!"

"Sounds really good, Libby." Chris was all sincerity. "But of course I expected that."

"Me, too." Gavin grinned. "Ya still give me chills, Libster."

"It was okay," Brandon remarked. "Not bad for an old gal." He blew her a kiss.

As the chattering continued, Nick walked over to a cooler and pulled out a beer. Libby watched him, waiting. For something.

"Anything wrong?" she asked.

He took a long draught of his beer. "Not a thing." He looked at her for a moment, then walked over and ran his finger down her cheek. "You still kill me."

Before Libby could react, Bridget rushed up to her mother with a squeal, practically leaping on her. "*You are so fucking awesome!*"

Libby laughed and pulled her daughter close. Dean video-taped the goings-on as Nick headed back to the circle.

"OK, beasts, what's next?"

★ ★ ★

As cars pulled out of the parking lot, Dean, Bridget, Gwen, and Libby confabbed over the next set of logistics.

"You've got our schedules," Nick said to Dean and Bridget. "Talk to your band, set a time, then holler back at me and I'll alert the rest of them."

"I'll try to make it next weekend," Dean replied, making notes on his phone. "I know that's best for you guys, so hopefully we can find a slot that works for them too."

Bridget, gazing at Nick with bona fide admiration, blurted, "You sounded so amazing, Nick. You're such a great guitarist." Her fandom was undisguised.

"Thank you, sweet pea. That's very nice of you."

"And your studio is awesome," Dean added. "I'd love it if you came out to SCC sometime to see my set-up; we could compare notes. I have a feeling I could learn a few things from you."

A Mercedes pulled up and Kyla waved to Nick from the driver's seat.

"There's my ride, kids. Yeah sure, Dean, let's do that. Just give me a call. See you all at the next one."

He grabbed Libby in a hug, leaned in and whispered: "You can't fool me, Liberty."

She looked at him, startled, but he was off to his lady.

Gwen, watching them, rolled her eyes. "Amazing. Thirty-five years and nothing changes."

CHAPTER 50

Libby and the guys managed one more rehearsal, which proved as exhilarating as the first. With everyone satisfied that they were ready to go, the meeting of the bands was scheduled for the desired Saturday, though not without some continued resistance from Minor Rebellion, who Dean and Bridget had gathered on a Zoom call to discuss the particulars.

"Basically the whole thing is a little weird," their lead guitarist groused. "We appreciate the money, and the tunes are great. But we're all experienced pros who know what we're doing, so it's a little insulting that you think we need handholding from some geezers."

Dean was about to answer when Bridget leaned in. "It *is* a little weird, I agree. But there's a very real possibility this A&R guy will take the next step with you guys, he just wants to hear more of what he heard on the recordings. He said he'd come back if we got closer to that sound, so isn't it worth doing whatever it takes to try to get there?"

"And like I said, once you're in," Dean added, "you can be as original as you want."

Maya, usually amenable to whatever was being asked, looked perplexed. "I get what you're saying, but if you want me to actually imitate the singer at this point, I'm not really comfortable with that. Nor do I think I could. She has her own unique sound."

"No, not mimic," Dean responded. "But could you use some of her phrasing, her inflections, that kind of thing? Remember, it's just for the next showcase, it's not something we'd have to—"

"Hey, guys," the drummer interrupted, "we're all here because the man liked what he heard on the record. If we get signed, that'd be major for all of us. So let's just do it like Dean and Bridget say and worry about the rest later."

Grumbles and sighs, but consensus was achieved.

With that fire under control, and various other tasks completed, Dean hunkered down for several hours of an academic recording job he'd booked, and Bridget headed to her mom's to spend the night, arriving to find Libby looking brilliant, with a hipper haircut and dressed to the nines.

"I swear, Mom, you look more like a rock star every day."

Libby laughed. "Down, Miss Mogul."

"No, seriously, you look fantastic."

"Thank you, daughter. Things are really nice right now and I'm having fun. Must be showing a little."

Bridget leaned in and gave her a kiss. "It is. So, fyi, Dean has the big battle of the bands set for next Saturday, eleven o'clock, and we've booked the room for six hours; S.I.R gave him a special deal. We probably won't need all that time, but we'd rather have it, since it's our only shot with everyone together. I called Nick, he called all the guys in your band, and everyone's on board."

"You talk about me shining, but, honestly, when are you going to start your own company? You're so good at this stuff."

"Thank you, but I've got enough going on with social managing my caterers and trying to get this project done. But while we're on the subject of my caterers and life changes, a couple of things I wanted to tell you. Heart to Table is moving into West Hollywood, and they've asked me to take on a bigger role, sort of a combination office manager, social media wrangler thing. It's a decent bump in pay, so I'm jumping on it."

"A lot less driving time too, so that's great, honey, congratulations."

"Yeah, it should be cool. They know about my school plans, assuming I do get in, so hopefully that can all get worked out when the time comes. And one more thing ..." She suddenly got coy. "I'm not sure how this will hit you, but Dean and I have been talking about looking for a place together."

"Wow. Really?" Though she already spent most nights with him, Libby found the news surprising, given the proximity of Bridget's divorce and the newness of their relationship, both points she articulated. "And beyond that, wouldn't it make more sense to stay here and save money while you're going to school?"

Bridget sat down across from her. "All worthy arguments, Mom, and believe me, I've considered every one of them, especially the 'not jumping into something too soon,' an old bad habit of mine. But I really have to start building my own life again. That whole 'finding my feet' thing, remember? And Dean is not Seth—"

"Not even close."

"So I have faith we can make something good of it. Dean does too."

The doorbell rang.

Libby stood up. "That'll be Jeff. Let's talk more about this later. It deserves a real conversation. But let me say this—I have faith in you, so if you have faith in him, I think you and Dean could make something good of it too."

Libby answered the door to find her very dapper dinner date.

CHAPTER 51

In a very crowded and contemporary Melrose Avenue restaurant, Libby and Jeff sat in a corner table, holding hands post-dinner. The mood was sweet and romantic.

"So this is your favorite restaurant?" Jeff queried, gazing around the noisy, crowded room.

"I wouldn't say favorite. Gwen brought me here once and I really enjoyed it. I thought you might too. What do you think?"

"Menu's good; service, very nice. It's a little loud for me, and I would have loved to have taken you to Morton's, but this ain't shabby."

"I think this is more my style," Libby demurred sweetly.

"Noted." Jeff smiled, squeezing her hand. "So tell me, how's it all going with the big rock and roll experiment?"

"Incredible. I swear, Bridget and Dean could go professional, they're so good at all this. And me, well, I'm in a little bit of heaven, singing again." She did seem to be sparkling.

"I have noticed you being bubblier and more excited lately. I hoped it was me but suspect otherwise."

"Maybe it's you *and* singing. Can you live with that?"

"I can. Listen, some news of my own: Michael is flying home for a few days, and I'm having a barbecue next Saturday afternoon. Just a few friends, some of his old classmates, that sort of thing. I want you to be there; it's time for you two to meet."

Libby stiffened. "Oh shoot, I can't next Saturday. The rehearsal with both bands is that day."

The waiter approached to take their dessert order; both ordered lattes, he got an apricot crostata to share, then they jumped back into the conversation.

"I didn't know that," he said, "but we're not gathering until one, so why don't you plan to come over for a while before rehearsal?"

"We're starting at eleven, and the room is booked for six hours. I could come over afterwards; could probably get there by sixish."

Jeff deflated. "No, he's made plans with some other friends for the evening, said he'll be taking off at five or so."

"Okay, so how about I swing by around ten, spend a half hour before I have to head back to Hollywood; is that possible?"

"He's at his mom's that morning, won't get to my place till around noon. He's trying to squeeze in everything he can in the short time he's here."

"Well, I don't what else I could offer—"

"Libby, I wouldn't push it, but this is important to me. I really want you and Michael to meet. Is there any way you could break away from rehearsal for a while and—"

"No, Jeff, that wouldn't work. I want to meet him, too, but given his schedule and mine, this Saturday is just not possible. How about we get together for a meal on Sunday? Any time; I'm open."

"He's back at his mom's on Sunday, then off to a conference in New York. Saturday afternoon is it."

The pause that followed was awkward. It suggested he thought Libby should somehow be amenable to rearranging her day. Which chafed her a bit.

"If it were anything else, I'd change my plans, but I can't. Not with this. I have to be there, Jeff, I'm sorry."

A beat. Then he patted her hand, neatly reining in his frustration. "I understand. We'll do it next time he's here."

Libby, wishing she didn't feel as guilty as she did, could only smile. Jeff scrutinized her tenderly.

"I love you, Libby."

The unexpected segue startled her.

"I've probably shocked you with that, I know, but I've been wanting to say it for a while now. I love you and I want you to think about making this a more permanent thing. I know you're not there yet, but I am, and I wanted you to know."

Libby was speechless. He filled the gap.

"We've been seeing each other for long enough that I know who you are, and love who you are. I want us to have a life together. I think we'd be happy. But I know I've taken you by surprise, so just let it sink in. When you're ready to talk about it, let me know.

She studied his face. He was very serious. "I will," she responded. "I promise."

★ ★ ★

Jeff's car pulled up to the bottom of the staircase outside Libby's house. When he put it in park, she turned to him sweetly. "Would you like to come up?"

He took a beat. "I think it might be good to end the night here."

She felt the heat of something. Rejection? Judgment? "Are you upset with me?"

"I just have a lot going through my head at the moment. I think I should be with my own thoughts tonight." He leaned over and kissed her. There was some sadness in it. "Sleep well, sweetheart."

He waited as Libby walked slowly up the steps. When she reached the top, they waved to each other as he pulled away.

CHAPTER 52

Libby, still in her dinner clothes, sat out on the patio illuminated only by the light from inside and the ambient glow of neighborhood streetlights. Her knees were pulled up to her chest as she leaned back in a deck chair, contemplating the sparkling night sky.

She was trying to capsulize her thoughts, but they were spinning with such ferocity she couldn't hold onto any of them long enough to find clarity. She felt myriad waves of emotion rising and crashing but the preponderant one was sadness.

Bridget came out to the patio, rumpled in her sweats, eyes puffed with sleep. "Mom? Didn't you hear the doorbell? Gwen's here. She said if it's too late she'll leave, but it seems there's a crisis."

Clearly impatient with the timing of this announcement, Gwen burst through the patio doors and unceremoniously plopped to the chair next to Libby. In her hand was a large manila envelope. Bridget slipped back inside as Gwen launched.

"I've been working with this writer friend of his, right?"

"That's what you said." Libby responded weakly.

"The guy's a bona fide teacher, but he's working with me privately because Otto asked him to. Anyway, I write my first ten chapters, which this guy thinks are hysterical, and I can't wait to share them with the love of my life."

"Oh, dear. He hated them?"

"*I don't know.*" Gwen wailed. "That's the problem. I sat across the room hiding while he read the damn pages. He had his back to me so I couldn't watch his face, but a back can be very revealing."

"And it revealed?"

"Nothing. Not a thing. It never shook, there was no chortle, not a snort; certainly no guffaw. The man never laughed."

"It's a comic novel, I presume?"

"It is."

"Maybe he doesn't get your humor."

"But he does. That's why we work; he thinks I'm hilarious."

"So what'd you do?"

"It's what *he* did. He put the pages down, turned to me, smiled sweetly, and said 'nice.' Then he went to the kitchen and made himself a damn sandwich. Can you believe that?"

"Very insensitive. What kind of sandwich?" She smirked.

"Fuck you. Probably ham, the asshole."

"Did you ask him any questions, see if he had more specific thoughts to add to his 'nice'?"

"No. I left. I took my first ten chapters and left. I've been circling the city for hours waiting for you to come home. Here they are." She slapped the envelope on the table. "Read them when you can, tell me if I'm delusional."

"I will be happy to, but understand that I know nothing about critiquing novels, so don't expect much. But I promise I'll go beyond 'nice' and if I laugh, I'll be sure to mention it."

"Perfect. Okay, I'm through. Now, you. Why do you look so glum?"

Despite not wanting them to, Libby's eyes suddenly filled.

Gwen sat up, surprised. "Oh no, Lib, what's wrong?"

Libby leaned her head down on her raised knees, wiping tears on her pants. "I know she did this for me, and I want it to be a success for her. But it's like she took the box I've had hidden under my heart all these years and opened it up. And now the dragon's out, he's out again, and this time he just might eat me alive."

"What are you talking about, Libby?"

"Remember that guy back in the day, Moody Haines? He was in a band with Nick at some point before we met, a great singer."

"Yeah. Yeah. I do remember him. Really tall, crazy good performer. He wrote a book or something, didn't he?"

"*Front Man*. Nicky gave me a copy for my eighteenth birthday, said he thought I'd find it relatable, which I did. It's all about his experiences as a singer, on the road, in the studio, the whole thing, and I remember this one paragraph he wrote about the act of singing, the unbelievable magic of opening your mouth and having music come out; of making people *feel* something, of making them move and cheer and dance. It blew my mind when I read that paragraph; I even made a banner with one of the lines because it so captured my own feelings as a singer. I've never forgotten it." She paused.

"Which was?"

"That moment when the crowd explodes. '*And when that happens, and you know it was you—your voice, your energy, your electricity—that inspired the joyful clamor, you rise up out of your body in pure exhilaration and sing louder.*' That's it. That's the whole thing, that's what I feel." Libby looked stricken.

"It's a beautiful line." Gwen struggled to understand. "But mostly I'm stunned you remember a random line from a book you got thirty-six years ago."

"I still have the banner. It's tucked inside an old photo album in my bookcase. I looked at it the other day, which is why I remembered that random line."

"Okay, and?" Gwen remained confused.

"Don't you get it, Gwennie?" There was anguish in her eyes. "After everything that happened, everything I lost, and even with everything I have, I *want* it again. I want the dream, the joy, the fucking volume of it all. I want to scream and dance and feel a bunch of sweaty guys behind me making great music together. I want to sing so loud I fly out of my body and don't come back until I have to. I want to be young again. I want to have a chance. And this time, this moment, *this* me doesn't have one."

Gwen sat silent, bereft of response. It was so quiet they could hear the breeze wafting through the palm fronds, the traffic from Hollywood down below, and the ever-present helicopters slicing through the night sky. It was peaceful and fraught at the same time.

"I get it, Lib. As much as I can, anyway. And it *is* sad. You lost a lot. I wondered if all this might excavate that dormant ambition of yours, that passion I always knew was part of you. I guess it has. I teased you about it, but I didn't want it to break your heart again."

"I just don't know what to do with it, that's all. There *is* nothing to do with it. My life has carved itself a place and a path, and it's a good life. But after all that's happened, *can* I just settle back into my old self now, the one that lives that good life? Does it fit me anymore? I'm not sure it does. It feels too small, somehow, too tight. Do you know what I mean?"

"Maybe. I think so. But maybe you can find, I don't know, some kind of—"

"It's okay, Gwen; you don't have try to find a solution to this. I don't think there is one. I just wanted you to know how I was feeling. I'll get over it at some point. It just struck me hard tonight for some reason."

Gwen's eyes glistened as she took Libby's hand. "You don't have to read my chapters. They probably suck anyway."

Libby burst into laughter, the kind that rolls out even when tears are flowing. When she couldn't stop, Gwen joined in.

Bridget stood inside, hidden by the shadows, taking it all in.

CHAPTER 53

It was the big day. Saturday, eleven o'clock.

S.I.R. Stage #2, one of the bigger spaces available, thrummed with the noise and activity of both bands working to create a stage arrangement that made sense in the rather bizarre circumstances in which they found themselves. Everyone was being civil, friendly. After introductions were made, any attitudes that might have been tempted to twitch or rebel were either nonexistent or well in check. Dean and Bridget held out hope that goodwill would sustain.

As this expertly managed set-up was underway, Libby and Gwen sat across the room nursing coffees, observing all that was unfolding with some amusement and much nodding approval.

"Wow. This could've been weird." Gwen articulated the obvious. "Egos abound in creative circles, and I know some of these people's egos very well. I'm impressed they're all playing nice with each other."

Libby threw her a sardonic grin. "Let's see how it goes when actual debates start about how and who to play what, and who should give in to whoever starts those debates."

"Ah, you cynic. But yeah, who knows with the oldsters. I have faith the young ones will behave."

"I'll have to defer to your opinion on that. I just met them today."

"They're all great kids, amazingly game for this game."

"It doesn't hurt that you pulled out your checkbook, which, I must say, was very generous. And very appreciated by the project director's mother."

"Artists deserve to be paid. You always said that. I've always believed that, so yes, money where the mouth is."

"You're such a mensch, Gwennie."

"It's completely self-serving. I've loved being involved in every minute of this. It's so outside the lines of my usual focus, like the best weird-ass reality show ever. If I wrote it, no one would believe it."

Libby jolted upright. "Damn, I'm such an asshole. I just remembered: I never got to your pages this week. It was so crazy with work that I—"

"Stop." Gwen held her hand up. "No need. *I'm* the asshole because I forgot to follow-up with the follow-up on that obnoxious plotline."

"Which was?"

"I got home that night and guess what was under my door? A four-page typed critique, pointing out what worked with every joke, every character, even the story structure. He thought it was brilliant. He even talked to his friend, and they discussed how brilliant it was, how brilliant *I* am. I could not be more shamed and chagrined for my miscalculation."

"Wow. Good for Otto. Serious points scored."

"No kidding. Oh, my man, I love him so."

"Well, I'm still going to read it."

"You should. I'm told it's quite brilliant."

Dean clapped his hands across the room. "Okay, everybody, let's get started. I figure it makes sense to have the old guys—"

"Hey, watch it!" August hollered.

Everyone laughed.

"Let me rephrase." Dean grinned. "Let's have the *original* guys run through the songs so you new guys can listen, see what they're doing, maybe make notes and stuff. Is that okay with everybody?"

Assent was given. The "original guys" went to their instruments, and Libby took the stage, a low hum of anxiety coursing through her veins. It was one thing to sing with the band, another to perform in front of a group of very hip young performers looking to capture their sound. Scrutiny would be fierce, she knew, which only exacerbated her nerves.

Brandon banged his sticks. "Let's start with, 'What Can I Do.'" He counted them in.

★ ★ ★

In a happenstance that was both bizarre and serendipitous, today was the day Aaron Leifer and his cohort, Tyler Williams, were hitting various rehearsal and recording studios around town to pick up on street vibes: who was standing out, what music was remembered; which bands seemed to be pulling from the pack. They hadn't been to S.I.R. in a while so they decided to make it their first stop.

"Hey, Norm," Aaron called out to the studio manager pecking his computer behind the desk. A '70s throwback with one gold tooth and the skinny, tattooed vibe of a street corner hustler, Norm nonetheless knew the music business inside and out and ran the space like a finely tuned corporation. Everyone at the labels knew him and he knew them. That guy.

"Hey, how you doin', Aaron, Tyler? Haven't seen you guys in a while. Everything copacetic in your world?"

"Yep, yep, just out on the street today seeing what's popping. Anything going on in here we should know about?"

Norm came over the counter. "Yeah, couple things. There's a ska band, Two If By Night, who seem to have their shit together. They're in #4."

"You're liking them?"

"Yeah, kinda wild. They've got people going in and out of here all the time, lots of gigs, guys in suits sniffin' around, so my guess is they're ready to roll. Might wanna get in there before they do. There was also this very happenin' girl group in a couple of times last week called Lightfoot. Real cute gals; sort of a mix of hip hop and Taylor Swift. Weird, not my gig, but they had everybody jumpin'. You might wanna check them out, too."

Tyler was taking notes. "Can you shoot me numbers for both their managers?"

"No prob." Norm went back to his computer, scrolled through his contacts, sent them to the printer. "Here you go." He handed the sheet to Tyler. "Oh yeah, that band called Minor Rebellion is in again."

Aaron and Tyler exchanged a look.

"You heard of them? Oh, wait, that's right. You saw them a while back, I remember."

"Yeah. What are you hearing about them these days?" Aaron asked.

"Not a ton, but I happen to dig them a lot," Norm continued. "That cool '80s vibe they got, with a very hot singer—not that you guys care about that sorta thing." He winked. "Anyway, they're in #2. Got a big crowd in there today; not sure why, but that's probably a good sign, yeah? Anyway, they just now got started so you should be able to hear them through the door."

"Thanks, man. We'll wander down and see what we can catch. And thanks for the numbers; we'll be sure to check them out."

Norm pointed them in the right direction and by the time they were standing in front of the big wooden door with a "#2" on top, the band inside was in full performance mode. When the vocal kicked in, loud and clear, Tyler turned to Aaron with a smile. "Holy shit. They got the sound now, right? Am I right?"

Aaron nodded with a pleased smile. "Yep. They got the sound."

CHAPTER 54

Rehearsal was wrapped; it went as well as could have been expected. The Minor Rebellion players had remained open to suggestions, implementing the various technical tweaks needed to get them closer to the original sound, and the Liberty crew seemed to enjoy playing the mentor role. Libby found Maya's interpretations of her songs somewhat unnerving, but there was no denying the woman was good and she made sure to tell her so. Maya was gracious in returning the compliment, adding for good measure that Libby's vocals, "were a lot to live up to."

As the players packed up, August flirted shamelessly with Maya, while Brandon and the younger drummer talked shop. Cords were rolled, the soundboard was shut down, and Bridget, exhausted and relieved, approached her mother.

"You were so good today, Mom. I can't believe it's almost getting routine, this thing of listening to you sing and being blown away every time."

Libby's smile was warm. "Thank you, darling daughter. It's all on you, I hope you know that. Despite the rocky road getting here, I have loved being involved. I'm going to miss it. But much like Cinderella, I will now take off my party dress and go back to the spreadsheets." There was melancholy in the statement.

Bridget sat down next to her. "Yeah." she said wistfully. "Well, anyway, Dean and I are going to a party at a friend of his, so I'll touch base with you sometime tomorrow. Do you have any plans for tonight?"

"Bed and TV. Go have fun. And really amazing job today, sweetheart."

Bridget stood up. "Thanks, Mom."

Dean suddenly clapped for everyone's attention.

"Listen, before you all leave, I wanted to thank everyone for putting up with this. It was a weird exercise, I know, but I think it's gonna help us out a lot."

Nods and "yeahs" chimed in agreement.

Dean turned to the Minor Rebellion band members. "We'll call you guys early in the week. Maybe one more rehearsal, then we'll bring Delgany back in; sound good?"

They chorused their assent.

As the young crowd headed out the door, August, Pat, Chris, and Gavin circled Libby.

Gavin spoke up first. "I thought this was a crazy fucking idea at first, but I have to admit: I had a blast. I'll play with you guys any time, any place, and Libby, I'm glad you're doing okay cuz you can still sing like a motherfucker."

The others hooted and hollered in agreement.

"Thanks." She blushed. "I didn't know it was still in there, so this has been a revelation for me too. More than I can say. And I hope you all know how much I've appreciated us getting past the past to make it happen. Your patience with me through-out this process has been just so ..." Her eyes welled up. "Just so really amazing. Thank you."

"Hear hear! And let's not take so long to get together again. I don't think any of us want to see what shape we'll be in if we wait another thirty years," Gavin chortled.

As goodbyes were said and the guys peeled off, Libby lin-gered, wistfully looking around the room. Gwen and Nick came back in from the lobby.

"Okay, commerce has been handled, boys are gone, kids are off." She turned to Libby. "I'm meeting Otto for dinner. Want to join us?"

"No thanks, I'm too tired for social expectations. I'll just grab an Uber home."

"Where's your car?"

"I drove here with Bridget; just sent her off to a party."

"I'm without demands at the moment," Nick spoke up. "I'll take you home."

Libby looked at Gwen. Gwen looked at Libby, grinned.

Nick looked at them both. "What? Kyla's out and I've got time."

"Some things never change." Gwen smirked.

"Ignore her. That'd be great, Nick, thank you," Libby rejoined.

He turned to Gwen with a wink. "'Night, Gwennie."

"Later, Nick Knack."

CHAPTER 55

As Nick maneuvered through Saturday night traffic, thick and slow-moving as he headed north, Libby leaned back, gazing out the window.

"Why are so many people out? Where is everybody going?" she mused. "I forgot how wild Saturday nights could be. Wonder if it's still fun."

"I've heard rumors that it is. You hungry?"

"Yeah."

"Pizza okay?"

"Sure."

Nick tapped a number on the dashboard screen, glancing over at Libby. "You got some throat left?"

★ ★ ★

Tucked behind the mixing board, Nick moved buttons and levers while Libby adjusted her headphones on the other side of the glass. He pushed the talkback button.

"That was good, but young it up a little more. It's a jingle for five-year-olds who like this inane show. Think airy, ditzy; young."

"I can do ditzy and young. I can. I really can." Libby rolled her eyes.

"I have faith in you. Okay, here we go."

He ran the track again. Very Disney-pop. Libby came in with an uncharacteristically chirpy vocal. *"Every day is Bennie's day, cuz we love Bennie."*

Nick stopped the tape and looked up. "Great. That's it."

"Seriously? Not too chipmunky? I think I sounded too chipmunky."

"Nope. It's exactly as chipmunky as they want. Check's in the mail. Actually, shoot me your Venmo. You got Venmo?"

"Um, no?"

He laughed. "Then good thing I still got a checkbook. Come on, let's go eat some pizza."

★ ★ ★

Seated around a coffee table, Nick on the couch, Libby on a floor pillow across from him, they wrangled a very large pizza in the quiet of the closed studio, both concentrating on their food.

"This is excellent pizza," Libby commented, her mouth full.

"Thank you. I always feel responsible for feeding my singers well."

"You're doing a fine job. Do you live near here?"

"Not too far. Up in the hills just west of the Hollywood Bowl. Have one of the original A-frames up there that I've tinkered with over the years; it's pretty cool. I'll text you my address so you can start sending me birthday cards again." He grinned as he pulled out his phone.

When hers pinged, she replied, "Thanks. Now you'll have to remind me when your birthday is."

"What? You never forgot it back in the olden days!"

She gave him a wistful smile and they quickly refocused on the meal. There was a humming tension between them, as if both were trying hard to act as if there was nothing unusual about being here together, in this moment, after so many years, all without really talking about why all those many years had passed without any connection.

He finally broke the moment. "I would have called you in before now, but the last time I saw you, back a million years ago, I got the impression singing was a thing of the past for you."

"Yeah. It was complicated back then. Hard to explain. I felt like the Fates were telling me to move on, so I did. Then all this got fired up."

"You've got quite the daughter there."

"She is something, isn't she?"

"Indeed. And she's all yours. Tough, pretty, determined. Happily, her DNA ignored Bart."

"Stop." Libby laughed, ignoring the compliment buried in there. "So, where's Kyla tonight?"

"Kyla's out with her 'crew.' Get that—a grown woman who calls her friends a 'crew.' 'Course, she thinks I'm dull as dirt because I spend most of my time here, so maybe I should give her a break. Clearly she needs a crew." He sighed. "One of these days I'll figure it out."

"Give yourself credit. From what I've heard you actually made a marriage work for a while."

"Emphasis on *a while*."

"What happened, if you don't mind me asking?"

"What, Gossiping Gwennie didn't tell you the whole story?"

"Not really. She does this thing where she throws out a nugget, then says if you want more you have to go to the source."

"I'm well aware of her technique. Anyway, what happened is a tale as old as time: we wanted different things. I was on the road when we met. When I got off, I put this place together and thought the stability would be enough for her. Turns out she was waiting for me to quit music altogether and get what she called 'a real job.' Hence, ex."

There was a beat. Libby put her pizza down, wiped her mouth. "Jeff wants to marry me."

Nick sat back, surprise crossing his face. "Wow. I didn't realize it was that serious."

"I didn't either."

"Are congratulations in order?"

"I don't know."

"No? Why's that?"

"I'm not sure I want to get married."

"In general, or to him?"

"In general. I think. Or maybe to him. I'm not sure."

"Huh. That's interesting."

The current running between them was palpable, but neither seemed to know what to do with it. He finished his pizza, took a sip of beer, gazing at her.

She gazed back. "What is it with us, Nicky?"

"Which something with us?"

"You know which something."

He closed the pizza box. "I always figured it was one of those things we weren't supposed to act on."

"Why is that?"

"Maybe because we never got the timing right, present tense included. Probably those Fates of yours telling us to leave it alone."

"You're probably right." She got up and started clearing the table.

Nick reached out and grabbed her hand. "Liberty, no matter what, we're friends again. I know some shit has happened and we'll need to talk about it at some point, but I'm really glad to have you back in my life, okay?"

"Absolutely. Do you want me to put the extra pizza in the fridge?"

"Sure. Put the pizza in the fridge." He got it. The conversation was over.

The ride back to Hollywood had a disquiet that wasn't present earlier, and Libby regretted spending the private time with him. Strange; somehow it still got sticky and complicated with them, even after decades apart.

Nick pulled into the cul de sac and stopped at the bottom of the stairs. He turned the car off, and they sat, looking at each other.

Libby broke the first ice. "What did you mean the other day when you said I can't fool you?"

Nick pondered for a moment, not sure he wanted to open the discussion. Then he did. "I was thinking about how easy it was for you to walk away from everything back then. You started another kind of life without missing a beat, like the rest of it didn't mean a thing, like *we* didn't mean a thing. Then watching you there, so happy to be with the guys, so happy to sing again; really coming alive, I knew that just wasn't true. Which makes it all the more inexplicable that you *did* walk away without a blink or a look back."

Nick's face was dead serious; they were finally right up to it, the looming behemoth in the living room. But his take, despite knowing that *would* be his take, left Libby feeling sucker punched. She tried to find a rejoinder, the right words to correct his misguided version, but nothing would come out of her mouth. Once again. She pulled the door open and leapt from the car.

As she ran up the steps, a flustered Nick followed. "Libby, stop. Come on, you knew we were going to have to talk about it at some point, didn't you? Why not now? Maybe the guys are okay shoving it under the rug and just being happy new friends, but that ain't us, Liberty, and you know it. So let's get it the fuck over with, right here, right now, so maybe, just maybe, we can have some kind of honest friendship at this stage of our lives."

She whirled around, her face a mask of turmoil. "You think it was easy for me to walk away? From everything I ever wanted my entire fucking life? You have no idea what happened; you never did."

"Is that right?" His eyes darkened. "Here's what I remember happening. We had a deal on the table. A deal we'd been working on for months. We were just getting ready to sign, and for some inexplicable reason, you walked away from it, you disappeared; you stopped talking to us, to me. You had your meeting with Eric, and then I never heard another word from you. Which blew my fucking mind. I mean, it was you and me. *You and me.* I could not figure out what in the fuck was happening, but then I finally got the whole story. And that's what *I've* been sitting on all these years."

Libby's eyes burned into his. "What *story* do you think you got?"

"Let's first establish that you would not answer your phone, return my calls, even tell Bart to talk to me. I was spinning. So I talked to Damon, who was being all cagey and stupid, and he said he was going to 'fix things.' I didn't know what needed to be fixed, and he told me to hold tight, he'd get back to me. But too much time passed, and I was done waiting. I decided to talk to Eric myself. Went down to his damn office and confronted him about it. And he laid it all out for me; all of it. Told me that, yes, we *had* a fucking deal. But you announced to him that you were pregnant and decided to turn it down so you could play house with Bart. He said they were willing to work around your situation, figure out how to tour with a kid, but you didn't think 'band life,' as he said you put it, would be good for a baby, so you told him you were out. And that killed the deal for the rest of us."

Libby dropped to the stairs at this point, sunk her head in her hands. Nick just kept ranting.

"Do you know how long it took me to stop hating you for that? How fucking angry, how outraged I was? All the guys tried to get to you, I kept trying to get to you, but you just disappeared, ghosted us, no communication at all. You left five people who loved you, who *believed* in you, in the fucking dust without a word. So yeah, I think it was easy for you to walk away, because I know how hard it was for me, and I didn't have a choice. You did. And you took it for yourself, fuck the rest of us." All sweetness was gone. Every ounce of the rage and resentment he'd felt seemed to have leapt the time gap to be here now, right in front of them.

Libby slowly lifted her face from her hands and looked at Nick standing a few steps below her. His expression was so hard, so set in stone, she couldn't help but soften, knowing he didn't know the truth, knowing the truth would hurt him, but knowing the truth had to be told, finally, in this unavoidable moment. "Sit down, Nicky, and let me tell you about my choice."

Nick hesitated, then sat on the steps, his face an inscrutable mask. She started from the very beginning, from the moment she got the results of the pregnancy test, to the ride in Damon's car, the meeting with Eric, his aggression and coldness, the step-by-step detailing of his assault and the crassness of his demands. She told him about having a hand-sized bruise on her stomach for over a week, about the threats of a lawsuit, threats he'd destroy her in the business. She told him about telling Damon, about his dismissiveness and, ultimately, his choice to believe Eric's lies that she was emotionally unstable and lied about him about assaulting and threatening her. She told him everything.

"I didn't know how you would all react, what you would expect me to do, if you would think I was lying or exaggerating too. And I was afraid. I was a terrified, pregnant nineteen-year-old who'd just had a big music business honcho grab my crotch and tell me he'd destroy me, with a manager who refused to defend or protect or even believe me, and he told me you'd all feel the same. I think I went into a dissociative state. I went silent. I couldn't even tell Bart right away. I thought, I hoped, that Damon would ultimately come to his senses and fight for me, tell you all the truth, because *he* knew the truth. When he didn't do any of those things, I completely splintered. And I couldn't come back from that. I was shattered and unsupported. And when I finally did tell Bart what happened, I made him promise to keep it to himself for all the reasons *I* couldn't talk about it. He fought me on that, but at least he supported me enough to do what I asked. So even he couldn't tell you the truth. For that, Nicky, I'm truly sorry. It was a chickenshit thing to do, especially to you. You all deserved the truth, but you—*you*, Nicky—deserved my faith in you, and I couldn't give it. I'm sorry. Even all this time later, I'm so sorry."

She felt like she caved in on herself then, but it was out. It was said. It was exorcised from her heart and soul. She was drained. Completely.

When she finally looked at Nick, the expression on his face was a panoply of anguish, regret, contrition, and pain. His own eyes had welled up, but words felt inadequate. All he could do was move up to her step and wrap his arms around her, enveloping her in an embrace that was the most visceral form of apology he could muster at that moment. She leaned into his shoulder and wept.

CHAPTER 56

Bridget and Dean were high on the adrenaline of success. In the midst of a sweaty and celebratory round of sex instigated after giddy analysis of their triumphant "battle of the bands," something that had never been assured and could have just as easily exploded into chaos, they were interrupted by the buzz of his phone.

He ignored it. They carried on. It buzzed again.

"Damn, who's calling this late?" he grumbled, disentangling himself from her limbs.

She rolled over, face flushed and glowing, and said, "Just check it real quick and then come back here as fast as you can."

When he looked at the screen, he turned to her, shaking his head as he answered the call. "Hey, Aaron. Wasn't expecting to hear from you; what's up?" He stepped outside the bedroom and shut the door.

Annoyed, Bridget wrapped the sheet around her and hollered toward the door, "Let's not forget this *is* my project, okay?"

Within moments Dean re-entered. "You are not gonna believe this."

"Oh God, what?" She sat up.

"He was at S.I.R. today. Said he got there just as we were starting. Norm pointed out our room to him."

"What was he doing there?"

"Apparently, it's part of the 'street crawl,' he called it, when A&R guys go out and see what's hopping in the world of music. I guess S.I.R. is on his regular route."

"Okay, so why is he calling you?"

"He said he was outside the door of Stage #2 listening, and he made a big deal about how we 'finally got the sound.' He said he wants to set up another showcase this week, bring one of the execs down."

Bridget was now pulling on her clothes. "That's incredibly exciting, right? Why do you look nauseous? Isn't that usually my job?"

"Because he didn't hear Minor Rebellion; he heard your mom."

Bridget stopped moving. "What?"

"He heard you mom singing."

She was stunned. "How do you know that?"

"He said he got there around 11:30. When Norm pointed out our room, he mentioned that we'd just started, which we did at just about 11:30. And we started with your mom's band. Which means if Aaron was standing outside the door of Room #2 around 11:30, he was listening to your mom, not Minor Rebellion."

Bridget dropped to the bed. "That's insane. And now he wants to come back this week to hear Minor Rebellion because they finally 'got the sound'?"

"Exactly. Kept saying he's always loved the tunes, loves the vibe, and now that the 'new singer has captured the sound,' he wants to move ahead. Normally that would be a good thing—"

"But if he comes back this week," Bridget continued, "he'll discover that Maya's not any closer to 'the sound' than she was last time, because though she's an amazing singer, she sounds nothing like my mom. So, once again, we're fucked."

"We just might be."

"How do we keep doing this to ourselves?"

"I don't know. It's a project that has repeatedly and persistently gone off the rails, that's for damn sure."

Bridget just stared off, mulling.

Dean watched her. "What are you thinking? You've got that weird look you sometimes get. I never know what it means."

"I never know either. But I *am* having a thought. It might be too crazy; it might be genius. Let me mull a little longer, and I'll let you know." She looked up at him coyly. "Of course, in the meantime, we could go back to what we were doing before Aaron Leifer so unceremoniously interrupted our evening."

He was in full agreement with that decision.

CHAPTER 57

"In all of my entire existence, I never thought I'd be Zooming with all of you old farts—excluding you, young Bridget and Dean. And maybe you, Libby. You're younger than us, right?" August blathered on as the players of Liberty popped up on the screen, one after the other, in a hastily organized Zoom call.

"Welcome to the modern world, Auggie," Brandon said with a wink. "Those of us still engaged with current culture are very familiar with this medium."

"I'll show you some current culture—"

"Okay, okay, fellas," Libby put an end to the banter. "I've only got a few minutes before I have to be back at work, so Bridge, if you and Dean could cut to the chase with whatever it is you want to talk about, it would be gratefully appreciated."

Bridget was at work herself, tucked in the break room for this quick meeting; Dean sat at the couch in his studio. The rest of the guys were lined up, ready and waiting to hear the "latest pitch," as Gavin had jovially framed it.

Since it was Bridget's idea, she and Dean had decided she'd be the one to lay it out: Aaron's call, the mistaken identity of the band he heard at the door; his desire for a quick return showcase, and then, Bridget's idea:

"I think we should set you guys up in a room down the hall from Minor Rebellion, and after they listen to them again, we bring them right over to hear all of you. I think you'll blow their minds."

There was a long pause as each of them digested this unexpected information.

"Wow. You are kind of blowing mine, sweet girl!" Nick exclaimed. "That is a pretty out there idea."

"I agree," Bridget nodded without resistance. "It is a completely, utterly crazy idea but you guys so deserve the shot. Why not take it?"

"Because it's basically pointless?" Brandon scoffed.

"Wait, so you want the young Turks in one room being all young and hot and hip, and us in the other room; old, fat, and original?" Gavin queried. "Have I got that right?"

"Whoa, harsh, Gav, and not exactly applicable to us all, thank you." Brandon countered.

"I get a little freaked thinking about how potentially embarrassing that could be," Chris mumbled. "I mean, I appreciate the intention here, but we are so far past our primes those label guys probably wouldn't make it through the door."

Libby, slightly panicked at the idea herself, leaned into the screen. "Bridget, I have to agree with Chris. I, too, appreciate your faith in us, but come on. They are not going be interested, no matter how good we are. Rock's a youth business, and we are, as Gavin pointed out, old!"

"Hey, not *that* old." Brandon snorted.

"Mom, I heard you say how much you wish you could have it all again. What if this is that possibility, that chance?"

Libby looked at her daughter tenderly. "Aw, honey, I say all sorts of things, but I'm not delusional. I've accepted where I am in my life. That night I was just swept up in it all."

Dean jumped in. "But the thing to remember is they already love the songs. We pitch that you're the originals, and how cool would it be to sign a band with chops, with history, with actual experience, *and* with the songs?"

"Even *The Voice* features older singers, Mom. They make a big thing about just listening to the voices, not looking at the people. It's a different time."

"Yeah," Dean chorused. "And maybe the times are a 'changing."

Nick laughed out loud. "Oh, Lordy, Liberty, they're quoting Dylan now. Maybe we gotta listen to the kids."

"Let's get real," Brandon groused. "How many of those 'older singers' ever get picked on shows like *The Voice*? None of 'em. I think the oldest was forty or something and nobody even knows who the fuck they are. It's a good gimmick, it's good PR, but in reality the old ones ain't got a chance in hell, and neither to do we."

"Yet my fear is we actually *might*. Damn!" Gavin exhorted. "Everything we always wanted, just thirty-five years too late. Now it would turn my life upside down."

Chris nodded. "Same here."

"Jesus, you fucking old fucks!" August yelped. "What's the downside to doing one little showcase? If we're blessed enough to get a deal we'd make some bread, get our tunes cut, maybe suffer through a few road gigs. Nice problems to have, right? If we don't, which we all realize is the likely scenario, we'd have the great good time of doing another gig together."

"I'm with Auggie," Nick leaned forward. "Realistically speaking, he's right; our chances are zip. But these two have resurrected a very dead horse and I think it's worth playing out, if for no other reason than perverse curiosity. Come on, guys, it'd be fun if nothing else and ain't that the point?"

The mood shifted as everyone discussed the options. A reluctant but growing consensus seemed to be coalescing. Libby pointed directly at Bridget.

"You're good. Evil, but very good."

Bridget grinned as Gavin slumped down in his chair.

"Shit, now I gotta lose ten pounds."

CHAPTER 58

After a long, exhausting day at work, the night eased into a quiet one. With Bridget at Dean's, Libby stretched out on the couch watching some inane show, thinking about all that was swirling around her these days, and just how she felt about it.

Since the night with Nick, that cataclysmic, emotionally fraught night, every single thing in her life felt different. There'd been subsequent conversations between them that triggered combinations of every known emotion; relief and regret, so much to understand, so much to reframe and let go. Nick struggled with retroactive guilt and decided to take it upon himself to sensitively (he promised her) and candidly bring the other guys up to speed on the actual facts of their shared history. Texts were sent back and forth with sweet sentiments and emotional apologies, promises of clean slates and new eras; invitations to get together. She was touched, and very much ready for them all to move forward with the past left firmly in the past. Where it now truly belonged.

She even heard that Nick reached out to Bart, the two of them talking through what had happened and the subsequent fallout. They were not likely to ever be good friends again, their lives too disparate at this point, but Libby was glad the rift had been breached enough for civility. Bart called her to say he appreciated the gesture.

As for her and Nick ... *her and Nick*. What did that even mean? There *was* no "her and Nick," there was just the pulse of electricity that always seemed to exist between them. She had to consider that it might simply be their unavoidable chemistry. Which made her wonder if they could have any kind of continuing friendship given that both were involved with other people who likely wouldn't appreciate the endurance of that chemistry. She decided it would have to be; they'd have to figure it out. Because she wanted him in her life again.

And, frankly, now they had no choice. There was this one more major event to manage: the magical, mystery showcase had been scheduled for tomorrow night. Libby's skin tingled every time she thought about it. It terrified her, titillated her; gave her something incredibly exciting to ponder. She had no delusions, as she'd insisted to her daughter, but it had been a very long time since she'd performed in a high-pressure situation like this, and she wanted to meet the challenge. She wanted the thrill of it. Even if for one last time.

She and Gwen had found the perfect outfit at one of her favorite vintage stores, Robbie had promised to take the train up to work the lights, Bart would be there to help with equipment; even Chloe and Martin said they'd be in attendance ("I wouldn't think of missing the opportunity to see my girl sing!" Chloe had exclaimed). It was evolving into a major event.

Her phone vibrated, and she smiled to see Jeff's name. Given all that was going on, they hadn't had much time together since the party. She knew he was feeling neglected, and she wanted to remedy that.

"Howdy, stranger!" she answered brightly.

"Hello to you. I'm so glad you picked up; I've been missing you."

"I know, me too."

"I might be able to remedy that if you can do something really last minute. I just talked to some very dear friends of mine who are unexpectedly in town for one night, and they'd love for us to meet them for a late supper at a place not too far from you. Would you be up for that?"

Libby, a wave of weariness being her initial response, looked at the clock. It was 9:25. "And here I was just thinking about how happy I am to be crashed out on my comfy sofa watching bad TV." She laughed, trying to lighten what she knew was going to be another disappointment for him. "Is this something that would happen, say, immediately?"

"They suggested 10:30 or so, given where they're coming from, so I figured that would give you enough time to get ready and get over there. I checked the restaurant, and their kitchen is open till 11:30. Let me text you the place—"

"Jeff, wait," she interrupted him, sitting up. "I'm sorry, I'd like to, but I really can't tonight, especially not that late. I'm completely and utterly wiped out. A 10:30 supper wouldn't get me home until far later than I want to be out. I've got the big showcase tomorrow, as you know, and I need to be well rested for that. I'm going to have a hard enough time getting to sleep as it is. I hope you understand. Plus, we'll be seeing each other at the showcase anyway, right?"

"Yes, yes, of course," he said, his voice somewhat muted. "I was just hoping you could meet these people; they're really dear friends and I think you'd like them a lot."

"I'm sure I would, and I hope we can find another opportunity before too long."

He sighed, not even trying to cover it. "No doubt we can, but I've got to say, Libby, I'll be glad when all this is finally over."

She froze in her seat. "All what, exactly?'

"I know you're having fun singing, which is great, but you have to admit our schedules have been really impacted by all this band stuff, which came right after all the CPA stuff, so I'm just looking forward to life finding its way back to some kind of normal soon. We could use it, don't you think?"

"Yes, but you do understand there's just the slightest chance this thing could happen, right?"

"What, the record deal part?"

"Yes. I mean the odds are very, very slim, I'm aware, but I don't want you to count it out completely and then be shocked if something amazing happens."

"I do understand, sweetheart." She thought she heard him sigh again. "And if it does, we'll deal with it then."

"Okay, good. You know the time tomorrow, right?"

"Yes, 7:30. I'll be there. Just don't expect me in black leather pants."

Libby had to smile. "Oh, I don't."

CHAPTER 59

The stage was set. Bart moved instruments and cords here and there, but it all seemed to be in proper order. Robbie was up on a ladder adjusting the spots, while Norm hovered nearby making sure no one broke or needed anything. A small table with fruit, cheese and wine was set up near the seats.

August, Chris, Brandon, Gavin, Nick, and Libby mulled around the stage area looking sharp and fired up. Occasionally Libby warbled a throat exercise, but otherwise, the group was quiet. The throb of music bled in from down the hall, but still they could hear the patter of rain on the roof.

Gwen rushed up shaking out her umbrella. "I can't believe it's raining. I hope that doesn't stop anyone from getting here. Otto is already late."

Libby was waving her arms and marching in place to help offset her nerves, but she had to smile at Gwen's concern. "Well, rest assured the men of the hour are here. They're already doing showcase number one in the room you just walked past. How did it sound?"

"Good, I think. I was too busy texting my delayed fellow." She stopped fussing and looked at Libby with a grin. "But they won't sound as good as you."

★ ★ ★

Aaron, Tyler, and the head of Delgany Records, Doug Bishop, were seated at a table set with wine and cheese, listening as the band powered through their set. Doug held the promo materials on Minor Rebellion; glancing through, he nodded at Aaron when he got to the very provocative picture of Maya, who looked particularly fetching tonight.

Dean and Bridget had stacked the room with their friends, and as instructed, the crowd was energized and participatory, hooting wildly after each solo, every song, particularly appreciative when Maya wailed.

Which was an easy ask because she grabbed the light in every interpretation of that phrase. Doug and Tyler were mesmerized. The rest of the band clicked, they sounded good, strong, but Aaron's face was set in an expression of confusion. When the song ended, the audience burst into raucous applause.

Doug leaned toward Aaron. "She's a fuckin' knockout."

Aaron nodded, but his eyes belied his enthusiasm.

When the set concluded, the band thanked the three men at the table, as well as the audience in attendance, exiting the room in dramatic fashion. Dean followed after, assuring them he'd be in touch while quickly getting them out the door. Back in the studio, the Delgany contingent stood chatting as the audience filed out. Aaron looked up as Dean re-entered the room. "You said you've got something else you want us to hear?"

★ ★ ★

In the studio down the hall, the players were at their instruments; the room was dark except for select stage lights. Robbie was at the lighting board; Norm controlled the sound. Another collection of Dean and Bridget's friends filled the seats, whispering and anticipatory. Band wives and children abounded. Chloe and Martin were at one table, Gwen, Otto, and Bart at another nearby, where there were two empty chairs.

Libby took a conference with Bridget at stage right. "Sweetheart, I would normally not want my daughter to hear me say this, but I am truly and fucking terrified."

Bridget put her hands on Libby's shoulders. "Mom, just know you're amazing. No matter how this turns out, you're going to show some people exactly who you are."

Libby appraised her daughter with unbounded tenderness. "When did you get so wise?"

"I think when I started managing a certain singer I know." She pulled her mother into a tight hug.

After Bridget slipped away, Nick quietly walked up and put his arm around Libby, whispering: "This ain't important, Liberty. Just remember that. Everything important you already have. This is just for kicks, okay?"

She nodded and looked out at the empty chairs. "Jeff's late. Which is weird. And no Kyla?"

He sighed. "She flew to New York this morning; said she's exploring 'new options.' Not sure what that means."

"But she's coming back?"

"Purportedly. I don't know. I have my suspicions."

"Oh, Nick, I'm sorry."

Dean had quietly slipped into the room. Voice hushed, he announced. "Okay, they're right outside. Robbie, dim the lights, everyone on stage. As soon as they're in their seats, Norm, I'll give you the cue and you announce the band, then, Rob, bring up the lights." Rob and Norm nodded.

Dean exited and everyone got into place.

Silence. Anticipation. Excitement.

The door opened, and Dean led Aaron, Tyler, and Doug into the room. Tension palpable, the men settled at their table, which was set with a different stack of pictures. Pictures of a band named Liberty.

Dean gave Norm the cue.

"Ladies and gentlemen ... Liberty!"

Wild applause as lights smashed the stage with color, and the band kicked into, "He Used To Know Me." Libby stepped up to the mic. Beautiful. Centered. Grounded. Gazing out, she smiled and started singing. Her voice was *on*—powerful, soulful, dynamic.

Bridget stood offstage right biting her nails. Robbie whooped with delight. Gwen and Bart glanced at each other with shared pride, shared history. Otto tapped his foot.

At the critical table, Tyler was clearly into it, head bobbing, eyes focused on Libby. Doug watched, intrigued. And Aaron could do nothing but shake his head, amazed and flummoxed by what was unfolding in front of him.

On stage, Libby was transformed. Her initial nerves gave way to stage magic. Unequivocally in her element, she felt the electrical rush Moody Haines had so eloquently articulated in his book those many years ago, metaphorically transporting out of her body. The energy and light that exuded from her was powerful, and there was no denying it was an extraordinary performance. When the song concluded, the audience roared, and before that sound could subside, Brandon counted the band into the next song, and the momentum continued.

★ ★ ★

The exiting crowd was abuzz with excitement; the chatter was loud, and smiles were bright. Clearly everyone had had a good time. Tyler and Doug strode ahead, promo materials in hand, while Aaron walked with Dean. He finally stopped, turned, and looked at Dean, perplexed.

"I don't know what just happened in there, but I want to think about it before we talk. You and Bridget come in tomorrow, ten o'clock. You've either made a total ass out of me or pulled off the best bait and switch I've ever seen. I'm just not sure which."

★ ★ ★

Back in Liberty's room, the mood was celebratory. It was over, and it had been good. Libby hugged Rob, who was duly impressed with his mother. Everyone crowded around her, pumped and exhilarated.

Chloe and Martin approached, both beaming. "You, my dear, were quite something," Chloe said. "I'm not sure how I'm going to ever ask you to bring me coffee again, now that I know what a star you are!"

Martin reached out and patted her shoulder. "Well done, Libby; very well done."

Suddenly Dean burst through the door. They all turned and stared, waiting for the verdict.

"Tomorrow morning, 10 o'clock, he wants to see me and Bridget. Don't know what it means, or what—or who—he wants to talk about, but we got a meeting!"

Loud, triumphant cheers erupted.

As Libby followed Rob toward the exit, Bart approached. "It's still raining, so I'm going to drive Rob back down. I don't want him dealing with trains and Ubers in this mess."

Libby smiled, touched by his generosity. "That's above and beyond the call. You're not going to turn around and drive right back up tonight, are you?"

"No, he's got me bunking at his mentor's house, a guy named Hewitt?"

"Yes, I met him. Nice guy. And that's a very sweet thing to do, thank you, Bart. It will relieve my concerns about him traveling in the rain."

Bart touched her elbow.

She stopped walking and looked at him. "What?"

"You were amazing tonight, Libby, you really were. Watching you up there I was so happy for you, but sad too. Because it made so clear what you should have had and what you should have been. It also proved that what you are now is still, really, the best chick singer in L.A. I say that with historical perspective and lots of love."

Her eyes filled as she put her arms around him for the first time in many, many years.

CHAPTER 60

The celebration continued at Shiplap Café, a popular bistro not far from S.I.R. Having commandeered the biggest table in the place, all the band members of Liberty, with wives, kids, and various friends, were in attendance. Chloe and Martin had begged off, but the remaining group, the core group, was bonded in their sense of accomplishment, and the mood was triumphant.

Libby stood near the doorway on her cell, gazing out at the pouring rain, hoping Bart and Rob's drive back down to San Diego would be safe and easy. She'd instructed Robbie to text when they got there, and he promised he would. Back on her phone, she said loudly, "What, Jeff? I can barely hear you, it's really crazy in here."

"I said I had a patient emergency. By the time I was done, it was almost seven, and I knew with the rain I wouldn't make it in time. I am so sorry, Libby; I know what a big night it was. How did it go?"

"Amazing!" She practically yelled. "The A&R guy wants to meet with Dean and Bridget tomorrow morning, so that's a really good sign."

"Very exciting."

Libby looked into the dining room to see Gwen showing Nick her engagement ring. "Why don't you come down? We're at Shiplap, and we haven't ordered yet. Besides, we're celebrating Gwen and Otto's engagement. Did you hear about that?"

"I did; great stuff, isn't it? I'm happy for them. But listen, sweetheart, now it's my turn for exhaustion. It's been a tough day and I'm not really in the mood for a lot of noise right now. Do you mind?"

"No, I completely understand."

"Though I'd be delighted if you came over afterwards." She could hear his smile through the phone.

"Okay, but not sure how late I'll be."

"Whatever time, it doesn't matter. I'll be here. Give my love to everyone. Can't wait to see you."

Libby hung up, brows knitted. Then she headed back to the table where she leapt into Gwen's lap with an enthusiastic hug.

CHAPTER 61

Rain battered the foyer windows at Jeff's house, as Libby stood outside, cold and shivering. Pushing the buzzer for a second time, she peered in the adjoining window as Jeff finally rounded the corner from the living room and opened the door.

"My God, Libby, you're soaked. Get in here."

He pulled her in and helped her out of her dripping raincoat, which revealed the quite fetching and fancy stage outfit underneath. He stood back and took her in like a museum piece.

"Holy cow; did not know I'd be welcoming my very own diva here tonight. This is, wow, quite the getup."

It was. With its mix of '80s irreverence and contemporary designer edge, the sartorial statement was fabulous and far afield from her usual wear. Add to that her teased hair, and makeup more creatively applied than usual, and she made quite the dramatic sight.

"It is. Gwen and I worked hard to find the exact right mix of sexy, sassy, and serious. I feel like we pulled it off."

He laughed as he wrapped his arms around her and whispered, "I'd like to pull it off too."

They stood in the foyer clinched in a warm, dedicated kiss. When he stepped back, he looked her over once more, chuckled, then took her hand. "Okay, fun entrance, but let's get you upstairs, diva, and out of this silly costume. Makes me feel like I'm with a stranger." He smiled when he said it, but she twitched at the comment.

"I'll have you know this 'costume' is rock chic, and definitely not silly."

He stopped and looked at her, cocking his head. "Okay, okay, I get it. But, Libby, cute though you may be in this get-up —and you are definitely very cute—I think we both know this 'rock chic' persona isn't quite *you*."

Mistake. She pulled her arm away, her face serious.

He looked at her, chagrined. "I'm sorry. Was that the wrong thing to say?"

"It was an odd thing to say. Because, quite frankly, this persona is probably more me than any *me* you've seen up till now."

He shook his head, laughing out loud. "Oh, come on, sweetheart, I don't believe that for a moment."

"Which is also odd because you once said you know who I am. I'm kind of curious what that means to you."

"Wait. Is that a real question?" His face got serious.

"Yes."

He paused, aware of her ire and searching for the right words to defuse it. "Okay. You're a sexy, intelligent, woman with two great kids, an admirable job you worked hard for, and a well-adjusted, successful man who wants to marry you."

Her face didn't shift. "And what do you think about all this music stuff?"

"Libby, for God's sake."

"No, seriously, I want to know."

A beat. "Well, given that this music stuff, as you put it, didn't exist when I first met you, you have to allow me a little leeway here. It's been a very unexpected addendum to your life, and, hence, to mine, but to answer your question: I'm glad you got to enjoy singing for a bit; I think you graciously helped make your daughter's admissions project a very inventive one, and I'm sure you both appreciated the chance to spend some time together doing it."

"Uh huh. And?"

"There needs to be an *and*?"

"What do you think about *me,* specifically, and this music stuff?"

Cornered, his back stiffened. "I'm not loving this interrogation, Libby, but since you seem determined to have it, let me think of how best to answer." There was an uncomfortable pause. "Okay, given the music I've heard, which I've very much enjoyed, I'd say you were no doubt a fine young singer who had a fun few years back when you were a kid. But then you grew up and got on with life, and you've made that life a very successful one, and, I might add, one I admire. So *I* personally don't think you need to harken back to the diversions of your youth to feel good about yourself. And I bet if you really thought about it, you don't either."

"That's what you think I'm doing? Trying to relive my youth to bolster my ego?"

At this point he was in the kitchen, pouring himself a shot of Scotch, something he'd never done in front of her before. He bolted it down, then looked at her with incomprehension. "What is happening here, Libby?"

"I guess I'm wondering now about the reason you didn't come tonight."

"Wait a minute, that's completely unfair. I told you why. I had a late emergency with a patient; it was raining, I wouldn't have made it on time. Why, do you think I'm lying to you?"

"No, I wouldn't have thought that, but you knew what a big deal it was for me, for Bridget. You knew I wanted you there. And now that I hear your honest opinion about how you see me in this world of music, it's hard not to wonder if your absence was intentional, even if subconsciously so."

His face darkened. "That's insulting and completely off base. I have been nothing but supportive of this effort—"

324 | LORRAINE DEVON WILKE

"Yes, you have been. The party was an amazing gift. Which is why I am completely flummoxed about everything you've said since I walked in tonight."

"Why am I suddenly the bad guy? For someone who doesn't even like rock & roll that much, I think I've been a pretty good sport about all this."

She stood at the kitchen counter, keeping distance between them. "Has it really been that difficult?"

"No. I've enjoyed watching you have fun. But it has *always* been with the assumption that it was temporary. I don't see myself playing stage-husband on a permanent basis. And surely, even *you* want to be doing something more dignified with your time than standing on stage with a bunch of has-been rockers screaming your lungs out."

Wrong. All wrong. Everything wrong.

As if a detonator had clicked, Libby flinched. Then she pulled in a sharp breath and ... screamed.

Loud.

Long.

Shocking.

She flung away from the counter and raced toward the front door.

Jeff, visibly shaken, rushed after her. "Jesus Christ, Libby, what the hell was that?"

She grabbed her wet coat, struggling to pull it on, her eyes flaming. "You *don't* know me. You don't know a fucking thing about me. You're clueless!"

The ashen look on Jeff's face made clear that this kind of drama, particularly directed at him, was completely out of his wheelhouse. "Libby, stop, please. You're overreacting, and there's no reason for that. I'm sorry if I'm saying the wrong things, but maybe I'm feeling a little cornered. If you'd just relax, you'd realize that all I'm saying is I liked where we were going, and I just want to get us back on track. That's a positive thing, don't you think?"

She whirled to face him. "But see, that's where this falls apart for us. I'm not *off* track; I'm right smack on the one I should be on. That you can't see that is significant to me."

Jeff reached for her, but she pulled away. She picked up her purse and, taking several deep breaths, attempted to calm herself. He could only stare at her, so rattled he didn't know what to do or say. She finally turned to him. "I'm sorry I screamed. You didn't deserve that."

"No, I didn't, but I'm trying to understand. Please come here, sweetheart." He opened his arms.

Libby, her anger drained now to sadness, didn't move. Standing silently, her head bowed, she finally looked up with tears. "Oh, Jeff. You are ... you are so sweet and, really, such a good, caring man. I've had a wonderful time getting to know you a bit, and I'm so grateful for all you've shared and done for me, especially the party. But we're at a crossroads, you and me. And I just realized—and maybe I've known since I saw your closet—I'm not the right girl for you." With that she opened the door and walked into the splattering rain.

Indignant now, he followed her out. "What the hell does that mean, Libby?"

She just looked at him, water and tears streaming down her face. "I'm messy, Jeff, my life is messy. I can't keep it neatly categorized; I don't *want* to keep it neatly categorized, and I'm still not sure how it's going to turn out. For you, that's an inconvenience. For me, it's a fucking revelation."

She leaned in, kissed his cheek, then turned and got in her car. As she drove off, he stood in the rain staring after her.

CHAPTER 62

The windshield wipers beat a thumping rhythm, struggling to keep up with the downpour. Libby sobbed in tandem with their racket, mascara cascading down her cheeks, her nose running, as she drove aimlessly down a rain-slicked street, not wanting to go home to her empty house, not wanting to call anyone; not wanting to go back to Jeff's. Definitely not wanting that.

When a text came in, she pulled into the brightly lit parking lot of a twenty-four-hour convenience store. It was from Robbie, letting her know he and Bart had made it back to campus, safe and sound, reiterating how *"phenomenal you were tonight, Mom, you totally blew my mind."* Those words worked to calm her, slowed her stuttering sobs.

After texting him back, she sat in the parking lot shivering, shaken by what she'd done, trying to think about Jeff. But she couldn't. Her mind wouldn't let her go there. It seemed only to pull her in one direction.

* * *

A dripping Libby stood at the door of a two-story A-frame on the tiny winding road of a hillside neighborhood. She knew it was late, too late. But she rang the bell anyway. A moment passed, two moments, then the outside light flickered on, and the door opened.

Nick. Who'd clearly been sleeping.

"Libby."

He immediately pulled her inside. The light of the doorway shone on her anguished face, ruined with dripping mascara and bedraggled hair.

"Baby, what is it? What's going on?" Closing the door, he pulled her out of her drenched coat. "Are you all right?"

"Is it okay to be here? Is Kyla home? I don't want to—"

"No, she's gone. *Gone* gone, I've been informed by a recent text."

"I'm sorry." She hadn't stopped crying.

"It's okay. We'd reached our end, it seems." He peered into her face, confused. "Do you just want to stand here for a minute? Or do you want to come in?"

"I don't know. I don't know what I'm doing." Barely above a whisper. "What am I doing?"

"I don't know, sweetheart. What happened? Did someone hurt you?" His concern was real.

"I thought I finally had it figured out. But I can't seem to get it right. I never seem to get it right. Who am I supposed to be now? *Who am I supposed to be?*"

His looked directly into her eyes, hands on her shoulders. "Just you, Liberty. Just you. That has always and only been who you're supposed to be."

Their eyes held on each other, questioning.

"I don't want the Fates to be right this time, Nicky," she whispered.

He caressed her cheek then, leaning in, he kissed her, long, deep, with no hesitation. In the cocoon of the darkened room, they fell into each other as if they'd waited the lifetime they had.

★ ★ ★

A pink dawn crept slowly through the windows. Libby lay curled in a pile of blankets, Nick snoring softly next to her. She turned gently, not wanting to wake him, and took the moment to gaze around his bedroom.

Nicky's room; a place she had never been but so often imagined. It looked lived in, chaotic, crowded with the elements of his life: guitars, several of them; cases, music stands, studio equipment. Shelves were piled with books and magazines haphazardly stacked. Photographs of the various and many bands he'd been in throughout his long career leaned here and there, some artfully hung, other tilting and curled. There were two gold records from some point, some band; she would have to ask him about those. Everything she could see in this space was *him*, his life, his work. It was colorful and eclectic, and it made her feel ... home.

Home.

That struck her, the sensation of *home*. She wasn't expecting it. But she hadn't expected anything when she drove here. She'd just been inexorably drawn.

She gazed at Nicky's sleeping face, following the lines that ran down his cheeks, the furrows across his brow. There were streaks of gray in his raucous head of hair, the scruff of his beard. The shape of his jaw remained strong and dominant. His eyelashes were still long, evidenced by their fan across his cheeks.

He is still so beautiful, she thought, even as he'd aged from the shiny young person he'd been when she met him as a shiny young person herself. They'd both grown older in body and spirit. Both survived heartaches and hardship. And now they were here. In this room, this bed, this moment. Which felt perfectly right, as if this was exactly, finally, the moment they were meant to be here together. Not before. Not then. Now. Exactly *now.* And for the first time in a long time, she felt like her heart was beating in the exact right rhythm.

Nicky stirred awake. He cracked an eye, taking her in, a slow smile warming his face. He pulled her into a swaddle of blankets, pressing his lips to her ear. "I was afraid I was dreaming and you'd be gone."

"I'm here."

"Is it too soon to tell you I've loved you almost all my life?"

No, it's the exact right time, she thought. Tucking into him, she whispered. "I've loved you the same."

CHAPTER 63

Bridget had researched the history and location of the now-defunct Mount Cloud Records, wanting to know where it had been, what building had been party to her mother's anguish. It was still there, the building, though now it was an office mall for lawyers and tech companies. The articles she'd found on Eric Burrows' catastrophic career implosion had been detailed and damning, appropriate, she thought, for such a despicable person. His death from cancer years later seemed only to have provided the media with opportunity to deconstruct, once again, his ugly professional collapse. By then, culture had become far less accommodating to the Weinsteins, Cosbys, Epsteins, and Burrows.

Now, driving down the same Sunset Boulevard toward a different building, a different record company, in a different time, Bridget hoped that whatever they were about to discuss would offer a different result for her mother.

★ ★ ★

"Your mother? For a school admissions project? Are you kidding me?"

They'd decided on the way there to come fully clean; there seemed no other option at this juncture, regardless of where the conversation might lead. Even Dean agreed that anything asked about the who, what, or how of the previous night's events required candor, so once inside the room and into the conversation, Aaron's continuing questions compelled them to lay out the somewhat astonishing evolution of all that had led them here.

Aaron was clearly stunned, his expression vacillating between shock and annoyance. Bridget and Dean sat opposite him at the large conference table, feeling degrees of their own unsettlement. Though they always understood there'd be no way to predict his reaction, they were both thrown by the terseness of his response, which seemed less forgiving than expected.

"I promise; we weren't trying to con you," Bridget insisted, her voice tinged with panic. "To be honest, we never thought it would get this far. And when it did, we weren't sure what to do, so we just kept going, and, well, here we are."

Aaron looked from one to the other. "And the two of you did it all? The band, the social media, the recordings, everything?" His incredulity was sharp.

"We had help," Dean answered. "Bridget's dad did some of the artwork, and her godmother paid for everything, but yeah, we basically put all the pieces together."

"Amazing. I should cither kick your asses out of here or offer you a job."

Through the windows of the conference room, Bridget saw Aaron's boss, Doug, in the vicinity. She was hit with an immediate rush of anxiety. When he noticed them in the room, he motioned for them to wait, grabbed some items from a nearby desk—it looked like their promo packs—and charged in.

"Wow. You two." He wagged his finger at them. "Very interesting experiment you ran on us last night. Clever, a little sneaky, but bold. I like that."

"Um, thanks," Dean mumbled, not sure where this was going.

"And I got the point. That second band—Liberty, was it?" He glanced at the promotional materials.

"Yes." Bridget nodded. Her hands were shaking under the table.

"Excellent band. Phenomenal, in fact. Clearly pros and, frankly, they kicked the young ones out of the room. And that singer ... wowser! A real dynamo. I bet she was hot in the '80s."

Dean shot a quick look at Bridget, whose face held motionless.

Doug started pawing through the photos in his hand. "Now, Aaron and I have been discussing what we saw last night, the songs we heard—which are fantastic, by the way—the presumed statement of your two-part presentation; though, to be honest, I'm not quite sure who, exactly, you want to win this race!" He laughed. "But let me be blunt, kids—and given that you're in the business, I assume you already know this—rock and roll is about two things: sex and youth. Youth and sex. Especially now, with social media bullshit, viral campaigns, stans and influencers who can literally make a group one night and cancel them the next, certain equations tell the tale. Especially with female singers. It's a simple one: Who do girls wanna be and boys wanna fuck? Sorry to be crude, but that's the way it's always been and will always be. Though, to be politically correct for this hyper-sensitive time we live in, that might amend to include anybody for either activity."

Aaron stiffened. "Doug, listen, I'm in the middle of—"

Doug held up his hand to quiet him, which Aaron clearly didn't appreciate. "See, Aaron wants me to sign your very talented vets. He thinks there's something noble and ironic in that. He's bought your pitch. But I've been around a long time, longer than him—" He shot a wink in Aaron's direction— "and I know the ins and outs of this crazy business. Success as a recording act is hard as fuck any day, but it's gotten a lot harder in these modern times when nobody wants to pay for anything, and what you wear—or *don't* wear—can snag more attention than the music. And let's not forget sampling, and AI, and global piracy that's robbing us all blind."

Aaron stood, still attempting to get in a word. "Doug, we've already—"

Again, Doug held him off. "I'll give you back the room in a minute, Aaron, but I need to make these points before I go. Your kids here went to a lot of trouble to showcase their two bands, and they deserve my perspective."

Aaron crossed his arms, defiant as Doug returned to his monologue. "I noticed you referenced *The Voice* in the old band's promo materials, and I get why you did. You're looking for rationale that makes your case. But the whole, 'we're not influenced by anything but *the voice*' might be good buzz for a reality show, but in real life, that's bullshit. In real life, *nobody* wants old. *No-bo-dy*. Unless it's famous old and called Cher."

Grinning at his joke, Doug held up the pictures of Libby and Maya with a look toward Bridget.

"Again, forgive my crassness, but let's be honest." With a casual flip, he dropped both photos on the table. Libby's landed so that it was half covered by Maya's, whose gorgeous face caught the beam of the overhead light. "Yep, right there, *that* tells the story." He looked around as if to gain agreement. The others were stone-faced. "Your old gal can sing, that's undeniable. But this one." He pointed to Maya's photo. "She's the whole package: young, a knockout, *and* a phenomenal singer. Regardless of any other thoughts or considerations, *that* fits the equation. So we sign her, build a band with some hot, young session players; do a deal with a couple of your oldsters' songs, get a quick album out, and *boom*, everyone wins." He looked at each of them and nodded. "You think about that. And thanks again." He grinned and shook his finger at them once more. "And you two, wow, really crafty."

After he exited the room, Aaron turned painfully to Bridget and Dean, who'd been stunned into silence.

★ ★ ★

The descending elevator seemed determined to stop at every floor. Bridget and Dean stood in the back corner, pressed tightly against the wall. Tears ran down Bridget's face, garnering furtive, sympathetic glances from other passengers. She made no attempt to react to any of them.

Dean's arm wrapped protectively around her shoulder; his face a controlled mask.

The doors opened and shut, over and over, as they proceeded down and Bridget's tears poured.

CHAPTER 64

As the main class day ended, and students and teachers rushed through the lobby to their lives beyond, the door to the conference room at South Coast College of Film and Media was shut, hung with a sign that read, "Presentation in Progress. Do Not Disturb."

Over the many weeks and months it had taken to inspire the hanging of that sign, Bridget's life had upheaved in myriad ways, both expected and unexpected. She'd assisted Heart to Table's move to West Hollywood, designing her new job to be a better fit given her skills and talents (she was now running the entire marketing department). She and Dean found a place in the same building where he'd been living, though one with an extra room for Bridget's office. And, perhaps above all, she'd worked tirelessly, doggedly, to trim, edit, and mold her admissions project into exactly what she wanted it to be. It had been a challenge.

The thesis remained the same, but the emotional heart and soul that emerged from the experience took it in directions she couldn't have imagined when she started. It got longer (currently at five minutes, six seconds), covering a wider range of elements related to the topic, and left her transformed in ways she seemed only able to articulate through this little film.

Which she was currently sharing with Ellie Scamehorn and the four other admissions faculty who watched with focused attention while making occasional notes. Seated behind their table in the darkened room, Bridget had supervised getting the large screen lowered from the ceiling, and setting up the projector where now, unfolding onscreen, were the concluding scenes of her long-awaited, hard-won, epiphanic admissions project. As it wound through a montage of shots—Libby at her desk at the store, her tentative first rehearsal, the lights and color of the big showcase—Bridget's confident voiceover narrated:

"This project began as a comparison of old and new. A chance to step into the world of music and technology and find the map. But in the end, it was more about my mother. About finding out who she was. Because, as it turns out, I hadn't paid much attention, and she'd forgotten. So we discovered some things together. Like what's important, what you need to be happy. Like the fact that success isn't always what you pictured. It might be later, smaller, even quieter than you imagined. But if it involves the person you truly are, it's the sweetest kind there is. I get to live my whole life knowing that. Lucky me."

The screen froze on an image of Libby and Bridget laughing in an embrace, the band in soft focus behind.

As Bridget let out a soft breath of relief, glad it was over and hopeful it achieved its goal, a tech across the room pulled the lights up, and the seated group leaned in toward each other to speak quietly for a moment.

A woman whose name Bridget had forgotten, earlier introductions having been quick and nervous, smiled. "Very nice work. Thank you. Once we're through with the process, you'll be informed of our decision. Good luck!"

Ellie Scamehorn rose. "I'll walk you out, Bridget." When they got to the door, she opened it with a warm smile. "Really beautiful work. I know it took a lot to get here, but I'm very impressed with the 'voice' you found. And, I have to admit, the twist of naming your young band Minor Rebellion was quite a surprise!"

"I thought you might appreciate that." Bridget grinned. "Though I have to credit Dean for that; it was his idea."

"It seems you two make a good team, so well done all around. We'll be in touch; know that it usually takes the group a week or so to go through all the applications that came in during this current period, but it won't be too long after that. I wish you luck—though I have a very good feeling."

Bridget did too. But she also realized that whatever was decided, she'd be all right. Just as her mother was when they reported what happened at the label. Despite Bridget's sorrow at being witness to a second round of career rejection for a phenomenal singer named Liberty Conlin, she'd come away with the lesson that bookended her documentary. It was a good one.

As she made her way across campus, Dean caught up with her. Without a word, he put his arm through hers and pulled her close. They walked together in comfortable silence toward the car. She looked up at him and said, "Let's go buy a couch. Then we'll go listen to some music."

CHAPTER 65

Though Bridget cried when she told her mother what had transpired that pivotal day at Delgany Records, Libby did not. Despite her excitement at doing the showcase, despite that tiny (miniscule) part of her that (hoped) wondered if some kind of strange magic really could happen in this transformative new chapter of her life, her heart of hearts told her it would be exactly what it was.

There was talk of keeping the band going, cobbling together a few Liberty gigs just for the sheer fun of it—and, of course, to promote the fact that two of their songs would be featured on an upcoming album by new Delgany Records artist, Maya Bell—but ultimately the complexity of family demands, work schedules, and, in ensuing weeks, waning interest, guided that idea quietly to the back shelf. Libby and Nick, widely applauded for finally making their way towards each other ("Damn, you two," Brandon had groused, "what took so long?"), suggested a barbecue and acoustic night at her house after things settled down. All agreed that would be good fun. It remained to be seen if they could get it on a schedule.

★ ★ ★

In a small club on the corner of some street and Santa Monica Boulevard, Happy Hour was merging with dinner time, but the performance room was where the crowd had gathered. Clustered around cocktail tables with drinks, hors d'oeuvres, and plenty of enthusiasm, the mood was jovial, the energy high-pitched.

A postage-stamp stage was tucked in the corner of the room, angled toward the crowd, and facing the large windows where passersby could be seen as they traversed the streets outside. Some gazed through the glass; others were drawn to come inside, and the tiny space was almost always crowded, even this early in the evening. Somewhere in the audience were Gwen and Otto, drinks in hand, smiles wide, attention fixed on the stage.

Libby and Nick were perched on stools in front of a microphone. Both appeared casual and comfortable, their faces lit less by the paltry stage lights and more by proximity to each other and the clear pleasure of performing together. They were mid-set, and the room was buzzing with appreciation.

"It's great that so many of you have come out this early in the evening." Libby's smile was infectious, her red tunic complementing the glow of her flushed cheeks. "We weren't sure if the 'blue plate special' time slot would be a good fit for our wild fanbase."

The crowd laughed. Libby joined them, keeping her eye on the door.

"But as it turns out," Nick continued. "Happy Hour music lovers seem to be more appreciative of geezers like me than that crazy late-night crowd—"

"Stop!" Libby playfully whacked him. "You're a *pre*-geezer." The crowd cheered. "Anyway, we're going to change the mood a bit here with a new song of ours, the first one Nicky and I have written together in a very long time, and we hope you like it. It's called 'That Time You Said.'"

Nick leaned back strumming his acoustic, leading Libby's voice, evocative and moving, into the song. The audience settled into the mood, listening attentively.

Somewhere before the chorus, she looked up past the audience and toward the window. The front door of the club swung open, and at the exact moment Bridget and Dean entered the room, a city bus clamored to a loud stop at the traffic light on the corner. Illuminated by the glow of a streetlamp, it was impossible to miss the huge billboard sign plastered on its side: "Delgany Records New Recording Artist, Maya Bell, appearing Friday @ The Wiltern."

Likely no one else noticed, their backs to the window, but Libby was jarred. She looked away, almost losing her place in the song. When she glanced back up, the bus was pulling away. Maya's luminous billboard eyes seemed to lock onto hers as the image moved slowly past the window and out of sight.

Taking a deep breath while Nick played his solo, she watched Bridget and Dean finally land a seat, waving to Gwen and Otto as they settled in. Libby smiled in their direction, trying to find solid footing again. Then she looked at Nick. She didn't know if he'd seen the bus, but his gaze was the touchstone that brought her back to where they were now, in this club, on this stage, singing this song. His eyes locked onto hers as he guided her into the second verse. They smiled at each other.

And she continued singing.

ABOUT THE AUTHOR

An accomplished writer in several genres of the medium, **LORRAINE DEVON WILKE**, a Chicago native and one of eleven children, has built a library of expertly crafted work with a signature style that exudes intelligence, depth, and humor. Whether screenplay or stage play, article or editorial, short story or novel, her work captures the edge and emotion of real life, incorporating original plots, jump-off-the-page dialogue, and thought-provoking themes.

In 2010, she launched her "arts & politics" blog, *Rock+Paper+Music*, and in 2011 became a popular contributor to *HuffPost* and other media sites. Her essays have been reprinted and excerpted in academic tomes, nonfiction books, and literary journals. She maintains a column at *Medium* and a popular Substack, *Musings of a Creative Loudmouth*.

She jumped into longform with her first novel, *After the Sucker Punch* (2014); her second, *Hysterical Love* (2015). Both won a slate of literary awards and garnered passionate readership. Her third novel, *The Alchemy of Noise* (She Writes Press, 2019), struck a powerful chord with its dramatic "ripped from the headlines" narrative, garnering an invitation to NPR's *1A* show to discuss "literature + culture," and awarded by an impressive roster of literary organizations.

Devon Wilke lives in Los Angeles with her husband, attorney/writer/producer, Pete Wilke; her son, and other extended family nearby.

To learn more visit @ **www.lorrainedevonwilke.com.**

ACKNOWLEDGMENTS

This story was birthed from one of those random "what ifs?"—the kind that sticks; the kind you can't stop thinking about, that tickles your brain until you follow the thread to some ultimately satisfying fruition. In this case, it was a prompt based on my rowdy, wild, exhilarating years in rock & roll, and went something like this: "What if someone secretly posted your old '80s music online and it went viral?"

I remember laughing, thinking that would, indeed, be random, but the idea sparked a bigger idea, one that carried me into the world of "Libby Conlin"—her band, her family, her life, her dreams, her secrets—all of which led to *Chick Singer*. It's not my story—that belongs to Libby—but it's one informed by my experiences, perceptions, and full-body immersion in the life of a female singer making her way in a creative industry that's, yes, exhilarating and life-changing, but also fierce, competitive, and occasionally brutal. It's percolated through various iterations, engaging the input of many wonderful readers, consultants, editors, and advisors, all of whom contributed to its "satisfying fruition," all of whom I want to acknowledge and thank.

First, always, my husband, Pete Wilke, my rock like no other. He's been an ever-constant support over my many years of artistic successes and struggles, wins and losses, ups and downs, and nobody knows me and my devotion to creativity better. He's kept the engine of our family running throughout, is the first person to read my work, listen to my music, attend my plays, or hang my photos, convinced there's always a reason to carry on no matter what the obstacles or disappointments. "Tomorrow's another day," is his mantra, and he not only lives by that resilience and optimism but has imbued it in me as well. I cannot imagine this journey without him, nor can I find adequate words to thank him for all he is and all he's done for me. I love you, Peter Jay.

The following lovely, talented people gave me their time, their opinions, and their estimable expertise, some more than once on this story; some with blurbs, some with critique, all with encouragement, and I am forever grateful: James Parriott, Pamela May, Tom Amandes, Fred Rubin, Barbara Tyler, Susan Morgenstern, Minda Burr, Joyce Jackson, Nancy Capers, Ann Werner, Debra Thomas, Judith Teitelman, Maureen Grammer, Perry Dunn, and Junior Burke.

Thanks to Rob Bignell for his excellent notes and editing. To Laurel Rund of *The Essence of Laurel*, and Barbara Bos of *Women Writers, Women's Books*, for their always-appreciated interest and support. To Katie Rose for her valued and life-changing guidance, and Rita Black for the path forward on chosen well-being goals, all of which contributed greatly to my forward motion.

Thanks and acknowledgment to the wonderful Sibylline Press/Digital First group: Publisher and Production Manager, Vicki DeArmon, for her belief in this project; Executive Editor/ founding partner, Julia Park Tracey, for not only reading the book once, but *twice*; to my editor Suzy Vitello, who offered fabulous notes, edits, and creative perspective, and Maureen Jennings, who was an early grammar and style checker. To Marketing Coordinators Hannah Rutkowski and Anna Wilhelm, for their incredibly helpful tutoring, especially in the arena of social media; to marketing guru, Pam Parker, for her expertise and wisdom in that most critical aspect of a book's success; designer and founding partner, Alicia Feltman, for the gorgeous cover; founding partner & licensing and rights manager, Anna Termine, for opening doors and opportunities for the book, to Sang Kim, Publishing Information Manager, Jenny McIntyre, Publicist, and all the staff who participated in getting

Chick Singer out into the world. I am delighted to be part of this passionate, enthusiastic organization of book lovers.

In the solitary working environment of a writer's life, one's close network of family and friends becomes essential, whether they read, critique, and review your work, organize and host book parties, MC your events, or just show up and buy those books. Some make book cookies for you, some come to your fundraisers; others are there to listen to you talk about your work ... your life ... your frustrations ... your hopes and dreams ... even your cat upon occasion. These people enrich my life incalculably, so I must acknowledge my "circle of wagons" with deepest gratitude: Pamela May, Tina Romanus, Joyce Jackson, Beth Anderson, Jason Brett, Lauren Streicher, Stuart & Carol Oken, Louie Rosen, Thom Bishop, Alan Rosen, Tom Mula, John Ahart, Eddie & Jennifer King, Nancy & Hedges Capers, Susan Morgenstern, Steve Sharp, Kimberley Ann Johnson, Amy Beth Arkawy, Julie Harris Oliver, Rick Kogan, Robert Batista, Mark Barry, Brenda Perlin, Diana Stevens, Suzanne Battaglia, Regina McCrae, Diane Cary, Jim Parriott, Debbie Zipp, Molly Cheek, Penny Peyser, Eric & Donna Krogh, Jeff & Ann Brown, Troy Evans & Heather McLarty, Sheryl & Dan Getman, Sandy & Dave Wilson, Jake Drake, Steve Brackenbury, Frank Ramos, Barb Tyler, Don Priess, Susie Singer Carter, Carolyn Sutton, Patricia Royce, Rick Singer, Renee Carly, Marian Hamlen, and Cindy Ritt. If I've forgotten anyone, forgive me.

And, of course, my cherished family who surround me with support and encouragement, many of whom have gone out of their way to read, review, help, share, and show up, especially Dillon Wilke & Marilyn Perez, Jennie & Jake Willens; Ben Amandes, Nia O'Reilly-Amandes, Meg Broz, Vicky & Larry Blanas; Steve Derebey, Marina Terzopoulos, Barb Amandes, Jamie O'Reilly, Meredith & Dave Kenyon, Ann Wilke, and my many and beloved sibs/in-laws: Peg, Mary, John, Paul & Angie,

Tom & Nancy, Eileen ♥, Gerry, Louise, Vince, and Grace & Noel, and my late parents, Virginia and Phil Amandes, who imbued my life with music, books, theater, and art, all of which led to my abiding love for the intrinsic and life-giving world of creativity.

Lastly, as a largely independent artist, I've been fortunate to have a robust, loyal, and long-term collective of wonderful people in my many social media circles who have stayed involved, supportive, and interested in my work over these many years. Whether fellow writers, musicians, artists of other mediums; readers, cultural and political activists, or tangential friends met online, the list is too long to name, but your connection and interaction with me on this journey is noticed and valued. Buying my books, reading my articles, subscribing to my Substack, sharing my perspective, reviewing my work, clicking "like," "love"; "friend," and "follower" have all contributed to my sense of community and the faith that what I'm creating, what I believe is important to convey through my work, is being seen, heard, and appreciated. Thank you, all, from the bottom of my heart … I hope you enjoy this book, too!

BOOK CLUB GUIDE

The questions and talking points that follow are intended to enrich your group's discussions about *Chick Singer*.

1. At the heart of this story is a complex, often fractious, mother-daughter relationship. Was Libby's decision to allow her daughter, Bridget, an unlimited stay in her home a wise one given the seemingly inescapable tensions between them? Is creating safe haven for boomeranging adult children compassionate parenting or an act of enablement?

2. It's often difficult for someone who was immersed in artistic pursuits as a younger person to adjust to a less creative life after marriage and children. Does Libby's generalized state of isolation and depression seem justified in the current circumstances of her life? Did you have empathy for her, or was it something you felt she should just "snap out of"?

3. Bridget is a sometimes difficult-to-like character who clearly has lifelong issues with her mother, expressing them regularly through hostility, snark, and regular doses of passive-aggressive communication. Does it take too long for Libby to set boundaries with her? Or is her patience, given the painful state of Bridget's life, an act of love?

4. The friendship between Gwen and Libby is a long one, built on decades of shared experiences, tremendous mutual support, good humor, and great love. Discuss the empowering and uplifting nature of "good girlfriends" and how essential those relationships are to women during every era of their lives.

5. Let's talk about the men in all three women's lives —Libby, Bridget, and Gwen. The inevitable components of love and passion, joy and hate; old and new, factor heavily into the stories of each featured relationship. What were your impressions of the more salient men, particularly Bart, Dean, Otto, Jeff, and Nick? Did you form an opinion of who was the best fit for whom while you were reading? Did Libby's ultimate choice surprise you?

6. The music business, both current and past, is a foundational part of this story, ultimately becoming an essential driver of the narrative. Did the descriptions of band life—recording sessions, performances; interactions amongst the players— enhance your enjoyment of the narrative? How did you feel about the denouement of Bridget's loving attempt to resuscitate Libby's singing career? Expected or unexpected?

7. The ultimate reveal that Libby's career was adversely affected by a MeToo incident turns the story on its head. How did that affect you as a reader and did it answer all the questions that bubbled up throughout the story as to why Libby walked away and what happened to those early relationships that meant so much to her? Did it change your feelings about Libby, impact your understanding and sympathies regarding her quirks, her choices, her personality in general?

8. It is said that "every woman has a MeToo story." Do you believe that? If you have one of your own, do you think the forum of a book club—having just finished a story with that as a central theme—is a safe, viable space to discuss such events?

9. Ageism, particularly as it affects women, is a throughline of *Chick Singer*. The struggles women go through in trying to advance and stay relevant in careers that celebrate youthfulness are brought to life, discussed, and, in some cases, overcome. Bridget's hope that, despite Libby's age, she could ultimately reclaim her dream of music success, sparks many thoughts about ageism in the music business, in the world at large; *everywhere*. Discuss how ageism may or may not have affected your life and work. And did you adjust, change, or evolve in ways to overcome that bias?

10. One of the most powerful take-aways of this story is the epiphany that real success can often look, feel, and be very different from what we originally imagined, yet what we step into can be so much sweeter and more satisfying than the original dream. Discuss the parallel trajectories and evolutions of the two main characters, Libby and Bridget, as their journeys track separately and together as they both grow, change, and learn to cherish and appreciate the lives and versions of success they ultimately embrace.

INFORMATION AND PRAISE FOR LORRAINE'S OTHER NOVELS

THE ALCHEMY OF NOISE
(She Writes Press, 2019)

- **2023** Indie Author Project Regional Contest Winner in California

- **2019** Readers' Favorite Awards Gold Medal Winner in Fiction (Literary)

- **2019** Best Book Awards Finalist in Fiction (Literary)

- **2019** International Book Awards, Finalist, Fiction (Multicultural)

- **2020** IBPA Benjamin Franklin Award Fiction Finalist in Multicultural

- **2019** Foreword Indie Finalist in Adult Fiction: Multicultural

- **2019** Nautilus Book Awards Silver Winner in Fiction

In a world so full of lonely people and broken hearts, Chris Hawkins, a Black sound engineer from Chicago's south side, and Sidonie Frame—white, suburban-raised, the head manager of one of the city's most elite venues—meet by work-related happenstance and fall quickly in love, convinced that by that act alone they can inspire peace, joy, and happiness in the world around them. The world, however, has other ideas.

Their unexpected relationship inspires myriad reactions amongst family and friends on both sides of the racial divide, and as day-to-day tensions, police disruptions, and persistent micro-aggressions become a cultural flashpoint, Sidonie's privileged worldview and Chris's ability to translate unfolding events clash. After a random and gut-wrenching series of police encounters shakes their resilience, it's the shattering circumstance of a violent arrest—one in which Chris is identified as a serial vandal and potential rapist—that sends their world into free fall.

He claims his innocence; she believes him, but with a looming trial, the dissipating loyalties of key allies, and unforeseen twists triggering doubt and suspicion, Sidonie and Chris are driven to question what they really know of each other and just whom to trust, leading to a powerful and emotional conclusion.

Lorraine Devon Wilke's third novel, *The Alchemy of Noise*, ventures beyond the humor and pathos of family dramas explored so cleverly in her first two novels to dig deep into the politics of contemporary culture. At its heart a love story, it explores the complexity of race in a suspenseful drama driven by issues of privilege, prejudice, police profiling and legal entanglements, and the disparities in how those provocative themes impact the various and diverse characters involved.

RICK KOGAN, Chicago Tribune & After-Hours W/Rick Kogan, WGN Radio 720: "A fascinating book, really, really quite something ... a real Chicago novel. I do find something quite courageous about this book. It's not only terribly provocative and moves like a freight train, but it's a very, very, very ambitious book."

Booked Up Girl Blog: "I absolutely loved this book and found myself engrossed in their story and journey. I felt a somewhat deep connection with Sid and Chris' characters. The story is just heart wrenching—I really couldn't put the book down, and it will stay haunting me for a long time to come. If you haven't yet read this—it must be next on your TBR!"

Barb Taub | Writing & Coffee: "The writing of *The Alchemy of Noise* is hauntingly beautiful, shocking, and compelling. I feel like I know so many of the characters, that they are the family and friends and fellow students I knew in Chicago. And yet I don't know them at all, can't believe they would react as the characters did here. But, as Sidonie points out, I've read the papers, listened to the news, heard the casually racist and discriminatory remarks. And even with a love as big as Chris and Sidonie's, I don't know how you get past that. Maybe reading this stunningly well written book is a good way to start."

Bookapotamus: "This book. Stop what you are doing. And read this book. It's heartbreaking, it's uncomfortable, and it's daring in the most important way ... This book haunts me—but it's a good thing. I cannot stop thinking about it. I feel as if Sidonie and Chris are real people, and in a way, they are—as the gut-wrenching brutality, tension, and racism is entirely plausible in this day and age ... I loved every minute of this story."

Georgia Rose Books: "The exploration of all the relationships in this novel is excellent. The characters rich and rounded, the way they react and interact absorbing. It is very well written. It's intelligent, educational, and eye-opening, though still easy to read, the prose flowing and drawing you in. *The Alchemy of Noise* is an excellent novel I thoroughly enjoyed and don't hesitate for a moment to recommend."

Janni Styles Book Blog: "From the challenge of loving narrow-minded relations to finding love without trust impossible, no matter your race or level of privilege, this book is rich with raw human experience. Deftly executed with grace and the author's own keen sensibilities, the story left me wishing it would never end. It is well-paced with moments of epiphany that had me feeling I was not just a reader but part of the story. In some way, we all are. Every single one of us can take responsibility for changing history for the better, lessons of yesterday are a chance to improve, to hate less, love more and a chance to be at peace with all people."

Words-A-Plenty Review: "*The Alchemy of Noise* was not what I expected. With each page I found myself becoming more and more intrigued. Then I had to step back for a minute and see the much larger picture she was painting with her words. Emotionally wrenching, well written and developed, Wilke has communicated the fears and doubts of being human in a world where intolerance of difference is rampant, where being humane is not extended to those who are different. This is not a light book; it is one that will stick with you for weeks if not longer. I finished this book about three weeks ago and just now sat down to write the review. Having come from a family from the deepest part of Indiana where racism runs unchecked and fueled by the past, I still feel the impact of this story."

HYSTERICAL LOVE
(CreateSpace Independent Publishing, 2015)

Dan McDowell, a 33-year-old portrait photographer wobbling toward an early mid-life crisis, is unceremoniously dumped by his fiancée after mentioning a years-earlier "ex-girlfriend overlap." Bunking next door at best friend Bob's for far longer than anticipated, Dan finds himself lost in existential confusion. His life is further upended when his father takes ill, and Dan reads an old story written by this enigmatic man about a long-lost love who haunts him still. Perplexed and inspired by this revelation—and incapable of fixing his own romantic dilemma—Dan sets off on a wild ride beset with detours, twists, and semi-hilarious peril to find this woman of his father's dreams, convinced she holds the keys to happiness for them all. A funny, thought-provoking tale of self-discovery and finding the true meaning of love.

- **2017** New Apple Books Solo Medalist Winner in General Fiction

- **2017** American Book Fest Best Book Awards Finalist in General Fiction

- **2015** indieB.R.A.G. Medallion Honoree

Kirkus Reviews: "Wilke is a skilled writer, able to plausibly inhabit Dan's young male perspective ... A well-written, engaging, sometimes-frustrating tale of reaching adulthood a little late."

Literary Fiction Book Review: "Devon Wilke manages to convey the male psyche with a good-natured humor that seems eminently believable. *Hysterical Love* is a deftly told tale."

Readers' Favorite Book Reviews: "I just finished reading *Hysterical Love*, the newest novel by Lorraine Devon Wilke, and I must say, I simply adored it! Her writing style is witty, pointed and funny, even hilarious at times."

We Magazine For Women: "One of the 8 Books Worth Reading This Summer, 2015."

Barb Taub Book Blog: "I never found a writer who was as good as DH Lawrence, but who could also get into a man's head and tell that story. Until now. Wilke is a kind of genius. Or a damn good writer doing a better job of getting into the head of the opposite sex than DH Lawrence anyway. She combines humor, terrific writing, and some none-too-gently acquired truths into a different kind of relationship story."

A Woman's Wisdom/UK Book Blog: "This is one of those books which exceeded all my expectations. I was expecting a romance with a couple of twists but what I got was something far deeper and more satisfying. If you want a book with many layers and to be thoroughly entertained by a cracking story then this one is for you."

Crossroads Reviews: "So worth the read. If you want a great laugh then pick this one up. The story was great, as were the characters. Unpredictable in so many ways. One to stick with you."

AFTER THE SUCKER PUNCH
(CreateSpace Independent Publishing, 2014)

They buried her father at noon, at five she found his journals, and in the time it took to read one-and-a-half pages her world turned upside down … he thought she was a failure, posthumous indictment that proves an existential knockout.

Tessa Curzio—thirty-six, emerging writer, ex-rocker, lapsed Catholic, defected Scientologist, and fourth child in a family of eight complicated people—attempts to transcend, but his damning words skew everything from her current relationship and the truth of her family, to her overall sense of self. In the tumultuous year that follows, it's her little-known aunt, a nun and counselor, who lovingly strong-arms Tessa onto a journey of discovery and reinvention in a trip that's not always pretty—or particularly wise—but one that leads to unexpected truths.

After the Sucker Punch takes irreverent look at father/ daughter relationships through the unique prism of Tessa's saga and its exploration of family, faith, cults, creativity, new love and old, and the struggle to define oneself against the inexplicable perceptions of a deceased parent. Told with both sass and sensibility, it's a story wrapped in contemporary culture with a very classic heart.

- 2015 Independent Author Network Finalist, Book of the Year Award

- 2014 IndieBRAG Medallion Honoree

- 2014 IndieAuthorNews Top 50 Indie Books

- 2015 Rosie Amber's Beach Reads Blog Tour Top 5 Beach Reads

Publishers Weekly/BookLife: "A realistic and profound journey of realization and forgiveness ... a solid novel that admirably explores the fragile, fraught relationship between parent and child."

Kirkus Reviews: "Wilke writes with razor-sharp wit and radiant flair, and the prose's high quality is the novel's principal strength. She also sensitively portrays how real love and affection can survive and even flourish in an otherwise dysfunctional family."

Tracy Trivas, author, The Wish Stealers (Simon & Schuster): "With bare-bone honesty and fiery dialogue, Wilke explores the loaded relationship between parents and their adult-children, examining the brave and lonely journey of self-discovery, reinvention, and healing ... raw and brave."

Junior Burke, author, Something Gorgeous (farfalla press/ McMillan & Parrish): "A keenly executed character study. The novel is tightly structured and holds its complex elements with a sure and skillful grip. The dialogue pops ... a thoroughly engaging and enjoyable read."

Mark Barry, Green Wizard Publishing/UK: "A great, sweeping, beautifully written, page-turning read, gripping from page one. A family saga with ambition and class. Meant to be absorbed over time, savoured by lamplight."

Sibylline Press is proud to publish the brilliant work of women authors over 50. We are a woman-owned publishing company and, like our authors, represent women of a certain age.

Made in United States
Troutdale, OR
06/11/2025

32058731R00218